BLADE BROKEN

THE ECHELON BOOK 1

NIRANJAN

First published by Geetha Krishnan 2025

Copyright © 2025 by Niranjan K

All rights reserved. No part of this publication may be reproduced, stored, or transmitted in any form or by any means, electronic, digital, mechanical, photocopying, recording, scanning, or otherwise without written permission from the publisher. It is illegal to copy this book, post it to a website, or distribute it by any other means without permission.

This novel is entirely a work of fiction. The names, characters and incidents portrayed in it are the work of the author's imagination. Any resemblance to actual persons, living or dead, events or localities is entirely coincidental.

Niranjan K (Geetha Krishnan) asserts the moral right to be identified as the author of this work.

No part of this text or cover design may be reproduced, transmitted, downloaded, decompiled, reverse-engineered, or stored in or introduced into any database for the purpose of training any model to generate text, including without limitation, technologies capable of generating works in the same style or genre without the author's express permission to do so. The distributor from which this text was obtained does not retain the right to sublicense, reproduce, or use this text or cover design for the purpose of training such generative text or art platforms without the author's express permission.

This text is the sole product of the author's imagination and creativity and has not been knowingly influenced by the assistance of or generated by the use of generative text commonly referred to as artificial intelligence or large language model. The cover art is likewise the product of the creativity of the artist listed below and has not been knowingly influenced by or generated in part or in whole by any generative imagery algorithm.

Editing by Fair Editions
Cover Design by Artscandare
Interior graphics by Leigh Graphics
Title Frame by Labyrynth Designs
Formatted by Fair Editions
Human Creativity Logo by Conrad Altmann

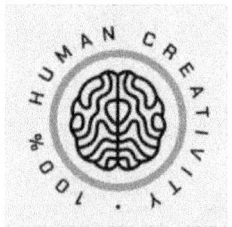

DEDICATION

TO MY SON

I MISS YOU MORE THAN I CAN SAY

HAPPY BIRTHDAY

FOREVER SIXTEEN

YOU WOULD HAVE BEEN TWENTY TWO

TODAY

CONTENT NOTES
THIS BOOK CONTAINS THE FOLLOWING CONTENT THAT MAY BE DISTURBING TO SOME READERS

DEATH, MURDER
POISON, BLOOD, VIOLENCE, TORTURE
DOMESTIC ABUSE
RAPE/ SEXUAL ASSAULT
GRIEF, LOSS, PAIN
ALCOHOL CONSUMPTION
DEATH OF A FAMILY MEMBER
TRAUMA, PTSD
SLAVERY
CONSENSUAL SEX WITH A SLAVE
NIGHTMARES
ILLNESS/ DISABILITY DUE TO TORTURE
BRITISH AND INDIAN SPELLINGS

A Note on the Units of Time and Distance

Smaller units of time are measured in terms of water.

A droplet would be equivalent to a droplet
A drop would equal a fifty droplets
A wave is approximately one and a half waves, or five hundred droplets

Weeks are called **griels**
Years are referred to as **farials**

The people of Castrial don't have months.

A week has nine days in it

Stephiel – Named after the deity of light
Madiel – Named after the deity of death
Astriel – Named after the deity of mountains
Rajiel – Named after the deity of animals
Kayiel – Named after the deity of plants
Flowiel – Named after the deity of water
Joniel – Named after the deity of fire
Niriel – Named after the deity of chaos
Liviel – Named after the deity of air

While the days are named after various deities, Castrilians, especially the upper class are not religious at all, and religion is not a part of their life.

Kar – A unit of distance that is twenty seven kires long
Kire – A smaller unit of distance which is fifty seven borits long
Borit – Even smaller unit of distance which is seventeen iodes long
Iode – A unit of distance, which is the measure of a hand, or equal to two hinors
Hinor – A unit of distance that is the length of a middle finger

BLADE BROKEN

THE ECHELON BOOK 1

NIRANJAN

LUCIAN AND ALARIC

PROLOGUE

ALARIC BREATHED IN the scent of the marketplace. How mundane it was! The stalls on either side of the wide paved street, the scents of food, fruits, and flowers, the stale scent of sweat underlying it, the clouds of perfumes that came off some of the people, the carriages, the press of bodies. It was all so ordinary, and yet to him, it was precious. To hear his native tongue being spoken after so long, to hear the lilting voices of the street vendors, was paradise.

He clutched the token he held in his hand, its edges cutting into his palm. Even now, he could not believe that it was over, that he was back home, in Castrial, his name cleared, his reputation restored.

His mother still lived in their old house, and as eager as he was to see her, he had to stop here first. Just to feel everything, to reassure himself this was no fever dream, no illusion brought on by the desperate hope in his breast.

Someone collided with him, making him lose his footing, and he had to clutch a street vendor's stand to avoid falling. The man apologised, his pale brown eyes concerned. Alaric was dressed in ordinary clothes today, his simple tunic and pants of an indefinite grey both mingling with the crowd and standing out. Though everyone around wore clothes of the same style, theirs was colourful, in a manner the Serenians or the Garanerians would have considered gaudy, but to Alaric, was home.

He wandered to a stall, where they were frying meat skewers, sprinkled with herbs and spices. He bought one, and bit into it, though it was taken out of the grill just then; even the burning of his tongue was pleasant after five farials of cold food with the barest sprinkle of herbs. The flavours burst into his tongue even as his stomach growled, reminding him that he hadn't eaten since the start of his journey.

His hired carriage waited at the side of the street, the horses grazing on the grass that grew there while the coachman looked on with interest, his Garanerian garb of loose flowing robes attracting some attention. Alaric was glad that the war was already over, since the gazes were only curious and not hostile. He turned to the stall and bought a couple more skewers, one with no spices for the coachman and one for him to savour. It had been a long

time since he had tasted food from Castrial and he wanted to remember it, to feel it in his bones again.
This is real. I'm home.
He tried not to think too much of everything he had done during the past five farials, everything he had been through. He had quite a few scars on his body, but his deepest wounds were not physical.
Lucian.
The name brought with it both an aching despair and a burning fury. His deepest scar even now was the one Lucian had caused, and Alaric didn't think he'd be able to heal from it so easily. He breathed in and out, slowly, savouring the breaths as he did everything else here. Biting into his skewer, he allowed it all to wash over him, the air of Castrial, the sounds, the sights, the tastes, and scents.
Tomorrow he would see Lucian again.
He pushed that thought to the deepest recesses of his heart and told his heart to be still. Why did the stupid thing get so excited about seeing the man again? After what Lucian had done to him? He finished his skewer, and let his magic out to clean his hands, to heal the burns inside his mouth. It felt even better to use his magic for simple things, instead of to fight, to defend himself, to survive, to kill.
Nothing would ever be the same again, and he was no longer who he had been. Yet, in this droplet, Alaric could fool himself that he was the same, that everything was the same.
One more droplet, he stood there, before he turned to his hired carriage and directed it to his old house and his mother.
He was back to his old life, but now he was the Shield of Castrial, second only to King Garret in the Echelon and equal in status to Lucian and above Lord Giles. Alaric breathed out again. It was time to show everyone that he was back, and that he hadn't

forgotten anything. If Lucian hoped for his forgiveness, he was going to be disappointed. Alaric was not in a forgiving mood.

As for Lord Giles, well, that was a grudge for another day.

Alaric settled back into the cushions, his gaze fixed on the outside, at the places that he'd never thought he'd see again. The tall buildings with white and blue walls reflecting the colours of Castrial blurred as the carriage picked up speed. There was the odd building with pink patterned walls, and a few yellow ones. Pale hues of purple also formed a large part of the city's colours. The buildings had tiled roofs which sloped upwards on one side and fell sharply on the other. Most had shapes of rectangles and a few squares, apart from the roof. Two storied buildings were the most common with a few single storied ones in between. Any building larger was either a noble's house or a commercial establishment.

The carriage passed by one of the public baths which reminded Alaric that he hadn't bathed either since he set out.

He sat back with a sigh. He would have time for all that later.

ONE

LUCIAN STARED AT himself in the mirror. He wasn't used to admiring himself, but today he wanted to see what he looked like.

Because today, he'd be seeing Alaric for the first time in five farials. When he heard that Alaric was back, Lucian's heart had leapt, and it was all he could do not to rush to Alaric's house. Only the memory of everything that had gone down five farials ago had stopped him.

Lucian had never wanted to be caught in the intrigues of the court nor in any deception, but he was privy to it, nevertheless. Not just privy, but part of it. As much as he wanted to set the record straight, he knew the necessity of maintaining this particular lie. It might break his heart, but it would keep Castrial safe.

In the end, Castrial was more important than Lucian's pain.

His reflection stared at him with judgement in his eyes. Lucian had to ignore it, however. He looked fine, which belied how he was feeling inside. His uniform fit well, the colours complementing his rich brown complexion and dark brown eyes. The insignia of the Blade of Castrial stood stark against the plain maroon of his coat, a blade wreathed in flames. He had tried to find out what it meant when he first took charge, but it seemed as if the meaning of that symbol was lost to time.

But whatever it had meant once, now it meant protection, defence, justice. Lucian was his King's blade, to be wielded by him against Castrial's enemies, both within and without. He was the master of spies, the commander of armies, and the leader of the military officials, second only to the King and equal only to the Shield.

The Shield of Castrial.

Alaric.

Lucian turned away from the mirror. It was pointless to waste time in front of it, trying to postpone the inevitable. Alaric was back, and Lucian would see him today. He had no excuses to stay away from court, and even if he did, the King had specifically asked for him.

Lucian took deep breaths. Inhale, exhale, and again. His heart was racing, but the focussed breathing helped calm it down. He made his way to the front door which was being held open by

Garth.

"Master Lucian," Garth said softly. "Good luck."

Garth and Davies were the only ones who knew what awaited Lucian today and how it affected him.

"Thank you," Lucian said. "I'll be dining at Lord Giles' this evening, Garth. Don't wait up."

Garth nodded. "As you wish," he said.

Garth might say it, but Lucian knew the man well enough to know that he would wait for him.

He went down the steps and climbed into the carriage. It was not his official one which was usually driven by Davies, though he had an official coachman from the Blade's Office. Lucian used him when he had to go somewhere from his office on official business. To and from home, whatever conveyance he used, he always used Davies.

Today, he was going in an open carriage, which was the latest in fashion, according to Bertram. It was his on his friend's insistence that he had bought it, but he found it much better sprung and more convenient than the closed carriages they usually used.

The wind was a problem, and if it rained, there would be a slew of other problems, but Lucian wasn't bothered. His hair was cut too short for the wind to do anything, and the magic imbued in his uniform would keep it pristine and wrinkle free.

Davies clucked to the horses and set them to a canter. The city was hardly a place they could gallop, but Lucian sometimes went out into the country, just to give the horses their heads.

He looked around him, trying to see the city from Alaric's eyes. Had things changed very much? Lucian had never paid much attention to his surroundings, not even when he was living with his father.

His father's death had hit him hard. Not because he had any affection for the man, but because he had been a larger than life figure for most of Lucian's life. It was so hard to accept he was gone, just like that. One droplet there and the next he wasn't.

At least he didn't suffer.

Things had changed after his death. Danae had taken on the title, but she didn't treat him like a pariah anymore. She acknowledged him whenever they saw each other, which was far more than his father had ever done. Percival on the other hand, was making a decidedly firm approach to mending fences with Lucian. It was a slow process, but Lucian was ready to forgive his siblings, if not to trust them fully. He knew that life was short, that things could change in an instant, and he didn't want to spend his life in more regret than he had before.

Tall buildings went past him, flowering trees and plants, a school and the public park where Lucian had first met Alaric. He swallowed and sat back, not wanting to see anything more. What was the point anyway? He would never be able to know what Alaric felt about all these; he could pretend to try to look through his eyes, but he would never be able to actually see through them.

Or hear Alaric tell him how he felt about coming home, about seeing the familiar places and the unfamiliar changes.

"I will be dining with Lord Giles tonight," he said, using magic to make sure Davies could hear him. He needed a distraction from his own thoughts. "Their coachman will bring me home, so you don't need to wait after taking me there."

"Their coachman?" Davies snorted. "More likely for it to be young Benjamin."

"Benji likes to drive," Lucian said, smiling despite himself, his mood lifting slightly. "And no coachman in Sir Giles' employ will dare say no to him."

"That youngster is too rash," Davies muttered, sounding disapproving.

"He's young," Lucian said, his smile widening.

Benji was Lord Giles' nephew, the orphaned son of his brother, who he had raised from infancy. The young man was entertaining to talk to, earnest about some things, and had an innocence about him that Lucian liked. Dew had thought of him as a young brother rather than her cousin, and Lucian felt the same.

"It will be Miss Dew's anniversary in a few days," Davies said softly.

"I know," Lucian responded.

Not like he could forget her or the day she passed away. It hurt him with a pain that was almost surprising even now, even after a farial. Dew had been one of the few people that he could be completely himself with, without masks or pretences. She had accepted him as he was, never asking anything of him that he wasn't ready for.

The only other person like that had been Alaric, but Lucian was under no illusions that things would be the same between them now. Five farials stood between them. Five farials where Alaric had suffered, and Lucian had a war to win.

Five farials of lies and betrayals.

Nothing was the same now, but Lucian's traitorous heart kept hoping all the same.

TWO

ALARIC BOWED AS the King entered, his heart giving a jolt as he noticed the man looked almost the same. Almost but not quite. There was something different about Garret today, more than the lines under his eyes and the nearly imperceptible loss in weight. He looked like a man with the weight of the world on his shoulders.

And perhaps he was. It was no easy matter to be King, to rule a kingdom like Castrial, to defend her against predatory neighbours like Garaner and Sarian. Alaric had the easier job, no matter how hard it was.

"Alaric." The King smiled, and there was genuine warmth in it, the smile reaching his eyes. "It's good to see you."

"Your Majesty," he said, taking a knee. "Thank you for your grace in pardoning me."

"Rise," the King said, sitting down behind his desk. "Have a seat, and no gratitude required. You are innocent and were wrongfully punished. I am only correcting a mistake."

All the same, Alaric knew how rare it was for a king to even admit he made a mistake. He had been in Garaner and had seen how the rulers there had brainwashed the people into believing they had the divine right to rule. The current rulers were benevolent in that they cared for the people, but they still had no hesitation in throwing away their lives when they had attacked Castrial five farials ago.

He bowed his head and sat down, looking around the room and finding no changes. The window to the side, the bookshelves lining one wall, the desk in front of him, the painting behind the King, the tapestries on the wall opposite the bookshelf, the rug under his feet, the curtains that hung heavy over the closed window, were all the same.

"You have suffered," the King said softly.

"I was glad to," Alaric said truthfully. "Castrial needed me, and I was... I wanted to do what I can. It was the least I could do."

The King nodded slowly. "You were needed there more than here at that time," he said. "I'm glad you're here now, however. We need our Shield, now more than ever."

The King turned to one of the guards who stood statue still and pillar like around the room. "Go, bring Lord Blade here."

Alaric shifted slightly, swallowing. Lucian. He hadn't attended court in the morning, the King having excused him, asking him to meet here in his office instead. He wasn't prepared to meet Lucian, but he had no choice. Alaric dredged up every last vestige of courage, every bit of acting prowess he had, and schooled his features into impassivity. He had to control himself. This was the King's office, and he couldn't afford to lose his composure here.

Lucian walked in through the same door Alaric had come through. He looked tired, shadows under his eyes, and the loss of weight was noticeable. Alaric's first impulse was to demand of Lucian what the fuck he had been doing to himself, but he bit his tongue.

"Your Majesty," Lucian said, taking a knee.

"Rise, Lucian. No need for formalities here. We're all old friends, are we not?"

Friend was pushing it; Alaric only had a passing acquaintance with the man when he was only Prince Garret. No one had expected him to be the King back then, not even him.

"As you can see, our Shield has rejoined us," the King said. "I want you to take him to your office, apprise him of the present situation and afterwards, introduce him to Astra. She has been taking care of your duties, Alaric, in your absence."

Absence. As if he wasn't exiled but had been on holiday or something. In a way, he supposed he had been on a mission, but would he have agreed that readily if his choice wasn't exile? If his heart wasn't broken?

Lucian bowed. "As you command, Your Majesty."

"These are trying times for Castrial," the King said, his voice edged with steel. "And I won't have any strife between you two. The Shield and the Blade must work together to protect and defend Castrial. Whatever issues the two of you have, you have to put it aside and work together. Do I make myself clear?"

Alaric bowed his head, inwardly seething. How easy it was to say to put it aside! As if Lucian hadn't betrayed Alaric's trust, his heart, their long farials of friendship. Still, he had no choice. The King had commanded this, and he had to obey.

"All right then," the King said. "Take him, Lucian, and tell him everything." He nodded to them both. "Dismissed."

He pulled a stack of reports to him and both Lucian and Alaric rose to their feet at the same time, bowing and departing from the King's presence. There was no attendant to show them the way this time, and Alaric followed Lucian who strode confidently ahead as if he was familiar with the palace and its magic. Perhaps he was. Resentment rose in Alaric in a tide. If he had a weapon, he would have stabbed Lucian then and there. Alaric had been in abyss and Lucian had been getting familiar with the palace.

He looked away, fighting his emotions. They were still in the palace, and he didn't want to be a criminal anymore. He had just got back, and if he did something to Lucian, he would be condemning, not just himself, but his mother and his servants as well.

Lucian paused at a door. "This is the portal," he said. "You can use it to come to the palace from your office and return without having to take the carriage. Only the King, the Blade and the Shield are allowed to use it."

Lucian took out his badge and placed it on a small receptacle on the door. The whole door lit up before changing to a portal, and Lucian stepped inside, Alaric following him. The disorientation of using a portal was there along with a suffocating sense of fear at the confined space. It was over in moments, however, as the next step they took brought them inside Lucian's office. Alaric had been here, times without count, and he took in everything that was still the same.

Except the man in front of him who was removing his badge from the receptacle inside the door and putting it back in his pocket. Lucian's desk looked as untidy as ever, and Alaric itched to clear it.

"Have a seat, Alaric," Lucian said. "This may take a while, I'm afraid."

Alaric sat down, staring at the sombre expression on Lucian's face and his gut twisted in something other than hatred and anger. There must be a reason why Lucian looked so worried and whatever it was, it had to be extremely bad.

THREE

SYLVESTER SIPPED SPARINGLY from the goblet of wine in his hand. No matter his high tolerance for alcohol, he couldn't risk getting inebriated tonight. It had taken a lot of manipulations and pulling invisible strings to get himself invited to this party and he wasn't going to risk anything by not having all his wits around him.

The guests were either drinking or dancing, but some sat around the smaller tables, talking or playing various games. His quarry tonight was at one of those tables, drinking steadily and losing whatever he was playing if Sylvester was to guess. He could only be thankful that the rulers of Garaner were not above nepotism. No one in their right mind would hire Lord Baldir for anything more serious than a wine taster. But here he was, minister of war, no less, holding the secrets of his kingdom in his hands, and behaving like the pampered child he was. Sylvester had met his sister, the female ruler of Garaner, who was a sensible person and smart as well.

But it did seem as if the rumours of how her brother was her weakness were true. Sylvester had met the previous minister of war, a man who was wholly befitted to his station. Perhaps that was why he was assassinated during the war with Castrial, the event that had started Garaner's slide into defeat. Perhaps the rulers hoped that by appointing someone as useless as Lord Baldir to this post, they could prevent such catastrophes in future.

Except they should have realised that it would open a whole new different can of worms instead. Sylvester didn't move as the man he had been watching lurched to his feet, pulled at his collar, causing a few buttons to come undone and one to pop off from his tunic, and started weaving his drunken way to the side table where the wines were.

And Sylvester stood in his way. He had chosen this position carefully. He stood next to a pillar, leaning one shoulder against it. The room was large, high ceilinged with arched doorways and floor length windows over which thick drapes were drawn now. The profusion of tables and chairs made it seem crowded; even the clear space in the middle where people danced was thronged.

Between where Sylvester stood and a table was enough space for a slender man to squeeze through without bumping into anything, and Lord Baldir was not a slender man. He wasn't corpulent, but well-built with height to match.

Lord Baldir straightened himself to his full height, which wasn't still as tall as Sylvester, an annoyed expression on his face, opened his mouth as if to say something, probably for Sylvester to move away, and closed it again as his eyes met Sylvester's.

"Do I know you?" he asked, a smile creeping on to his face, and a faint stirring of lust.

Sylvester smiled back. "I don't think so. This is the first time I'm attending a party here. It's all been formal dinners before this." He bowed. "Sylvester Giles. Assistant to the Castrilian Ambassador."

Lord Baldir grinned. "I'm Reswick Baldir, the Minister of War and brother to Her Majesty. I don't remember seeing you with the ambassador at the dinner last griel."

Sylvester had missed it on purpose, though he couldn't say that. "I was indisposed that day," he lied smoothly. "And I wouldn't have come today, but Silian insisted."

"You know Silian?" Lord Baldir's smile turned to a chuckle. "What am I saying, of course, you know Silian. Everyone knows Silian."

"It certainly seems so," Sylvester said with a rueful smile. "When he said a party, I didn't expect this."

He gestured with his chin to the people all dressed in elaborately embroidered robes or ankle length tunics. Sylvester himself was dressed in a pair of pants and tunic over which he wore a rather plain over robe. Despite the lack of colour in the robes everyone else wore, the embroidery made up for it, depicting mythical beasts and beautiful gardens.

"Don't blame you," Lord Baldir said, moving closer. "But your robe is nice. Suits you. Brings out the brown of your eyes."

Sylvester looked down at his drink. "Thank you."

"So, Sylvester," Lord Baldir said, all but purring. "How long have you been in Garaner?"

"Oh, quite a long time," Sylvester said, meeting the man's eyes again. "More than a decade now. But I don't socialise much. Meeting Silian was an accident, and he... He kind of adopted me, I think."

Lord Baldir laughed. "He tends to do that. He likes people and is always willing to help."

Sylvester, who knew very well the kind of 'help' Silian specialised in, smiled. "That he is. I am very grateful to him."

"So," Lord Baldir said, sidling even closer to him. "Maybe we can get another drink, and go somewhere private?"

Sylvester didn't have a chance to reply because a heavy hand fell on his shoulder and a smooth voice said. "Reswick, here you are! I've been looking all over for you. Please introduce me to your new friend."

The man let go of Sylvester's shoulder and moved near to Lord Baldir who looked sour, but he muttered. "Alyswin, why are you even here?"

Sylvester wanted to know that as well.

"Why? Can't I be at a party thrown by my dear cousin?" The man called Alyswin asked, brows lifting.

"Whatever," Lord Baldir said, looking sulky as he moved away and back to the table where he was earlier. Alyswin's narrowed eyes met Sylvester's.

"Rather odd place to see you at, Sylvester."

"Lord Gwayir," Sylvester bowed to him. "As I was telling your cousin, this was unexpected."

"Oh really? And I suppose it's accidental that you happened to accost my cousin too?"

"Accost?" Sylvester raised his own brow. "I didn't accost anyone. Your cousin came to me."

Alyswin stepped closer but Sylvester stood his ground. "I find that hard to believe. I have my eye on you, Castrilian. Whatever you want from my cousin, you aren't going to get it."

Sylvester frowned. "Not even wine?"

Alyswin's face reddened with rage, and he turned around and walked away, going to where his cousin was, and sitting at one of the empty spots at the table.

Sylvester moved to a corner, where he could still see his quarry and sipped his wine. He was patient, after all, and there were other parties and occasions.

Besides, if Sylvester knew people, and he did, there was no longer a need for him to do anything at all. Lord Baldir would come to him. And not just because of the charmed make up Sylvester was wearing. It was barely discernible, but its effect was unmistakeable. It would not affect anyone who didn't care for men or hadn't thoughts of finding someone for the night, but it would affect anyone who liked men and who had sex on their minds.

The effect would wear off in an wave or so, but even so, Sylvester knew that Lord Baldir was not likely to let him go. He was a hunter, after all, for all his foppishness. He would never let a prey get away, especially due to what he saw as his cousin's interference. Lord Gwayir couldn't have done better, to be honest. In his well-meaning bluster, he had done exactly what Sylvester wanted.

So, he would soon have Lord Baldir in his bed, and once there, it was a small matter to get the information he needed from the man.

The thought gave Sylvester no pleasure.

FOUR

LUCIAN CHECKED HIS surroundings, making sure he was alone before going towards the street corner where he could get a hired carriage to take him to the riverside docks. It was a quick trip, needing only a couple of copper marks. He strode into the inn by the docks and went to the inn keep.

The man nodded at him. "The boat is at the back," he said.

"You'll be fine?"

He asked that every time, as if Lucian was a novice. But Lucian didn't mind it.

"I'll be fine," he said as he produced a gold mark and placed it on the man's outstretched palm. "Thank you. You never saw me."

The man bowed and Lucian departed by the back door, where a small boat nestled close to the docks. Lucian untied it, and got into it, pulling up the anchor before using a pole to push himself away from the docks. Once the boat was into the open waters, he took the oars and began rowing.

Soon, the faint light that marked his destination was on sight. As Lucian rowed closer to the shore, the source of the light became clear as a man holding a lantern. He made no move to assist as Lucian leapt from the boat and pulled it up and tied it to a railing that had begun to rust.

"One of these days, that thing will fall down, and I'll be stuck here with you," Lucian remarked as he dusted his hand on his cloak.

The man chuckled. "I think you'll swim to avoid that fate, my lord Blade." He held out the hand not holding the lantern. "It's good to see you, Lucian."

Lucian grinned as he took the hand. "Good to see you too, Hansen."

The man let go of Lucian's hand and turned to lead the way through a wilderness of grass and shrubs, a small path, just enough for one person becoming visible in the dim light of the lantern.

"You know, of course, that Sarian is mustering their armies," Hansen said as he stopped and waved his hand. The air in front of him rippled and a wooden cabin came into view. He opened the door and stepped inside, and Lucian followed him.

Inside was warm and cozy, unlike the chill outside. The room was lit by magical orbs that floated on the ceiling and a fire crackled on the fireplace. Every time, Lucian was amazed at Hansen's magic which ensured that not even smoke from the chimney was visible past his illusion.

The whole island had an enchantment laid upon it which rendered useless his own magic. Once Lucian would have hesitated to set foot on a place like this, but over the farials, this had become familiar ground for him.

"I know what Sarian is doing," he said. "They didn't actively involve themselves in the war last time and Garaner had to go at it alone. This time, they're hoping to crush us. They know we can ill afford another war."

"They do, but more than that, they have a secret weapon that no one knows about." Hansen took a tome from a pile in the corner and held it out to Lucian. "I know you can read the Serenian script."

Lucian took the book, sank on to a stool, opened it and began to read. It was a book on a creature native to Sarian. Something they called a dragon. It was highly magical, intelligent and vicious. There was a picture which looked like a cross between a bat and a lizard. Large wings, scaly skin, long tail and a snout which was open and breathing fire. A human was depicted as standing next to it, reaching barely to its large toes.

"It's that big?" Lucian demanded. "And it breathes fire?"

Hansen nodded. "The Serenian royals have a way to control the beasts. For some reason, the control slips if the beasts are outside Sarian."

Lucian stared, eyes wide. "The burned villages at the border," he said, his voice barely a whisper. "It was this creature."

Hansen nodded again, face grim. "It was. Somehow they got it over the border, but well, there's very little can be done against it."

Lucian looked at the picture again. "Something this big... Someone should have seen it!"

"Your spies, you mean? Not unless they are spying inside forests, and as you know, half of Sarian is woodlands. The royal palace itself adjoins a forest at the back. They're keeping the beasts under control there. But there are plenty of wild ones too, if one wanted to go to the woods."

Lucian sighed and ran a hand through his hair.

"It appears that your informants are much better than mine," he said, rising to his feet. "May I take the book? The King may need to see it."

"Be my guest," Hansen said. "And Lucian, be careful. This war, if it happens, won't be like the last time. Sarian is not Garaner."

Lucian nodded, sombre. "I know," he said. He took out a pouch from his tunic and placed it on the stool he was sitting on. "The usual payment."

A scowl appeared on Hansen's face. "I've told you before, I'm not doing it for money."

"I know." Lucian smiled. "But even magic can't create food or clothes out of thin air, and you need to live."

As he tucked the book inside his tunic and stepped out of the door, Lucian shivered as the cold slammed into him. He pulled his cloak tighter around him and walked to the boat. At least he could warm himself with magic once he was on the river. What he learned today was worrying enough. Lucian knew he would have to seek a meeting with the King soon.

As soon as he got home, he would send a message to the palace. If Sarian was indeed going to be using these dragons to fight them, they had to find a way to defeat them without going to war.

Lucian could only hope that such a way existed.

FIVE

BEING BACK HOME was something Alaric had never thought he would have when he was in exile, despite all of Sylvester's reassurances. After all, Sylvester had his own agenda, something for which Alaric couldn't fault the man. They had a war to win, and Alaric was useful for that.

He wasn't angry with Sylvester or for the King for the use they put him to. He was only one man in the end, and they had the safety of all of Castrial to think of. Even so, despite the fact that he was just a tool, they had, in the end, come through on their promise to vindicate him. His name had been cleared, and he was allowed to come home. But more than that, he had been given the position of Shield of Castrial. That was something Alaric had not even dared hope for.

As he walked to his carriage, following morning court, whispers followed him. He was used to whispers, had learned to ignore them, but these hurt for some reason.

"Criminal." "Son of a slave." "Bastard." "His father-"

Except the first, it was nothing he hadn't heard before, but when he was merely Alaric, a minor official, it was something he could shrug off. Now, he was the Shield of Castrial, he found himself unable to do so. His steps slowed and his fists clenched. But before he could turn around, a familiar voice spoke.

"Do you want to say that again, Lord Hadel?"

"My lord Blade." Lord Hadel sounded flustered. "I was just... It was just..."

"Just what?" Lucian's voice was like the crack of a whip, sharp and stinging. "It sounded very much like you were implying His Majesty's judgement was wrong."

"My lord Blade!"

The man sounded panicked, and Alaric allowed himself a small smile as he walked to his carriage, not bothering to listen further. It was familiar, the way Lucian would jump into his defence over insults Alaric had ignored, but this time there would be no Lucian hurrying after him, throwing an arm around his shoulder and guiding his steps.

Alaric didn't want to miss that past, or that Lucian, but he did. The Lucian he saw every day these days, looked different from the man he had seen before his exile. He looked careworn, tired, and thinner.

As much as Alaric wanted to believe that his absence had contributed to that, he wasn't ready to open his heart to that thought. If he did, if he allowed Lucian in again, he might be setting himself up for an even larger heartbreak, and he couldn't afford that. Not when he held the position he did, and had duties to Castrial that he couldn't forget for anyone, even Lucian. Keeping Lucian at arm's length and holding on to his anger was the only way for him to move forward.

Because Lucian had a propensity to fill Alaric's mind to the exclusion of all else, to be the centre of his world in a way that made it impossible for Alaric to think of anything else, and he could ill afford that.

Astra was waiting by his carriage, her posture straight and stiff. She nodded to him, and they both climbed into the carriage, sitting on opposite sides as it moved towards the building that housed his office. Astra looked outside, and Alaric studied the woman. She was usually quiet, never speaking unless spoken to. She had been helping him for the past few griels since she had been taking care of his duties these past farials. She seemed relieved to be rid of them, but Alaric knew she was no simple soldier.

"Captain," he said. "You went to the royal academy, didn't you?"

She nodded, not looking at him, tension radiating off her. "I was a few farials below you and Lord Blade."

"I apologise if I'm making you uncomfortable," Alaric said. He had no idea why the woman was so on edge, but he wished he could change it. "Is there anything I can do?"

Astra's shoulders relaxed fractionally. "It's fine," she said. "You will know anyway. It's in the files."

Alaric frowned. "Is it necessary for me to know?"

She shrugged. "I guess not."

"Then I don't want to know," he said. "Your life is yours, and I don't want to pry, not unless it affects Castrial's safety."

Astra chuckled but turned to look at him. "Not many share your views on the matter," she said.

"I'm sorry to hear that," Alaric said.

Unfortunately, he knew well how people were, but whatever it was had Astra feeling unsafe and frightened, he was not going to add to it.

She looked at him still, her eyes full of emotions he couldn't read. "Thank you," she said softly.

He shook his head. "You shouldn't have to thank me for behaving with common decency," he said. "It's something you are owed and whoever doesn't, you should put them in their place."

A laugh burst from her. "I never thought of that," she said. Her eyes regarded him gravely. "Have you done that?" she asked. "To people who treated you badly?"

Alaric didn't smile. "No," he said. "But I... I had people who stood up for me."

"Lord Blade," she said softly. "I remember, back in school... I guess back then you couldn't have done anything either... So it's good that he did. He had nothing to fear from any of them."

"And now, I find that if I retaliate, I may be held to be abusing my position," he said quietly. "That's not what I want."

"I feel the same, but perhaps I shouldn't be so hesitant to stand up for myself." She paused. "Nor should you, you know. His Majesty is not unreasonable and supports his people, especially those he appointed himself."

Alaric felt a surge of gratitude for her understanding. Before he could say anything, the carriage stopped. Alaric waited for Astra to descend before following her.

"My lord Shield," one of his assistants said as they entered. "The head of the city law enforcement is waiting for you."

The woman standing next to his assistant bowed to him, her uniform dusty and eyes filled with caution. Alaric frowned as he looked at her. He remembered her from before. She had been holding that position long and had been doing a good job too.

"Come inside," he said, indicating the open door of his office. "If I may trouble you, captain?"

Astra nodded as she followed him and the other woman.

"Chief Lorelei," Alaric said. "Have a seat and tell me what I can do for you."

"There's been a murder," she said, after sitting down. She fidgeted. "A pimp in a brothel. I know that it's under my jurisdiction, but... Eyewitness reports say it's a nobleman who did it."

Alaric frowned, wanting to say that that shouldn't be a problem, but unfortunately, it was. No noble would defer to a commoner, and they were all well-guarded by soldiers who wouldn't think twice about driving away law enforcement officials or guards.

"Who?" he asked.

The Chief fidgeted again. "It's Lord Giles from all reports. They said he used to frequent the establishment, but he had some words with the deceased yesterday... He pushed the man and when the deceased said that he would complain, he stabbed him with the sword he carries everywhere."

Alaric stiffened, unable to help it.

Lord Giles.

Sylvester's father.

Dew's father. Dew who had been betrothed to Lucian before her death.

Alaric might have been away, but that didn't mean he didn't know what went on in Lucian's life.

But Lord Giles was more than just that, and even though

Alaric hated him, he didn't hate him enough to want him to die.

"Are you sure it was Lord Giles?" he heard himself ask, his voice steady despite how his insides was a storm of emotions–anger, despair and something he couldn't put a name to.

"That's what the eyewitnesses say," Chief Lorelei confirmed. "I want your advice, Lord Shield, and assistance. I can't go to Lord Giles' house and arrest him."

"I can," Alaric said. "Captain, do you mind accompanying me?"

"I'll be happy to," Astra said. "Where are we going?"

"To the crime scene, and then we'll decide," Alaric said. "If it's indeed Lord Giles, we may also need to inform His Majesty."

Though the laws held no distinction between a noble and a commoner when it came to crimes, in actual fact, nobles got away with more. It was a state of affairs the King was not happy about. All the same, Alaric wanted to apprise the King of the facts before he made an arrest.

There was also the matter of Lord Giles' family. Usually, criminals' families were also given the same punishment, a law that Alaric had been thinking of changing. Why should innocents suffer for the crime of someone? But as it stood now, Lord Giles' family would be executed along with him if he turned out to be guilty.

That was something Alaric couldn't allow, and he hoped the King would listen to his plea for leniency. Even so, worry coiled tight inside his gut as he hoped that Lord Giles hadn't actually done it.

SIX

THE NIGHT WAS SILENT, and Sylvester lay still, his breathing regular as he listened to the snores of the man in his bed. Lord Baldir was snoring softly, mouth partly open, an arm around Sylvester's chest. Sylvester didn't want to take any chances as he kept still, kept his breathing even and regular, forcing his body to relax.

If Lord Baldir was not sleeping, he would know when Sylvester cast his spell and that was the last thing Sylvester wanted.

Bit by bit, Lord Baldir's body relaxed even more, the hand across Sylvester's chest was withdrawn, and he curled up on a side, hand under his head, and sighed.

Sylvester waited. He had the whole night. There was no need to be impatient. He found himself studying the pattern on the ceiling, though it was too dark to see it clearly. It was some geometric design, one that made the eyes grow heavy and mind confused. Sylvester withdrew his eyes and looked at the young nobleman at his side. Lord Baldir was not as useless as he had imagined.

Did he know who Sylvester was? Sylvester hoped not. No one in Garaner who knew his real identity was alive now, and Sylvester had kept a low profile since the war. If the situation wasn't so urgent, he wouldn't have taken direct action. But after Lucian's message, he had to know if Garaner was gearing up for another war, if they were supporting Sarian.

If so, Sylvester would do everything within his power to stop them. He was one man, but Alaric had already proved what one man could do, with enough determination.

Guilt reared its head at the thought of Alaric, and Sylvester squashed it ruthlessly. He had used Alaric, but he had done so at the behest of his monarch. He had done it for Castrial, and he wouldn't give way to regrets. In any case, Alaric was home now, and in no danger. He was the Shield of Castrial, and nothing was going to hurt him anymore.

Sylvester half rose on one elbow, but Lord Baldir didn't move. Sylvester placed a finger on the sleeping man's temple and wound a tendril of his magic to seep inside the other man, careful not to do lasting damage, but probing his mind, even as he kept him asleep. Sylvester breathed deep, the strain of keeping that delicate thread of magic taking up all his concentration. It was more difficult than people imagined, this slow trickle of his magic, which had to sneak past the other man's mental defences and lay bare the secrets of his mind. People's minds were usually disorganised chaos, jumble of thoughts, emotions, desires, and to find what he wanted from that mess required patience as well as skill, something Sylvester had in abundance.

Lord Baldir's mind was well ordered, however: disciplined, and that made the task even more difficult because such people were used to keeping secrets. The more important a secret, the harder it was to find, but if he was not careful, he would end up alerting the other man, and then Sylvester would have to kill him. He didn't want to. He was a spy, not an assassin.

He found what he was looking for and withdrew his magic, again slowly so as not to make the other's mind aware of his presence. It was excruciating, and sweat beaded on Sylvester's forehead, ran in rivulets down his chest and back, but even so, he couldn't hurry. Once he had withdrawn his magic, Sylvester mopped his brow with the edge of a bed sheet, got up from the bed and padded across to where a jug of water was, chugging it down.

"Sylvester?" Lord Baldir's voice was sleep slurred. "Why are you there? Come back to bed."

"Had a nightmare," Sylvester said as he placed the jug of water down, his thirst quenched somewhat. He was right to be so careful.

Lord Baldir rose from the bed and came towards him, wrapping his arms around him. "Come to bed, and I'll make you forget."

Sylvester grinned. This was familiar territory after all.

"After last night, you still want more?"

Lord Baldir chuckled.

"Perhaps I want to hear you beg so prettily. Come to bed."

Sylvester complied. After all, getting his brains fucked out was one way to deal with his problems.

If only everything in his life was that simple.

Morning came, faster than he had anticipated, and Sylvester woke in an empty bed. Raised voices outside the room and the door was flung open violently and Lord Gwayir walked in, an expression of fury on his face, his glare on Sylvester.

Sylvester sat up, allowing the sheet to slip from his body to pool at his waist, his naked torso on full display, with the various marks Lord Baldir had left on him the night previous.

"Lord Gwayir," he drawled. "What an unexpected pleasure. What can I do for you?"

"You can leave my cousin alone!" Lord Gwayir snapped, his fists clenching at his sides. "Do you think I'm a fool? That I don't know what you're up to?"

Sylvester smirked and stretched himself languidly. "Your cousin is an adult as he proved to my satisfaction several times last night." A choked laugh came from Lord Baldir and Lord Gwayir's face became mottled with rage. Sylvester continued, "Really, I can't see what has you so wound up. Unless you're jealous?" He raised an eyebrow. "If you wanted him to share, you could have said it."

Lord Gwayir turned on his heel and walked off, the stomp of his footsteps loud and Sylvester heard a door slam somewhere. Lord Baldir sat at the edge of the bed, clad only in a loose robe and pants.

"He's probably going to tell my sister," he said. "As much as I enjoyed it, and you, I fear she will tell me off."

"It's fine." Sylvester smiled at him. "We both enjoyed ourselves. No hard feelings. If you can give me a droplet to get dressed, I'll get out of your hair."

He had to behave normally, to hide how eager he was to leave. He had got what he had come for, and he shouldn't have stayed so long anyway. All the same, he had no regrets. After the tension and stress of invading Lord Baldir's mind without his knowledge, the sex had helped him relax.

"Sure." Lord Baldir rose. "I'll leave you to it then. You know where the bathroom is, if you want to freshen up. Your clothes have been laundered." He pointed to them on a chair.

"Thank you," Sylvester said, and raised a brow when the other man stayed, fidgeting. "Is there anything else?"

Lord Baldir sighed. "No, not really, just... My cousin isn't all bluster... He's dangerous... You should be careful."

Sylvester nodded. It was nothing he didn't already know, but he appreciated the warning all the same.

"Don't worry, I'm always careful."

Lord Baldir left the room and Sylvester got out of bed, stretching again, before going to the bathroom. He needed to leave as soon as possible, and he needed to get back to the embassy so he could send a message to Lucian.

Garaner was in talks with Sarian, though they hadn't committed to anything yet.

SEVEN

IT STARTED AS rumours, and by the time Lucian heard of it, it was already everywhere, and the day was more than half over. Lucian still had a lot of work to do. There was the message from Sylvester, for one. If Garaner was going to ally themselves with Sarian, they had a lot more problems than whatever Lord Giles was accused of doing.

Still, this was Lord Giles, Dew's father. He was the one member of Dew's family that Lucian liked the least, for all that the man had been kind to him. His dislike of the man had stemmed much earlier than his engagement with Dew, however, and Lucian could never get over it.

All the same, he couldn't ignore this. If it was simply rumours, he would do what he could to scotch them. If there was any truth to them, however... If they were true, there was little Lucian could do, since such crimes didn't fall under his purview. It was Alaric's duty to investigate them, and Lucian didn't want to go to Alaric. Not unless he had no other choice.

Once he wouldn't have hesitated, but too much had happened between them since. The five farials of Alaric's exile stood between them, a wall so tall and strong that Lucian had no idea how to scale it or pull it down. He didn't think he had it in him to break down the walls Alaric had built around his pain, not when Lucian was part of that hurt.

So, right now, he had no plan but to seek out Lord Giles. Lucian told one of his assistants, Rhen, where he was going to be, and left his office. The streets were busy at this time, but his destination wasn't far. His uniform covered by a nondescript cloak of grey and with its hood pulled up, he didn't look like anyone important.

The tavern that Lord Giles patronised was busy, but Lord Giles was in his private room, getting steadily drunk before he would leave for one of the brothels in the city. Disgust curled low in Lucian's belly as he entered the room. The man's bloodshot eyes took him in, widened as recognition struck, and Lucian closed the door, casting a spell of privacy before confronting the man who would have been his father-in-law.

"Do you know what people are saying in the streets?" he

demanded. "That you killed someone?"

"He was only a pimp," Lord Giles said as he poured himself another mug of ale and leaned back on his chair, head held high. "Also, a commoner. No great loss to the world."

"That's not the point!" Lucian grated out. "Did you kill him or not?"

"Of course I did," Lord Giles said, dashing all of Lucian's hopes. "What of it? He was irrelevant, unimportant. I did a public service by killing him. Disgusting cheat."

Lucian stared at him aghast. "Have you any idea what will happen when the investigation reveals your guilt?"

Lord Giles' brows knitted. "What investigation?" he asked. "I'm a noble. Yes, some people came by to ask some questions, but that's just routine, Lucian. Don't worry. I'm a noble and no one would dare touch me. Not even that bastard whom His Majesty appointed as the Shield."

"You will not talk of Alaric that way!" Lucian snapped, his hands itching to punch the man, and he gripped the edges of his cloak tight to stop himself.

"Ah, you were friends with him once, weren't you?" Lord Giles asked. "I'm glad you saw his true colours, however. He killed Lord Hark, but then–"

"Shut the fuck up!" Lucian snapped again. "Alaric is innocent, unlike you, who seems to take pride in killing a man much weaker!"

He turned and left the room, slamming the door behind him. He rushed out into the street where he had to lean on the post of one of the streetlamps to get himself under control. Both his anger and his breathing. It was a struggle, but bit by bit, he managed to wrestle his emotions and body into submission.

He sighed and looked for a hired carriage. Lord Giles might be a fool and not worth his time, but his wife was not. Dew's mother had suffered enough, and Lucian hated to add to it, but he couldn't let her be taken by surprise.

Estella looked happy to see him, her face lighting up. She hadn't had many chances to smile since Dew's death, but she always had one for Lucian. Today her smile was strained, and Lucian sensed she was hanging to her composure by a thread.

"Lucian," she said, kissing his cheek. "This is a surprise. Shouldn't you be at work?"

"I had to come," he said. "Did you know what Hamin had done?"

Her face clouded, and she bit her lip, her voice shaking as she spoke. "I do... Hamin seems to believe nothing will happen to him, and he doesn't listen to whatever I say." She paused. "I haven't told the children yet... I don't want them to know he's guilty, Lucian... Don't tell them, please!"

Lucian couldn't deny her, but he had to try to get her to understand the severity of the crime and its impact. It wasn't something Estella would know because Giles never attended court and paid no attention to what went on. Estella wasn't interested in politics, unlike Dew and Keylin.

"His Majesty had been looking to make the nobles abide by the laws of Castrial since he took the throne," Lucian said. "Most nobles who are aware of His Majesty's ire have taken special care to do nothing to bring his wrath on them. But Hamin had never... I fear His Majesty may do something to make Hamin an example."

"Oh," she said, going quiet for a few moments. "So, that's it then," she said finally. "Hamin has crossed one line too many and now he will have to pay the price."

She sounded resigned, which wasn't what Lucian wanted.

"The law isn't going to spare you either," Lucian said. "You know that families are punished along with the perpetrator." He paused. "I can arrange for you to leave Castrial before the matter comes to trial, Estella. Hamin may refuse to leave, but you should. You, Keylin, Elda, and Benji. You have to save yourselves."

She studied him for a droplet, a soft smile breaking over her face. "You're so much like your mother, did you know that? She was fiercely loyal too." She sighed deeply. "I can't leave, Lucian. Hamin may have cheated on me and broken my heart, but he's still the father of my children and I can't... I can't run away when he's in trouble. He may need me."

"You know Keylin will never leave without you," he said. "Neither will Elda nor Benji."

A look of fear came to her face, but she shook her head again. "I'll try to convince them... But where can we go, Lucian?"

"To Sylvester," Lucian said without hesitation. "He will protect you, and His Majesty will be glad to ignore you as long as Hamin is punished."

She looked thoughtful. "Maybe, but may be not... I've heard that you and the Shield are not on the best of terms."

"Alaric has a grudge against me," Lucian said honestly. "And he's justified in it. But that's not important, Estella."

"But it is." She took his hands in hers. "If the Shield bears a grudge, he may not let the King let it be, and I'd rather not bring any trouble on you or Sylvester. Thank you, Lucian, but... I... I don't know that we can escape this... I'll talk to the children... You can get them away, but me... I can't leave him, Lucian. I'm sorry." She paused. "Perhaps Betram would marry Keylin so she would be safe even if she stays."

Lucian didn't think Keylin would agree to marry Bertram to save herself when her mother and the rest of her family was going to be in trouble. Estella spoke of loyalty, and Lucian wasn't the only one who had it.

Keylin might love Betram, but she would share whatever fate

her family was going to suffer.

Lucian knew he would have to talk to the King, even though he hated to. He had never made any requests of the King, had never asked anything for himself. To his mind, it would have been an abuse of his position, because in the end, the King owed him nothing. Lucian had promised himself he would never ask Garret any personal favours, but this was one time he might have to break that.

But before that, he had to go to Bertram, to let his friend know what was happening.

Bertram was home, and his mother chatted with Lucian about inconsequential things as she insisted on taking him to her son's office. Lucian made appropriate responses, keeping his impatience in check.

Bertram was going through some reports when Lucian was ushered in, likely related to his estates. Being a nobleman also came with a lot of responsibilities, and while people like Lord Giles chose to ignore those and leave it to others, Bertram was more hands on. He had once told Lucian that he had time anyway and he hated being a social butterfly, so better for him to be useful.

Bertram rose from behind the desk, dropping the sheaf of papers in his hands on it, his face wreathed in smiles.

"Lucian! This is an unexpected surprise! What brings you here?"

Lucian waited till Bertram's mother had left and the door closed before telling him everything, Bertram's face grew pale as he listened, and he ran a hand across his hair.

"Can anything be done?" he asked.

Lucian shrugged. "I don't know," he said, unwilling to give his friend false hope. "It's not likely. His Majesty has always been very insistent that the laws are for all, that even he is not exempt from them."

Bertram turned away, clutching his head. "If I ask her to marry me now... Will she?"

Lucian shrugged. "You know her," he said.

Bertram's laugh was hollow. "I do... She won't... Not if she can't save the rest of her family... Damn Hamin, why did he have to be so so..." He turned to Lucian, eyes full of hope. "Can you make a representation to the King?"

"I can try," Lucian said. "But don't expect anything to come of it. Like I said, His Majesty is all about the rule of law. He won't make exemptions, not for anything."

But Lucian had to try all the same.

Betram raked his hand through his hair, clutching it. "I should kidnap her and all of them," he said. "Get them away... You will help me, won't you?"

"If you really mean to do it, you know I will."

Bertram nodded and then looked towards the door. "What do I do about my mother?" he asked quietly. "I can't leave her, and she probably won't agree... I may have to kidnap her too."

Lucian chuckled. "Let's have a large quantity of sleeping potion available then," he said.

"We can take them to Garaner," Bertram said. "I still have friends there, and Sylvester is there as well. You do what you can to influence the king, and I'll make arrangements for the kidnapping."

Lucian nodded, feeling relieved. In the end, abductions might be the only way out. As tempted as he was to leave Hamin behind, he knew it was not an option. At least, they had a backup plan if nothing else worked.

He would also have to let Sylvester know and give the man permission to return to Castrial. He hoped that the King would show some leniency to the family, for Sylvester's sake, if not for anything else. After everything Sylvester had done for Castrial, to spare his family was the least the King could do.

All the same, Lucian didn't allow himself to hope for the King's pardon.

EIGHT

ALARIC'S HEART HAMMERED in his chest as he was led into the King's office. His Majesty's desk was clear today, and the King sat behind it, face impassive.

Alaric bowed low. "Your Majesty."

He was dimly aware of the attendant who had led him in

leaving, closing the door behind him. He raised his head to realise that none of the King's guards were there. He was alone with the King, and that made his heart pound even more.

"Well?" the King asked. "Why does my Shield wish to see me in private?"

"There has been a murder," he says. "The local authorities referred it to my office since the culprit is a noble." He paused, feeling like the collar of his uniform has suddenly grown tight. He resisted the urge to tug at it. "Lord Giles is the culprit."

"And?" the King asked, his voice cold and eyes sharp. "Have you come to plead for a noble?"

"Not for him, no," Alaric said. "For his family. If you can spare them…"

"Why would I?" the King asked. "The law doesn't ask me to spare the family of the guilty. The law insists that they be punished too."

"Laws can be changed." It came out before he could help it. "There was a time the son of a slave wouldn't have been able to be the Shield of Castrial, but here I am. This law is unfair, Your Majesty."

"Maybe," the King acknowledged. "But changing a law isn't something that can happen at the drop of a hat. It will take time. You know that."

"They don't have time." Alaric felt bleak. "They're not just Lord Giles' family… They're Sylvester's as well."

"I'm aware," the King's voice sharpened.

"And mine," Alaric whispered.

The King was silent for a long droplet. "You know I owe you," he said finally. "The entire Castrial owes you, but I can't break the law, even for you, Alaric."

"I'm not asking you to break the law. The King has the right to give pardon, to offer leniency… That's all I ask."

The King sighed. "It's not so simple, Alaric. You know that." He paused. "Let it come to trial. I will do what I can. And if you disagree, you can appeal."

Alaric nodded, knowing himself dismissed and he bowed again. "Thank you, Your Majesty."

It was a start at least. One he had to be content with. Alaric might be angry, he might want something more, but he well understood the realities of the situation.

Once outside the royal study, he paused, taking a few deep breaths to calm himself down before he directed his steps outside, the attendant at his heels like a shadow. He ran into Astra who smiled and nodded at him, and he greeted her back.

The magic of the palace led him directly to the entrance hall where the King usually held his morning court. It was empty right now, since it was well past noon. Only the guards, standing at regular intervals like silent sentinels. The attendant who had been behind him had vanished somewhere, and Alaric went outside, passing stone columns carved with flowers and fruits.

Outside, the sky had turned dark, and Alaric climbed into his carriage. "To the Blade's Office," he said quietly.

"Official business?" Travers asked with the familiarity of someone who had known him all his life.

Travers had been his neighbour after his mother had been freed and had been kind to both of them. When Alaric came back and took office, he had hired the man since he had no job and was forced to live in a poor house. While such places took care of people, they were also crowded more often than not. Travers had been more than happy to accept Alaric's offer.

"You could say that," he said, grimacing. He was not looking forward to the meeting, but he still cared enough about Lucian to tell him what was going on.

Perhaps Lucian would have a better chance of convincing the

King than him. He could hope so, anyway.

Lucian was absent, as it turned out. One of his assistants, a man Alaric was unfamiliar with, called Rhen, told him they didn't know when to expect him back. He ushered Alaric into his own smaller office and bade him sit.

"Is there anything we can do for you, my Lord Shield?" he asked, perfectly polite and courteous.

"I wanted to ask an update on the situation with Sarian and Garaner," Alaric said. "I have co-ordinated with the various ministries to do whatever repairs are needed to the roads and other infrastructure. The route to Sarian goes through the Deneld woods and reports of attacks by magical beasts are common. There's nothing we can do about it, though. But the route to Garaner goes near Skull Cap and I've heard some reports about bandits there. Before I tackle the issue, I want to make sure it's necessary."

A grave expression crossed Rhen's face. "I'm afraid the news is dire, my lord," he said in a hushed voice. "Sarian is mobilising their troops, but we have no idea what they're planning as of now. My lord Blade has apprised the King already and His Majesty will no doubt be calling a meeting of the council to decide on the next course of action."

Rhen was high enough in the Echelon that he would be privy to things that most others didn't. The people in the Blade's office, especially Lucian's assistants, were just below the major ministers in the Echelon.

Alaric hid his dismay. He didn't have enough people to take on the bandits if reports of their numbers were true. The strangest thing was they seemed to attack only soldiers and royal messengers. It made him suspect they weren't bandits at all, but trained soldiers sent by either Sarian or Garaner.

He would have to meet with Astra again and get her to bring some of her people to supplement his. That took priority, if a war was imminent. He would ask his assistant to compile the evidence against Lord Giles and present it to the magistrate to get a warrant for arresting him.

Once he was back from dealing with the bandits, he would lead the arrest himself. As much as he hated it, he couldn't let someone else do it.

He left Lucian's office and made his way back to his own. He had to send someone to meet Astra first. The captain had become someone he trusted, someone he cared for, almost a friend. Alaric never had any friends besides Lucian while growing up, and it was odd to have someone now.

He had thought that he and Lucian would always be friends, but he knew better now. All the same, he found himself trusting Astra. At least, if she were to betray him, he would know she did it for Castrial and not for any other reason.

He could tell himself Lucian had done the same, but it was so difficult to believe that.

It's all in the past.

Lucian was in his past. Now, there was only the Blade of Castrial with whom he had to work.

Nothing else mattered.

NINE

SYLVESTER WAS AT his desk in the embassy. Though the ambassador had no idea about Sylvester's other job, he would be a fool not to have any suspicions. He was more lenient towards Sylvester than the other staff, but that could just be because he was noble born. Sylvester couldn't be certain, and anyway, it didn't matter.

"You have visitors," the ambassador said, causing Sylvester to look up from the reports he was going through.

He rose to his feet. "Visitors?"

Was it Lord Baldir? Sylvester couldn't think of a reason why the man would be here. He couldn't think of anyone else who might walk into the embassy with impunity and have the ambassador look so flustered.

"In my office," the ambassador said. "Come. It's best not to keep them waiting."

Them?

Sylvester followed the ambassador into his office, which was more spartan than his station warranted. The ambassador, Lord Velenk, was a man of simple tastes. When he had first walked into the office, Sylvester had been surprised because Lord Velenk was also one of the richest nobles in Castrial.

The room was nearly bare, with a simple rug on the floor, a very utilitarian desk and chairs. Lord Velenk used candles instead of magic for light, and the ornamental candlesticks on the desk and sconces were the only thing that wasn't starkly simple.

The two visitors who stood waiting inside had Sylvester go to his knee, head bowed.

"Your Majesties," he said.

What were they doing here? He kept his expression neutral and steadied his unruly heart. The rulers of Garaner weren't a couple, despite popular perception. They were cousins who had formed an alliance when the previous King had passed without direct heirs and the kingdom was on the verge of civil war. For the last decade, the two had ruled Garaner well and had ruthlessly suppressed all dissidence. Apart from the disastrous war against Castrial, their rule had been an unmitigated success.

The queen had her own paramours, who were not in the

public eye and seemed to prefer it. The King was a more secretive man, and even more private, but he was single and seemed to not want to change the state of affairs.

"Leave us, Lord Velenk," the queen said, her voice sweet, belying the core of steel the woman had.

"Yes, Your Majesty," Lord Velenk said, bowing, though he paused a droplet to give Sylvester an anxious look.

Sylvester looked down, not meeting the man's eyes and Lord Velenk stepped away, closing the door behind him, leaving Sylvester on one knee in front of the rulers of the people he had been spying on. He didn't move, gave no outward signs of discomfiture. It was an odd custom that the Garanerians had, of being on one knee before their monarchs. Sometimes in Castrial, they would be on their knees before their ruler, but both knees, never one.

"Rise, young lord Giles," the King said, and Sylvester rose, not without difficulty, wobbling a droplet before straightening and standing still, though he still kept his eyes lowered. He was discomfited by the use of his title but again schooled his expression to neutrality. "You may look at us," the King added.

Sylvester raised his eyes and lowered them again. "I would ask what I can do for your majesties," he said.

"Indulge us," the queen said, taking one of the straight backed uncomfortable chairs in front of Lord Velenk's desk. "Have a seat."

Sylvester sat down, wary, as the King took the third chair, sandwiching Sylvester between the two rulers. He stayed silent, not asking anything more, keeping his gaze lowered despite the permission he had been so graciously given to look at them.

"We are curious," the queen said contemplatively. "About why you are really here."

"I'm part of Lord Velenk's staff," Sylvester said stiffly.

"We are aware," the King said. "But you are the only son and heir of Lord Giles, I believe. You have a sizeable inheritance waiting for you in Castrial, and a life of luxury. Yet, you're here." He looked around the room, brows furrowing. "One might wonder why."

Sylvester swallowed. "My father and I are estranged," he said flatly. "We had some disagreements that are rather irreconcilable."

"We've heard something of that," the queen said delicately. "But would such disagreements be enough, we wonder, to drive a young man who had lived in the lap of luxury, someone who was born as a noble, to brave the difficulties of being a—forgive my plain speaking—glorified attendant to Lord Velenk in such inhospitable surroundings."

"I enjoy my work," Sylvester said, again stiffly. "I'm used to being here, and Garaner has never seemed inhospitable to me."

"Of course," the King murmured. "We are known for our hospitality. But still, we wonder, Sylvester—I may call you Sylvester, may I not?—why you prefer such drudgery over a life of luxury in Castrial?"

"This is important work," Sylvester said coldly. "I'm helping the citizens of Castrial who live in Garaner and who may need help. It's far more satisfying than a life of dissolution."

"Admirable," the queen purred. "Truly admirable. We are full of envy for Castrial that their nobles are so high minded. Ours aren't so, you know. But you do know. You have been attending some of the parties thrown by those who seek—what did you call it—a life of dissolution. In fact, I hear you have even been in bed with my brother, for all your high minded talk of serving the citizens of Castrial."

Her voice had sharpened at the last that they could have been daggers piercing his flesh and Sylvester had to fight hard to prevent himself from flinching.

"Lord Baldir and I are both adults who enjoyed each other for a night," Sylvester said, striving to keep his voice steady. "I didn't see any harm in it and neither did Lord Baldir. Even so, after Lord Gwayir's interference, Lord Baldir and I have decided we would not repeat our dalliance." He paused. "No emotions are involved on either of our parts anyway."

"We're aware," the queen said. "Who my brother takes to bed is not my concern usually, but when it's you... A man we suspect of spying for Castrial... We have to be cautious."

Sylvester lifted his gaze to look her straight in the eye. "I'm no spy," he asserted. "I'm only a diplomat who was trying to alleviate my boredom and loneliness for a night."

"Sylvester," the King said, sounding amused as he placed a hand on Sylvester's shoulder. "Do you take us for fools? You who can sit here and look us in the face and instead of quaking, you're calm, measured, each word spoken with thought. We've had many diplomats from various nations here. Even your ambassador would have quailed by now."

"Maybe I'm just that reckless," Sylvester said calmly. "Or fearless. Take your pick, Your Majesties."

"You're certainly steadfast," the queen said with a sigh. "I'm sure if we arrest you or cause you to be harmed, Castrial would raise hell."

"I doubt it," Sylvester said, calm even now, though his palms had begun to sweat.

He could escape, kill them both, but that would serve no purpose. Garaner was looking for an excuse to declare war, and Sylvester was not going to give them one. The death of the rulers might plunge Garaner into a civil war, but then it might not. Sylvester couldn't take a chance, couldn't risk war.

"I'm just a lowly diplomat. My kingdom wouldn't risk alienating a neighbour for me."

"Somehow, I find that hard to believe," the King murmured.

He shook his head, his hand dropping away from Sylvester's shoulder. "What do I do with you, Sylvester? We can't touch you without risking war, and believe me, we don't want one." He paused. "Let me make you a gift to speed you on your way, Sylvester. Your presence is no longer welcome in Garaner. Tomorrow morning, a contingent of my guards shall arrive here to escort you to Castrial. You are no longer welcome in Garaner and should you return, you will be put to death. If you're not here tomorrow, we will consider that an admission of guilt." He smiled at Sylvester. "But to make the journey easier, let me give you a piece of information. Sarian is going to declare war on you. Garaner is not going to be part of it."

He rose and the queen did too, both graceful and elegant.

"We shall inform Lord Velenk that he has to let his assistant go," the queen said. "Tomorrow, Lord Gwayir himself shall come to take you back. Have a nice day, Sylvester."

Sylvester sat straight and still till the royals were out of the room and out the front door after a brief talk with Lord Velenk. Once he was sure they had left the embassy, he allowed himself to slump and to rub a hand across his face.

For all his care and caution, he had still fucked everything up. He had no idea how to make this right. Lord Velenk entered the room, and Sylvester looked up to see the man looking at him with concern.

"I'm sorry," he said. "I trust you, Sylvester, but I have no choice but to let you go."

Sylvester nodded. "I know, sir," he said.

"A message came for you when you were with their majesties," Lord Velenk said. He handed over a large gem that Sylvester recognised as a communication device. The spell on it was wearing off, as evidenced by the lack of lustre. "The Blade of Castrial has asked you to contact him urgently." He looked around the room.

"I'll give you some privacy."

Sylvester drew a deep breath. He didn't know how to tell Lucian that he had been kicked out of Garaner, but did he have a choice? He fed a tendril of magic into the gem, focussing on Lucian. Soon, the gem emitted a beam of light in which Lucian's face was visible.

"Sylvester," he said. "I've some urgent news for you."

"Before that," he interrupted. "Their Majesties have asked me to return to Castrial, never to return, under pain of death." Even as he was opening his mouth to apologise, Lucian spoke.

"I see. Well, never mind about that. Your father has killed someone and will be arrested soon. I fear he and the rest of the family will be punished. You should come back to Castrial."

Sylvester felt the blood drain from his face, but he shook his head. "I can't. The rulers of Garaner have decreed that I have to be accompanied by their guards and if I leave before that, they will declare war on Castrial." He paused. "They said they have no intention of joining Sarian, but Sarian is going to be declaring war any time."

Lucian muttered, "Fuck!" under his breath and Sylvester agreed with the sentiment.

"It doesn't matter," he said after a droplet. "I'll be there in five griels, most likely. Can you hold off the trial till then?"

"I'll see what I can do," Lucian said. "But I think it will be better if you delay your arrival. His Majesty may show leniency to the family at least, but we can't have your name linked with theirs before you return."

"Because I may have to share their punishment," Sylvester muttered.

"Yes," Lucian said. "It doesn't matter that Garaner has exiled you. You're still an asset, and I can't have you compromised at this time. Take care and be back as swiftly as you can."

Sylvester bowed his head. "Of course," he said, his fists clenching, the gem's edges digging into his right palm, the stinging pain indicating that it had probably drawn blood.

"I have sought an appointment with His Majesty," Lucian said. "I'll do my best for them, Sylvester."

Sylvester nodded. "I know."

The light faded and the gem lay inert on his bloody palm. Sylvester wanted to fling it to the wall, to create a portal and rush to Castrial, to get his parents, his sister and the rest of his family away.

But where could he take them? He was no longer welcome in Garaner and Sarian was Castrial's enemy. He slumped to the floor, clutching his head. He had to trust Lucian here and hope that the King remembered Sylvester's contributions.

He feared it wouldn't be enough.

TEN

LUCIAN WAS BUSY the rest of the day, so busy that he barely had time to leave his chair, let alone his office. With Sylvester having been ejected from Garaner, they had to find a replacement. He couldn't blindly trust what the rulers of Garaner might have told Sylvester. He saw that Sylvester felt guilty, that he blamed himself, but Lucian didn't. Sylvester had been there too long, and someone was bound to get suspicious sooner or later.

Finding a replacement for someone as well trained and experienced as Sylvester was not easy, however. Lucian couldn't help but think of Wayan, and a pang of sorrow shot through him again. His brother had died in a foreign land, but at least no one had known he was a spy. That was cold comfort for Lucian.

Hadn't he lost enough already? He couldn't lose any more people. No matter what, he had to protect Lord Giles' family.

Dew's family. Sylvester's family, and most important of all, Alaric's family.

But right now, he had to find someone to replace Sylvester in Garaner, which was no easy task.

"What about Hyacinth?" Rhen asked. "She's experienced enough and has already requested for a transfer."

Lucian frowned. "She's in Ihweith now, isn't she?"

Rhen nodded.

"All right," Lucian said. "We can send Charlotte to Ihweith. It's a safe assignment where she can gain some experience. Authorise the transfer and posting and authorise Hyacinth to use a portal stone. We need her in Castrial yesterday."

Rhen looked hesitant. "What about Sylvester?" he asked. "Are we retiring him?"

If Lucian had his way, he would, but the King had already turned down his request once.

"He's too good and not old enough to be retired," Lucian said. "Let's allow him to have a holiday. We would need someone in Sarian, and Sylvester is the best choice."

"They may suspect him," Rhen warned. "They are Garaner's ally."

"We'll have to cross that bridge when we come to it. Besides, there's no such thing as a permanent ally. Garaner is not used to sharing intelligence with Sarian, and they may still be holding a grudge for how Sarian left them in the lurch during the last war."

Rhen nodded. "All right. Should I draft a posting order for Sylvester?"

"Not right now," Lucian said. "Let's wait for him to return. In the meantime, contact our spies already there. We need to know Sarian's plans."

Rhen left the office and Viola entered. She was also his assistant, junior to Rhen, but no less competent. She took a seat without asking.

"Lord Shield has asked for any intelligence regarding bandits in the Skull Cap area. I've given him what we have." She paused. "Lord Shield feels that it could be something other than bandits." She placed the sheaf of papers she was carrying on his desk. "After looking through the reports that he gave us, I agree."

Lucian pulled the papers towards him. They were local crime reports, but as he read, he saw the pattern that Alaric and Viola might have seen.

"Fuck!" he muttered. "How did they manage to escape our attention for so long?"

"By pretending to be bandits," she said. "But you know what this means, don't you?"

"They know that local crimes are the Shield's purview," Lucian said slowly. "And that even the Shield isn't likely to see that information unless he asks for it."

"And that that information is never passed on to us unless it's during wartime," Viola added. "Lord Shield had to take special permission from His Majesty for sharing of information during peace time."

"We have a spy," Lucian said flatly. "Someone high up in the Echelon, someone who knows well the powers of the Blade and the Shield and the areas where they never overlap."

"That's my conclusion too," Viola said. "What do we do

now?"

"We have to find them," Lucian said, rising from his chair, suppressing a groan as his back and legs protested the movement after being on the chair all day. "I have to seek a meeting with His Majesty and apprise him."

Viola nodded. "I'll tell Rhen. We'll take care of matters here."

"Charlotte and Hyacinth will arrive here any droplet," Lucian said. "As soon as Hyacinth is back, you and Rhen should debrief them and prepare them for then new roles. Have Rhen contact Sylvester as well, but ask him to be careful."

"Of course," Viola said as she accompanied him to the front door. "Should we send a message to the Shield's office? I assume His Majesty will want to discuss it with him as well."

"Sure," Lucian said, hiding his trepidation. He was not looking forward to meeting Alaric, not when Alaric was likely to ignore him as he had been doing.

ELEVEN

ALARIC REINED HIS horse in, the soldiers and guards with him doing the same. His eyes swept the area. It was low hills and woods, with the King's Road running between them. The road was wide and paved, newly repaired. It ran up to the Garaner border, this road. They were close to Skull Cap, the supposedly haunted rock formation that had the shape of a human skull. A few kars past

Skull Cap was the border between Castrial and Garaner, which had guard posts on both sides.

Alaric didn't want to think of Garaner and his time there. It was in the past. But with a war with Sarian looming near, he wondered if it was better for him to go back to being what he was back then. For Castrial's sake.

But the King hadn't asked it of him. He had to think of what he had to do now. The task at hand. Getting rid of these bandits or rather the spies who pretended to be bandits. They had chosen a good spot, he had to admit. Other than royal messengers and merchant caravans, not many passed through here.

Merchant caravans mostly passed through unmolested, except those who carried reports to and from Castrial. It was as if they knew who to target. Today, Alaric and the ten guards with him were all in the guise of messengers. Unless someone from the Shield's office or Royal guards was the spy they were looking for, they would pass on the information to the pretend bandits.

It was disturbing to know there was a spy high in the Echelon and none of them had any idea who it was. Alaric could say it had nothing to do with him, that it was Lucian's job, but he would only be fooling himself. This was everyone's business and fury surged in him at the thought of someone betraying Castrial and everything they valued, everyone they loved.

Still, perhaps he would be able to find the traitor through these spies today.

"They're likely to be closer to Skull Cap," he said softly. "Ride quickly as if we're in a hurry. Remember that we need at least one of them alive."

The guards nodded, Astra tense next to him, eyes hard. "We'll follow your lead, Lord Shield," she said.

Alaric inclined his head before moving, his horse's strides lengthening as he gave it its head. It was a war horse, the type that messengers in Castrial used, known for speed and endurance. This one was named Valin, the name of the wind god. Most horses were named after him and his sons.

Alaric was not religious, and Castrial had no official religion. The Ancient's Creed that was followed in Garaner was not as prevalent in Castrial, except when it came to naming horses. He supposed Garaner must have seen it as an insult, naming horses after a god they revered, even if it was only a minor deity. But religion had never been a reason they had given for war. It was always for other reasons.

Sarian on the other hand was motivated only by greed and the desire to dominate. There was never any ambiguity in their motives. In a way, that was more honest. Though Alaric would have preferred if neither of the nations chose to attack his country. War was an ugly affair, and he had no desire to see it happen.

They rode single file, him in the lead, Astra just behind him, their dark green cloaks with the insignia of the messenger corps of Castrial flapping behind them. As they passed the next line of woods, there was a shout and the thunder of hooves from behind a hill. Soon, they were surrounded by people on horses, dressed head to toe in black, masks hiding their faces, swords drawn.

"No need to let this get ugly," one of them shouted, voice smooth and cultured, only the faintest of Garanerian accent to their words. "Just give us your valuables and we'll be on our way."

"What if we refuse?" Alaric asked, keeping his horse under control, one hand on its neck and the other still holding the reins.

"Don't try to play hero," the same person said, but there seemed almost an excitement to them now.

Alaric drew his own sword. "We work for the King and Castrial, and we refuse to surrender to you."

Astra drew abreast of him, drawing her own sword, hand steady, and eyes like flint. Behind them, the rest of their group too unsheathed their swords.

The one who had been speaking gave an exaggerated sigh. "Don't say we didn't warn you," they said before charging, but Alaric saw the fleeting glance they gave another one who stood at the back, and the infinitesimal nod in response.

So, the one at the back was the real leader. This other one was there to confuse them.

Alaric's horse danced out of the way, and he parried the thrust of the bandit's sword. The bandits' mounts were not as well trained as theirs, Alaric realised. He sent a fire spell close to the speaker's horse, and as he expected, it spooked, whinnying and rising on its hind legs. They tried his best to hold on, but their riding skills were lacking. They leapt from the spooked horse and landed on their feet and Alaric charged towards them. Their mask had somehow untied, and Alaric met the shrewd gaze of a man who brought his sword up to defend against Alaric's strike. Alaric used his sword as a conduit to send another fire spell which went through his chest, cauterizing the path through his body, leaving a smoking hole in his middle.

The man stood there for a droplet, eyes wide and uncomprehending before he tottered and fell. Alaric turned to the rest of the bandits who were still fighting, unaware of the fate that had met their leader. Alaric rode towards one of the two who were harrying Astra, who was holding her own but barely. One of them was the real leader he had noticed earlier. He drove his sword through their shoulder as Astra thrust hers through the heart of the other bandit.

The injured bandit cursed and lunged at Alaric, but Alaric was ready. He raised the hilt of his sword and knocked him out. The bandit crumpled on top of his own horse, and Alaric caught its reins to prevent it from bolting.

The man had cursed in Serenian. Interesting. It seemed that

they had been pretending to be Garanerians to confuse them.

"Kill everyone else," he said, raising his voice and turned away from the fray.

Screams and sounds of steel rending flesh filled the air, and soon, there was silence except for harsh breathing, the sound of a horse's hoof as it shifted and the jangle of the mail shirts that they had all worn under their coats.

"It's done, Lord Shield," Astra said from behind him. "We have gathered the corpses and the horses as well. Shall we leave?"

"Thank you," Alaric said, relinquishing the reins of the bandit's horse to one of the guards. "Take him to the Lord Blade. They are better at questioning spies. We still have our work to do." He looked at Astra. "Ask the backup team to make sure there are no more of the bandits hidden somewhere. No need to leave anyone alive."

Astra nodded. "I'd already sent the message," she said. "Let's go home."

Home.

Castrial.

Lucian.

Alaric didn't want to think too much of anything, especially not Lucian, but it was as if his heart didn't get that. It insisted on reminding him of Lucian at every possible time, making him want to just go to Lucian, to talk to him, to kiss him, to–

Alaric shut the train of thoughts down. Thoughts of Lucian was more luxury than he could afford right now. There was still the matter of Lord Giles, and his trial and arrest. He couldn't afford to get sidetracked.

He followed Astra and the guards as they rode towards Castrial.

TWELVE

THE ROAD STRETCHED out ahead, the sun shining overhead, the trees on both sides of the road standing like sentinels, providing not much in the way of shade. The carriage and its escort of horses moved fast, even though Sylvester knew they didn't have to be. He was under an armed guard by a division of the Elite troops of Garaner and was being accompanied by Lord Baldir.

There was no possibility that he was going to make a break for it. It had been a surprise when Lord Baldir had turned up to escort him instead of Lord Gwayir. No explanation had been forthcoming, and Sylvester didn't ask for one. What did it matter anyway? Whoever escorted him was all the same.

Under normal circumstances, Sylvester wouldn't have minded going slow or taking his time or even riding in the carriage with Lord Baldir as he was expected to do, but after the news about his father, all he could think of was getting home as early as possible. He was the only one on a horse without an armour, and the soldiers kept him in their midst. It wasn't out of any desire not to see him hurt, but because they feared he would escape.

At the fireside during the night, whenever they had to stop by in the wilderness, Sylvester had heard snatches of conversation which seemed to indicate that these soldiers at least believed he was a spy and seemed to believe him to be possessed of some extraordinary magic that enabled him to escape any situation. Utter nonsense, but superstition was something that ran rampant in soldiers, no matter which nation they belonged to. Sometimes, listening to them made Sylvester remember that all three nations were once one. One empire under the monarch of Sarian.

Even though it had been centuries since, Sarian hadn't been ready to let go. There had been bloody wars between all three nations over the centuries till finally, they had settled into this uneasy peace with Sarian and Garaner more allies than enemies and Castrial having to struggle by herself.

Sylvester's butt was numb and this thighs chafed from all the riding even though he was no novice on the saddle. He just wasn't used to long travel without magic. Eyeing the carriage, Sylvester wondered what Lord Baldir would say if he went in there. The carriage was supposed to be for both of them, but Sylvester had staunchly refused its use till now. One reason was he didn't want to stay in a confined space, and certainly not with Lord Baldir. He wasn't embarrassed; Sylvester had enough of a thick skin that being in the presence of the man he had lied to and slept with and stolen from wasn't something that bothered him. He just wanted to avoid the man's questions.

Lord Baldir was more than he appeared. Of that Sylvester had no doubts now. The man's mind had been too well ordered, the wards around his room too complex and carrying his magical signature for him to be the fool and hedonist he appeared to be. Sylvester had thought it was nepotism that he held the post he did. He was the queen's brother, after all. But he had worked under the former Minister of War, and his presence here was probably to discover what Sylvester knew.

There would be no torture or mind magic tricks involved. It would be a conversation between gentlemen. The kind Sylvester hated the most. Had always hated. Nobles used words to play political games, and it was something he had been exposed to from his cradle. He was certain he could hold his own, but he still hated it and wanted to avoid it.

But right now, sparring with words with Lord Baldir was beginning to sound attractive, compared to riding on this dusty, hot road for one kar more. His body ached too much, and his eyes stung. The handkerchief that he had wrapped around his nose and mouth and the one he had wrapped around his forehead protected somewhat, but not fully. The dirt roads in Garaner were a far cry from the cobbled streets of Castrial or the stone paved roads of Sarian. Despite how tightly packed the dirt was and devoid of any breaks, it still threw up dust in clouds.

He could have used magic, but he just didn't have it in him to divide his focus. His anxiety for his father and his family was eating him from the inside already.

Fortunately, they reached a town as the day dwindled and the leader of the guards called a halt at the biggest inn in town. It had rooms to spare, luckily, and Sylvester was happy to get out of his travel stained clothes and to sink into the large tub of water the servants had brought up.

He had spare clothes in the large chest that had been brought into his room. He was looking forward to finishing his bath and then change into clean clothes and sleep in a proper bed.

He closed his eyes as he leaned against the edge of the tub, sinking into the hot water. It was heaven. The servants scrubbed his back and chest and changed the water when it got too dirty. Sylvester sank into the water again and asked the others to leave. Sighing in pleasure, he closed his eyes again.

Twelve days on the road already and he was wearier than he expected. He would be in Castrial in another sixteen days at the most. He knew that it wouldn't matter. His father's trial would be over by then. Perhaps it was already over. He didn't know, and with him being on the road and travelling in the company he did, Lucian wouldn't be able to contact him. If the rulers of Garaner or Lord Baldir had any proof about his being a spy, he would be executed without a trial. As things stood now, they had no proof and Sylvester was part of the ambassador's staff, not to speak a nobleman of Castrial. They could escort him out of the kingdom, but if something happened to him, they would have to answer to Castrial, and Garaner was trying too hard to avoid another war.

Killing a spy was legal, killing someone they suspected to be a spy was entirely different. The rulers of Garaner might be autocrats, but they still believed in the rule of law.

So, Sylvester had to endure for another sixteen or seventeen days, make sure no one found out he was a spy, give them nothing. No matter what happened to his family back home, he was unable to help now. Once he was home, he could perhaps do something. Appeal to the King, maybe.

He wished his father weren't such a fool or so uncaring. But if he was, if he was anything except the man he was, Sylvester wouldn't have left home, wouldn't have become a spy, wouldn't have risked his life every damn day. He would be with his family, and they wouldn't be in the situation they were in now.

The awareness of someone's gaze on him was what made him open his eyes. Through the fog of steam in the bathroom, he could only see the silhouette of a man. Sylvester's weapons lay within easy reach, his escorts not yet divesting him of them, and the servants taking care not to move them out of reach.

"Who is it?" Sylvester asked, even as he leapt out of the tub, water flying everywhere as he grabbed his sword and pointed it at the intruder.

"Relax," a familiar voice drawled. "I only want to talk."

Lord Baldir waved away the steam and fog, the spell barely seeming to need any effort. The man had already bathed and changed, his hair damp and his clothes rich and with nary a wrinkle.

"Could you point that thing elsewhere?" he asked, wrinkling his nose as he stared at the sword which was pointing at his chest.

Sylvester lowered the sword, grabbed a towel and wrapped it around his waist. "Why are you here?"

"To talk," Lord Baldir said, crossing one elegant leg over the other as he deposited himself on a stool. Despite his best efforts, he still looked completely out of place.

"I don't know what we have to talk about," Sylvester said drily. "Your sister and cousins have exiled me, made the ambassador fire me, and I'm leaving Garaner branded as a spy."

"If you weren't a spy–" Lord Baldir began.

"If I were a spy, I would be dead now, and we both know it!" Sylvester snapped.

"Come now, Sylvester," Lord Baldir said. "We have no proof,

and you know it. But that doesn't mean you're innocent. We both know you aren't."

"I need to get dressed," Sylvester said.

"I've more than seen you naked," Lord Baldir said drily. "You don't have to be coy. To be honest, I am more afraid of letting you out of my sight than how you feel about my presence."

Sylvester sighed. "I won't run," he said. "No matter how badly I may want to. Your sister and cousin made their position very clear. I won't risk a war."

"They won't just because you choose to run, no matter what they may have said," Lord Baldir said.

"It still has repercussions," Sylvester said as he moved behind the folding screen with his clothes hanging from them on hooks on the inside. He took another towel and started towelling his hair. "I can't let my kingdom pay the price for my selfishness."

"Mmm... Why are you in such a hurry, though?"

"My family is in trouble," Sylvester said briefly. "I got the message the same day your rulers exiled me. So, I would have left Garaner anyway."

"I'm sorry." A pause. "May I ask why you did it, though? You must have known getting close to me was never going to be worthwhile."

Sylvester made no answer as he hung his towels on the free hooks and started pulling on his underclothes.

"I don't know what you mean."

A sigh. "Of course, you don't. You were just looking for a good time."

"Naturally," Sylvester said as he started to dress. "It's not my fault you people are paranoid."

"Of course, it has to be our paranoia. Not because you're guilty." Frustration tinged Lord Baldir's tone. "Let's not play this game, Sylvester. We can't prove it and even if you admit it to me here, that's not actually proof."

"I told you I'm innocent," Sylvester said as he started tying the laces of his tunic. "If you can't believe it, that's your problem."

"I thought you were the Red Shadow."

Sylvester frowned, his hands fumbling with the final two laces. "The what shadow? Who is that?" He was genuinely curious. It was his first time hearing of something like that.

"Oh, it's nothing you would have known," Lord Baldir said. "It's just what we call the assassin who killed my predecessor."

Sylvester's hand stilled briefly on the way to his coat. "Oh." He took the coat and slid his right arm into the sleeve.

"You don't know who it is, by the way, do you?" There was a strange tension in Lord Baldir's voice.

"I've never heard of a Red Shadow before," Sylvester said, as he stepped from behind the screen, the coat with the insignia of his family around him. It was warm and soft, but Sylvester was beginning to be a bit suffocated. He walked past Lord Baldir and entered his bedroom, going past it to the dining room beyond where the table was already laden with covered dishes.

"I grant you've never heard of the Red Shadow. That doesn't mean you don't know their real identity."

Sylvester snorted as he seated himself at the table and started ladling food on his plate. Rice, lentils, leafy vegetables, chicken slices, some vegetable stew, and flatbread both of which he left alone.

"Join me, since you're here anyway. It's too much food for one person."

"Agree," Lord Baldir said as he sat down and took the flatbread and the stew. "Surprised a noble of Castrial should feel so, however."

Sylvester snorted. "Most nobles don't, I agree, but there are exceptions." He sniffed at a meat dish. "I would be happy to have spicy food again, though."

Lord Baldir chuckled. "Ah yes, the famous Castrial cuisine. I've never tried it."

"With your rank, I suppose you don't need to go to other countries for any reason," Sylvester said as he bit into a piece of chicken.

He was used to Garanerian food, and too hungry to care for how bland everything was anyway. The chicken was well cooked and still juicy, which made up for the lack of anything to flavour it.

"Not really," Lord Baldir said, eating delicately. "I was part of my predecessor's staff, you know. He mentored me." He paused. "He was something very rare in this world."

"And what is that?" Sylvester asked, taking a sip of water.

"A truly kind man." Lord Baldir shredded the piece of flatbread in his hand. "It's not easy to fill his shoes, not just because I'm not as good as him at the work, but because he was such a good person."

Sylvester picked up a piece of fried vegetable and bit into it. "I'm sorry for your loss."

"I will avenge his death," Lord Baldir said as his eyes met Sylvester's squarely.

"Have you considered that whoever killed him must have been someone who was acting on orders? That they probably didn't want to do it, but had no choice?"

The droplet he spoke, Sylvester wished he could take them back. So stupid, but he had got alarmed by Lord Baldir's expression when he spoke of revenge. Fear for Alaric who deserved better than to be turned into a weapon filled his heart, and the words he spoke from that fear were truly foolish.

Lord Baldir's gaze never left his.

"So, you do know who it is, and you care for them," he said

softly. "Who are they? A friend? A lover?"

Sylvester forced out a light laugh. "How would I know an assassin? I'm just assuming, of course. Maybe they're someone who revels in death."

"It's likely, judging by the state of the bodies left behind," Lord Baldir said quietly.

Sylvester swallowed, dropped his eyes, and ladled some gravy on to his plate.

"Do we have to talk of it at the dinner table?" he asked plaintively.

Lord Baldir laughed, but there was no mirth in his eyes.

THIRTEEN

LUCIAN GOT INTO his carriage, telling Davies to take him to Hamin's house. Hamin had been arrested yesterday, and his family was put under house arrest till the trial. What happened after that would depend on the outcome of the trial. Perhaps he should be going to the Shield's office, examining the evidence against Hamin, but Lucian wanted to see Estella first, to reassure himself that she was all right.

The carriage moved swiftly over the cobbled street which was more or less empty so early in the morning. Lucian knew that Estella would be up already. She had set routines which never wavered. It hadn't changed even in the days following Dew's death, even though she had been devastated. So Lucian wasn't expecting something like Hamin's arrest to change anything.

As expected, guards surrounded the house, the royal guards, not the ones from the Shield's Office. His Majesty had granted a contingent of royal guards to Alaric, to be used for the Shield's office till they had numbers enough to not need them. Lucian hoped the guards wouldn't stop him, even though it would be within their rights to do so. Without a written order of permission from the King, no one was allowed to meet people under house arrest.

Perhaps he should have gone to see Hamin, examine the evidence against him, but what would have been the point? Hamin didn't seem bothered by what he did, and he had freely admitted he was guilty to Lucian. He had no doubt that the man would have done the same to Alaric, if he even deigned to talk to him. His fists clenched, and he breathed out slowly, counting his breaths, allowing his anger to dissipate.

He tolerated Hamin for the sake of his family, a part of him even cared, but he still quite intensely, savagely, disliked the man, and he always would.

A guard stepped on to his path, spear blocking his way as he walked in through the open gates.

"Lord Blade," the man said quietly. "No one's allowed inside."

Lucian had expected it, but all the same, he had to try.

"I just want to see them. I don't even have to meet them. Please."

"Apologies, Lord Blade. It cannot be done."

Lucian was mustering arguments when a familiar voice spoke. "And what is the Blade of Castrial doing here, I wonder. Has he forgotten the law or is it that he thinks himself above it?"

Lucian wanted to close his eyes, but he couldn't, not here, with the eyes of the guards trained on him. He schooled his features to neutrality as he turned to face Alaric who appeared to have just arrived.

He bowed. "Lord Shield."

Alaric bowed back. "And what, if I may ask, brings you here, my lord Blade?"

Lucian's heart spasmed, as the memory of Alaric calling him that teasingly came to mind. He kept himself from wincing, but barely.

"I wanted to visit them," he said, gesturing to the house behind him. "Can I beg your indulgence, my lord Shield?"

Alaric's eyes remained cold, his expression remote. "My indulgence cannot be above the law. Unless you're part of the family, you're not allowed in. But then, if you were part of the family, you'll be in there with them and this conversation would be moot."

Lucian was about to plead again, no matter how useless it was when Alaric spoke again.

"They're all well, if that would put your mind at ease. They are only detained, not ill-treated, and they're allowed to leave the house with a few guards to accompany them."

The laws regarding house arrest didn't stop the detainees from leaving the house with a sufficient number of guards to ensure they wouldn't escape or make plans for such. They were not allowed to visit anyone, but to leave the house to buy necessities and such only.

Lucian bowed his head. "Thank you for letting me know." He paused. "I would like to review the evidence against Lord Giles and to speak to him."

"That's your right under law, and his too, if he wants to see you."

Lucian frowned. "Why wouldn't he?"

"I'm not privy to his thoughts, but so far, he has refused to see anyone who has attempted to visit including his wife and daughter."

Lucian's heart sank. "I see."

Alaric sighed. "He did it, Lord Blade. He admitted it when asked, seemed not to care about confessing such a thing. He still seems to think that he won't be convicted. Shows no remorse whatsoever, and His Majesty most abhors unrepentant criminals. I fear he and his family with him will likely be given the highest possible punishment."

On the surface, the words could be construed as taunting, and Lucian had no doubt that the guards would see it so. But Lucian knew Alaric. Even now, even after everything, he knew Alaric, and this was his way of letting Lucian know that he should attempt to convince Hamin to show some remorse at the trial so as not to anger the King. He despaired of his ability to do so, however. If only Hamin would see his family! They might be better able to convince him. He doted on Keylin. Surely, he would listen to her?

Of course, with Hamin, doting meant he gave her money and never asked what for. Lucian doubted if the man ever spent time in her company other than at dinner, and if he even knew what she was like.

He hadn't known anything about Dew either.

Memories of Dew were like an old scar that still ached from time to time. She was his friend at a time he needed someone, and he would always be grateful for that. There was a part of him that would always love her. Losing her had been painful, and there had been days when he missed her so fiercely, his chest ached with it. It still felt like a piece of his heart was missing.

Dew's death had taught Lucian that there were degrees of grief. The grief of losing Wayan had been more intense, more terrible than the grief of losing Dew, but both had shattered his heart, left him with invisible scars that ached.

But missing Dew or missing Wayan was nothing like the yawning chasm in his soul whenever he had thought of Alaric these past five farials, and Alaric wasn't even dead. Lucian knew it, even though he had been unable to find him. Whenever he had time, he had gone looking, but he had never been able to find any traces to his whereabouts.

Till one day the King had summoned him and told him about Alaric, about his plan. Lucian should have been angry, should have felt disgusted, but he wasn't. He had suspected when the King had commanded him to write that letter and ordered him to not to save Alaric back then. He didn't suspect what the King had in mind, but he knew that he had plans involving Alaric.

Knowing what those plans were after all these farials... Lucian's heart ached for Alaric, and he wished he'd risked it all back then, but what good would that have done? If Lucian had acted based on his feelings, perhaps Garaner would have won the war and all Castrilians would be suffering now. What was one or two people's suffering set against that of thousands?

Besides, the past didn't matter now. All that mattered was that Alaric was safe, that he had a future. The King had asked Lucian to assist Astra in finding the real murderer of Lord Hark, to clear Alaric's name.

And now, here they were, him and Alaric, and no matter how deep the chasm that was between them now, no matter the disdain on Alaric's face when he looked at him, no matter how Alaric preferred to ignore him whenever they met, it was enough that he was here, back in Lucian's life where Lucian could see him every day.

But he couldn't afford to think of Alaric or Dew or Wayan right now. There was war brewing, and he had bigger problems than Alaric's attitude. Bigger problems, if he was honest, than Hamin's fate or the fate of his family. But Lucian had to try to save them at least.

One of the guards spoke from behind him. "Are you going out, miss?"

He turned to see Keylin who looked startled to see him.

"Lucian!" she exclaimed, coming towards him.

The guards made no move to stop her, and though he held out his hand for her, she surprised him by hugging him. He hugged back, his worry for her overshadowing everything else.

"How are you?" he asked. "Is everyone holding up?"

"Nothing else we can do," she said quietly as she disengaged herself. "What are you doing here?"

There was hope in her eyes, and Lucian hated that he would have to dash it.

"I came to see how you're doing," he said.

"Oh," she said, as her eyes dimmed. But she smiled brightly even then. "We're well, Lucian. Don't worry about us." She turned to the guard who had spoken earlier. "Yes, I'm going out. Can I be accompanied by Lord Blade?"

Alaric sighed from next to Lucian.

"I'm sorry," he said quietly. "But laws are laws. You cannot go out without guards from the Shield's office."

Lucian noticed for the first time that Alaric wasn't wearing his cloak of office. He looked rather dishevelled and dusty, as if he had just arrived from some distance. He was also wearing the uniform of a royal courier.

How had he not noticed this before? He wanted to ask Alaric what he had been doing, why he was here now, but this was neither the time nor place.

"I see," Keylin said. "I... I want to visit my fiancé, if you don't mind."

"Once again, I'm sorry," Alaric said. "You can't visit anyone, not even with guards."

Keylin's face fell, but she turned a beseeching glance on Lucian which reminded him that she was probably aware of the laws as much as he did.

While normally, she wouldn't be allowed to visit anyone, she could if Alaric himself were to escort her. Or if he allowed Lucian to. Their status in the Echelon allowed them privileges not afforded to others.

But Alaric had already refused, and Lucian was not going to argue with him in public over it.

But even if Keylin wasn't allowed to visit Bertram, there was nothing preventing Lucian from doing so. He could perhaps talk to Bertram, have him send a message to Keylin, to persuade her to marry Bertram before Hamin' trial so that she wouldn't have to share whatever fate befell the rest of her family. It was selfish of Bertram and him, but there was nothing they could do for the rest of the family whereas Keylin could be saved.

And yet, here was Alaric who, he was certain, was here for him. Because there was no reason for Alaric to have hastened here in the state he was in unless it was something vitally important. He must have gone to Lucian's office and upon being told where Lucian was, must have hurried here. He would have stopped to change otherwise.

"I'm sorry, Keylin," he said. "I can't come with you anyway. I have something urgent to attend to. I just stole a droplet to come here to see how you're all doing."

Her smiled faded, and she bit her lip, looking away.

"I see. It's fine, Lucian... I... I think I don't want to go out now."

She managed a shaky smile before she went back to the house.

Lucian turned to Alaric. "Why do you want to see me?"

"Follow me," Alaric said, dropping his voice to a soft whisper. "Too many eyes and ears here."

Lucian nodded as he followed Alaric.

FOURTEEN

THE DUNGEON WAS cold but well lit, and the prisoner hung from his manacled wrists. He was stripped down to his undergarments. Alaric's people had searched diligently for weapons before handing him over to the Blade's office. There had been no poison on him or inside his mouth either.

The man's hair had been shaven off, but aside from that, he

was unharmed, the injuries he had sustained in the fight already healed by the prison healers. As Alaric had suspected, he was Serenian, but the one who had spoken was Garanerian. Some letters they had found in his clothes indicated that he was a Garanerian spy to Sarian, who had joined this group's mission.

But their mission had to be more than stealing confidential information. But so far, they hadn't made much headway with their interrogation.

Alaric looked at Lucian. "So, you're unable to find anything? No hint of who the spy in our ranks is?"

Only he, Lucian, and Astra were there. Today was the best opportunity for them to interrogate the prisoner without anyone else noticing. Lord Giles' trial was going on, the King presiding. It was unthinkable for the Blade and the Shield to be absent, but the other officials wouldn't know that. The King was the only one who knew since they needed his permission.

Lucian shook his head. "Not unless we resort to torture. His mind is well protected against intrusions."

They spoke in the dialect of Castrial's language that the common people spoke, and which was rather difficult for non-natives to follow. Lucian had picked it up from Alaric when they were both boys, and Astra had been exposed to it from the servants at home. They were certain that no spy would have been able to learn the dialect unless they had lived among the common people for farials. With how the common people were seen by the nobles till recently, it seemed unlikely for any spy to seek a home among them.

"His Majesty doesn't approve of torture," Astra said. "Are you sure there's no other way?"

Torture had always been against the law, but other kings had closed their eyes to it. Whatever his faults, Garret wanted things done by law. Mind magic was permitted, but not torture, either physical or mental.

"He's too disciplined and too determined," Lucian said. "And yes, I'm well aware that His Majesty frowns upon torture. I'm not eager, myself, but there doesn't seem to be another way."

Alaric studied the man. He had been rendered unconscious by a spell, but even then, his mind was a fortress.

"Is he like that when asleep as well?" he asked.

"As far as we were able to determine, yes." Lucian's eyes held a speculative gleam as they met his. "You have an idea."

Alaric both hated and loved that Lucian knew him so well. "Yes. I'm not sure it will work, but what have we to lose?"

Lucian chuckled, a rich sound, and Alaric hadn't realised just how much he had missed it. It made him lose focus for a droplet as he stared, mesmerised, at Lucian. He drew his eyes away the next, bringing his mind back to focus.

"Get him drunk," Alaric said. "Perhaps his mind would be more amenable then."

Most people trained to keep their mental walls up even when asleep, but there weren't many who took into account the effects of alcohol and the few magical herbs that lowered inhibitions and constraints and made them lose focus.

"Good plan," Lucian said. "I'll ask–"

"Lord Blade!" someone called as hurried footsteps approached. Lucian tensed and Alaric stared as well. Had someone discovered their absence? If so, who?

A man in the uniform of the Blade's office appeared, eyes wide. Lucian relaxed.

"It's Desmond," he said quietly. "I'd asked him to contact me here when the trial was over."

Alaric was startled. The trial was already over? They hadn't noticed time passing.

"The trial is over, and His Majesty is deliberating the

sentencing now." Desmond panted. He held out three rings. "He asked that the three of you portal in so as to avoid anyone suspecting you weren't there." His eyes flickered to the prisoner. "I'll stay here, be on guard."

There were guards outside the prison too, but having someone here helped. After all, they couldn't be sure someone wouldn't attempt to kill the prisoner to silence him. Not many were informed of him or his arrest, but Alaric knew they couldn't take it for granted that the spy in their ranks didn't learn of it.

They took the rings; it was expressly forbidden to portal to the King's side, and there were wards linked to his blood that prevented anyone from doing so. Yet, the King had asked them to, which meant these rings were supposed to get through those wards. Alaric couldn't help but be concerned by their existence, and from their expressions, he knew Lucian and Astra felt the same. But they had no choice now.

They put on the rings. Alaric sent a tendril of magic to the ring, visualising His Majesty's face. The world blurred around him, and he lost his footing, staggering next to Lucian as they were in front of the King. The only other person there was Astra's second, Darla.

"You're here," the King said, waving Lucian and Alaric to their seats while Astra took her position behind him. "I was about to pronounce the sentence."

Alaric was alarmed at the King's tone. His Majesty looked angry, lips pressed together and face red. His form was stiff.

"Your Majesty," he said.

"I've never seen a prisoner behave as that man did today. Not only did he admit to committing the crime, but he also didn't seem to think there was anything wrong with it!" The King's hand gripped the sceptre set on to the side of his throne tightly. His voice was hard and cold. "He had no remorse for what he did. A human life was cut short, and he seems to think of it as no matter. Because the man was a commoner. As if that's what matters!"

Alaric bit his tongue, stopped himself from speaking. Anything he might say now would cause more harm than good. Lord Giles was not the kind of man who deserved anyone's sympathy. All the same, Alaric was worried about his family. The King had promised leniency, but with how Lord Giles behaved during the trial, how much could he depend on it?

Lucian seemed to be under some internal struggle himself. Alaric recalled that Lord Giles' family was as good as Lucian's own now. If the King sentenced him to death or exile, he would have to arrange for Lucian to smuggle them out of Castrial. But with Sylvester compromised and not able to live in Garaner anymore, where could they go? There was always Ihweith, or another nation across the ocean which were on friendly terms with Castrial and where an immigrant Castrilian noble and his family would be safe.

Why didn't Lucian or Sylvester do it? Was it because they feared Alaric wouldn't let go? That they thought his hatred of Lord Giles was so intense that he would pursue them no matter where they went? No other explanation presented itself and he couldn't help how his lips twisted at the thought.

He wished that Lucian had trusted him enough to know that he wouldn't have pursued them if they had escaped. Not even Lord Giles. Did he really believe Alaric had become so vindictive?

The King made a gesture that opened the curtains that hid them all. He stood up and walked to the edge of the stage.

"My dear subjects," he said quietly, his voice amplified by a spell. "We have tried Lord Giles and have found him guilty of the crime he is charged with. He deserves the worst punishment for his crime, but his son, Sylvester, has been selflessly serving Castrial for farials and deserves consideration. I exempt Sylvester Giles from the punishment meted out to his family. Lord Giles and his family are hereby sentenced to slavery for life, to be sold in public auction to the highest bidder within two days."

He stepped back, the curtains slid back, and the spell dissipated.

Alaric couldn't speak or move. Slavery. Public auction. He wasn't sure if the King was being merciful or vindictive. It was better than death, better even than exile, but that didn't make it all right. It would depend on the master, after all.

And Keylin and Benjamin... Both of them were young, beautiful, and Alaric couldn't be certain that they would be safe in any noble's household.

"Alaric," the King said. "Stay. All the rest of you, leave."

Lucian, Astra, and Darla bowed to the King before leaving through the door at the back. The stage was set with so many wards that no one outside would be able to hear anything they speak in here, not even if they were listening at the door or used magical means to eavesdrop.

"I want you to buy them." The King's gaze was hard. "Bid first. No one will bid against you."

"Your Majesty!"

Not that he hadn't thought of it, but he would not have expected the king to take a hand in an auction.

"I know it revolts you, that there are no slaves in your household, but you have to do this." The King paused. "I know I promised to be lenient, but this is the extent of my leniency. If he had shown any remorse..." The King shook his head, pressing his lips together. "All the same, the family is innocent and must be protected. There is no one else I can trust."

"There's Lucian," Alaric said, just for arguing.

"Lucian's status is different," the King said quietly. "His relationship to Hamin's family is different as well. There will inevitably be talk about Keylin Giles and whoever owns her, but only if she is in your house can those rumours be refuted completely."

Alaric couldn't gainsay that, but he also knew there had to be more. It came to him suddenly and he was ashamed he hadn't realised it.

"You're trying to appease Sylvester."

"As I said, he has toiled hard for Castrial in a foreign land. Protecting his family is the least I can do for him. Between you and Lucian, who do you think he would prefer to have control over his family?"

"Lucian is his direct superior," Alaric said quietly. "I see what you mean."

"I'm glad. You will do it?"

Alaric nodded. "I will do it, Your Majesty." He paused. "I would have even had you not asked, but you asking makes it easier for me. Thank you for your grace."

The King's lips twisted in a grimace. "My grace," he murmured before rising. "Walk with me."

Alaric bowed and rose to his feet, following the King out of the room, Lucian, Astra, and Darla, who were waiting outside, trailing behind him.

FIFTEEN

SYLVESTER LAY AWAKE in the early waves of dawn, the curtains of his bed and room both closed. It was one of the more luxurious inns they had stayed at and likely to be the last they would stay at since the rest of the way was through farmlands and forests. There might be an inn or two, but Sylvester wasn't sure.

Eleven days more and he would be back at Castrial. He wasn't sure where he would go next, whether he would even be able to leave. He hoped that his family was safe, but it wasn't something he could be certain of. The laws of Castrial were strict and the King was impartial when it came to meting out punishments. The days when a noble could get away with whatever he did were long past.

All the same, he could hope.

Despite the closed curtains, the room slowly brightened, casting light on the chairs, the chaise longue, the chest of drawers and the clothes strewn haphazardly on them. Seeing the clothes reminded Sylvester he wasn't alone in the bed or in the room. Reswick was fast asleep, curled up on his side and close enough for Sylvester to feel his warmth, but not so close that their bodies were touching.

Lord Baldir, not Reswick.

But it didn't seem right to call the man Lord Baldir after fucking him every chance he got. At least the nights were entertaining, and the sex was fantastic. All the same, Sylvester had to wonder why either of them were doing this. Reswick and he both knew where the other stood, and even though he had no proof, Reswick seemed certain of Sylvester's status as a spy.

Which begged the question why he wanted to do this. Sylvester was worried and in need of distractions, but what was Reswick's angle? That he had an angle, Sylvester didn't doubt. But what? It wasn't clear to him and that made him warier than ever.

A knock at the door made Reswick startle and sit up on the bed, eyes wide, but with no trace of drowsiness. Like Sylvester, the man had trained to be fully awake the droplet he opened his eyes.

How had he ever thought him to be useless? Sylvester knew best how masks worked since he had been wearing one for countless farials now. And yet, he had failed to recognise Reswick's. It was an error in judgement, and he had no doubt that it was that which led to the present situation.

"Who is it?" Reswick called out.

"My lord," a whiny voice spoke from outside. "There's a message for a Sylvester Giles."

Sylvester was on his feet and started to pull on his clothes. "Give me a minute," he said.

Reswick didn't move from the bed, watching him from underneath his hooded eyes.

"You're expecting a message?"

He wasn't. Lucian wouldn't risk it, and if he did, that meant– Sylvester had no idea what that meant, but his heart hammered in his chest, his hands shaking as he fumbled with the laces of his shirt. He shook his head and ran a hand through his hair, trying to make it look less dishevelled before opening the door.

He saw the knife too late, and it plunged into his gut. Pain exploded from within him, and he fell down even as Reswick bounded from the bed and had snatched his sword to run the man through.

Sylvester saw his killer fall next to him, eyes wide with pain and panic and Reswick knelt next to him, his hand on the man's temple.

"What..." Sylvester gasped, looking at Reswick's hard eyes. "What are you doing?"

"Finding out who sent him," Reswick said. He raised his voice. "Get a healer in here, quickly!"

"Oh." Sylvester didn't know what to make of it.

Reswick didn't send the assassin, and as someone rushed into the room and knelt by him, hands poking at his wound, Sylvester grimaced and lost consciousness.

WHEN HE CAME TO, he was still in the inn, in his bed. Pain lashed him when he attempted to move. A pair of arms came to support him, helping him sit up before pushing a glass of water at him which he took in hands that were still not quite steady and drank, sipping slowly.

"How long was I out for?" he asked as he gave the glass back to Reswick.

"Three days," Reswick said. "We feared you might die, but the healer here is skilled, and you were lucky. The knife went through your belt so the wound you sustained was less fatal than it might have been."

"Three days," Sylvester said, voice hollow.

"And you have to stay in bed for another three at least," Reswick said, sounding apologetic. "If you want to live, that is."

"Did you find out who sent that man?"

"He's a Serenian spy. He had orders to kill both of us, it seems. He didn't know we were both in the same room or he would have used some other method. He had poison gas pellets on him when we searched him."

Sylvester frowned. "I thought Garaner and Sarian were allies. Why would they target you?"

"Because I advised my sister and cousin against supporting Sarian in their war efforts against Castrial. The last time, Sarian left us in the lurch, and we suffered a defeat, not to mention, losing the most experienced of our ministers and generals. This time, I said it's better for us not to get involved. We still need to build up our strength and our infrastructure both. The people are also tired of war. The last war lasted a long time, after all, and the soldiers' morale is already low. Pushing them to another war would be inhumane."

Sylvester said nothing, staring at the man, surprise robbing him of speech. When he finally found his voice, he asked, "You advised them against war?"

"I don't know why that's so hard to believe. I may be minister of war, but I'm a peaceful man. I abhor war."

Sylvester drew a deep breath, releasing it slowly. "If only everyone felt that way," he said quietly.

"You don't like war either, do you?" Reswick asked.

Sylvester shook his head. "Would any sane man?"

"By the way," Reswick said, taking a tiny tube with a scroll within. "This came for you when you were unconscious. A courier from Castrial brought it." He held it out. "I didn't open it if you're wondering."

Sylvester took it, hand shaking again, voice wavering as he asked, "Why not?"

The tube was sealed with Lucian's personal seal, not the Blade's. Sylvester didn't dare speculate what it contained. The fate of his family for sure, but what that fate was, he was afraid to know.

"Pretty sure if it was something I would want to know, it wouldn't be sent this way."

Sylvester opened the seal and the tube and took the scroll which too was sealed.

"You wouldn't have been able to open it anyway," he said. "The seal has a spell on it and so does the scroll."

He read the message, aware that Reswick had leaned over to

read it over his shoulder and that he probably could read Castrilian.

"Hamin found guilty of all charges against him. Angered His Majesty by being unrepentant. His Majesty has ordered Hamin and his family to be enslaved and sold at public auction. Alaric bought them. Because of your work with the embassy, you have been exempted from punishment. Come to my home when you reach Castrial. We have much to discuss.

Lucian."

"Lucian?" Reswick asked. "The Blade of Castrial? And yet, you claim to be an ordinary nobleman?"

"He was engaged to my sister," Sylvester said.

"Was?"

"She's dead."

Sylvester couldn't stop his voice from breaking, his eyes from stinging, and he turned his face away, blinking furiously. Dew's absence was a physical hole in his being, a place where her laughs, her smiles, her pouts, her voice, everything that made her who she was, once existed. That emptiness that he was getting used to in slow increments threatened to suffocate him once more and he swallowed in an attempt to dislodge the lump that took residence in his throat. His chest was tight, and he absently rubbed it, as if that would alleviate his grief and pain.

"I'm sorry. Hamin is?"

"My father."

Reswick winced. "I'm sorry again."

"Thank you," Sylvester said.

"And who is Alaric?" Reswick asked. "Will your family be safe with him?"

"He's the Shield of Castrial," Sylvester said. "And yes, they will be safe with him."

As safe as they would be with Sylvester himself. At least, that was a blessing that it was Alaric who bought them. Lucian probably knew it too, that it would put his mind at ease. He appreciated that Lucian had taken the trouble to write to him, to inform him.

"I know now why you were in such a hurry earlier," Reswick said. "And I can imagine you want to get to Castrial as soon as possible, but in the state you're in, you shouldn't be travelling and even using a portal could kill you."

Sylvester closed his eyes, slumping, pain flaring again. "I know."

Reswick placed a hand on his shoulder. "Take rest. Once you're recovered, we'll go as quickly as possible."

He squeezed Sylvester's shoulder before leaving. Sylvester stared at the sheets that covered him, at the bandage that was wound around his middle. As much as he wanted to rush home, what Reswick said was true. Besides, his family were already slaves, and Alaric wouldn't treat them badly. Sylvester's arrival wasn't going to make any difference.

The thought didn't stop the tears that started welling in his eyes.

SIXTEEN

KEYLIN WAS UNCOMFORTABLY aware of how clammy her palms were and of the sweat that trickled down her back. Her heart hammered in her chest, and she could imagine she must stink by now. She couldn't remember the last time she had a bath, and being in this stuffy carriage wasn't helping. Her dress had been fashionable once but now was caked in dirt and blood. The places where it had been torn and mended by her own inexpert hands stood out to her eyes. The once vibrant blue of it was now almost a drab grey.

Keylin was tempted to use her magic to clean it, but she had never been too good at cleaning spells. Her magic was strong, but she was more used to using it for organising her desk, her bookshelf, and in growing her garden. She could even use it to fight off a thug or two, but she was hopeless at mending and cleaning.

That had all been Dew, and Keylin's chest tightened at the thought of her sister. She would never be glad her sister was dead, but she was glad Dew didn't have to be a slave like her.

Of course, if Dew had lived, neither she nor Keylin would have been in this situation since both of them would have been married by now.

But her family would still have been slaves: her parents, her aunt, and her cousin at the mercy of a stranger.

She risked a glance at the man sitting opposite her. He was not looking at her, which was a relief, his mouth set in an uncompromising line that she didn't know the meaning of. There was a faint whiff of something sharp and citrusy in the carriage, probably from the closed incense burner that hung from the ceiling, high enough not to brush against any heads, and swaying with the motion of the carriage, a whiff of smoke curling from it. She gave one more look at the man, who sat so still that he might have been a statue.

Keylin didn't know what he wanted, this hard-faced stranger who for some reason looked familiar, and who was now her owner. Her heart hammered so hard against her ribs at the thought and her stomach churned. She wished that he had let Lucian buy her. She wished she were not a slave. She wished she could go back to a time when she was one of the nobility. She wished a lot of things, but none of it mattered. This was her reality now.

Her mind still couldn't fully process the change in her circumstances. Far easier to speculate on why Lucian had not even bid for them as soon as this man entered the fray. No one else had bid, and so she had ended up here, with her new master.

Alaric, Shield of Castrial, and His Majesty's left hand. In the Echelon, he and Lucian ranked the same, next only to His Most Exalted Majesty, the King of all Castrial.

This was also a man with a notorious grudge against Lucian. He must have bought her and her family almost certainly because he wanted to get back at Lucian through them. They were the closest Lucian had to a family, after all.

Keylin felt her throat close up, and eyes prickle as she remembered Dew again. Lucian would have been her brother-in-law if Dew had lived. Her sickness had been so sudden, and no one had been able to do anything. It still was the worst day of Keylin's life, and that was what gave her strength right now.

Even this didn't compare to the loss of her sister. She had survived that. She would survive this too.

Lucian still treated her like a sister, and her family had always treated him like a son. He must have suffered and yet, he had been a rock for all of them at the time of Dew's death.

A small sigh escaped Keylin. She wanted to pull the drapes behind her which covered the back window and look at the other carriage carrying the rest of her family. She had suspected that her owner had something nefarious in mind when he isolated her and chose her to accompany him in his carriage. The doors were closed, and all the windows covered with drapes. No one would have noticed. Not that they could have done anything. He owned her, just like he did her family. He could do anything he wanted to her, and no one would turn a hair.

Her family had never mistreated their slaves, but she was old enough to know that wasn't the same everywhere. There were laws in place to protect slaves from extreme forms of torture or death, but for some reason, rape was something everyone turned a blind eye to. Not even a law to protect her. If she bore her master's child, she would gain her freedom, and her child would be educated properly, but even then, would never bear their father's name.

But Alaric sat unmoving, looking straight ahead, not even looking at her. His coat was a sober blue, his tunic white, and he wore pants a shade lighter than his coat. The emblem of the Shield of Castrial—a plain unadorned shield in a white background—was displayed on his chest; a larger one would be on his back too. His clothes were finely cut and expensive, and Keylin was certain they were comfortable too.

She wished she knew why he bought her and what he planned to do. Why she was in his carriage, and above all, why he hated Lucian so much. She had seen him when they were under house arrest, but not often, and he had always behaved politely, but indifferently.

"Why?" she asked, because the silence was unbearable, and she could no longer hold in her questions. "You bought us to spite Lucian, didn't you? He told us you had a grudge against him."

"Is that all he told you?" Alaric's voice held no emotion.

"That you were exiled for five years after a wrongful conviction and returned only now and given the position of the Shield." She could pity him, but what had she and her family ever done to him? "You targeted us because Lucian is close to us," she said. "You just wanted to get back at him, so you framed my father for murder."

"You speak as if you were present at your father's trial." His tone held mockery now. "As if you heard every evidence against him. If you did, you would know that it was no frame up. Your father should have been executed along with the rest of you. You should thank His Majesty's mercy that you're only to be slaves."

He looked at her for the first time, and there was something contemptuous in his dark amber eyes, eyes that were so familiar and yet, Keylin couldn't recall where she had seen them.

"And you're wrong. I didn't target your family to get back at Lucian. Your family was always my target. Yes, I could have let it go as any predecessor of mine had done. After all your father was a noble and the victim just a commoner. But I chose not to, I chose to investigate, to bring the truth to light, and I'm sorry that it doesn't suit your reality." He paused. "Commoners have rights too, and no matter how despicable he was, he had a family that depended on him. I don't expect you to understand that."

"And if it had turned out that my father was innocent, you would no doubt have let him go," she said, her tone laden with sarcasm, though a twinge of unease pierced her mind.

Had her father really killed a man because he was uncaring of consequences? Because he believed nothing would happen to him?

Alaric lifted his brows, and his mouth twisted in a sardonic smile. "Whatever you choose to believe of me, I don't fabricate evidence or cause harm to innocent persons," he said. "Your father is guilty, and there is enough evidence pointing to that."

"You just now said you targeted our family," she pointed out, though she didn't ask why. Her father had enemies, after all, and perhaps he had wronged Alaric at some point.

"I won't deny that I was looking for an opportunity," he said calmly. "And your father was good enough to provide me with one. But that doesn't mean I would have framed him for something he didn't do. As I already said, he is guilty."

"If my father killed someone, there must have been enough justification," she said stoutly, even though her heart was hammering inside her chest. "There must have been a genuine reason."

"The whore that man supplied was not up to your father's

standards, and she blabbed about how small a certain part of his anatomy was." Alaric sounded derisive. "I suppose he considered it reason enough to do murder."

She flushed. "You're lying!"

Except she knew her father's philandering ways, but how was she to admit it to the man opposite her?

"I have nothing to gain from lying and to you," he said drily. "Your opinion of me hardly matters to me. You're free to think what you want, to delude yourself how you want if it will make you feel better."

She flushed deeper, knowing that he was goading her and dismissing her in the same breath.

"I hate you!" she spat.

"I already told you I don't care," he said. "Now be a good slave and be quiet, or I'll gag you."

Fuming she looked at the window. "Can I pull the drapes?" she asked frostily.

"If you wish but be quiet."

She pulled the drapes and looked outside. They had left the city behind and was now passing through a wooded area. He must be taking them to his country estate then. It filled her with relief. No one they knew would come to visit them here. Even if not for her master's job and reputation, the place was far enough away from the capital and from the centre of all that was fashionable in the kingdom. She knew the world she lived in. Everyone who had smiled at them and sucked up to them would now laugh and rejoice in their ill fortune. That was how it always had been, and she didn't know how it could be different now.

Evie might not, but Keylin didn't think she would ever see Evie again. Would she see Bertram again?

Her heart ached as she thought of Bertram. She understood why Bertram couldn't have come to bid on her. It would be odd indeed to wish to purchase the woman he had been betrothed to just a few griels ago. She wondered if she would ever be free again, if she would ever see Bertram again, if he even wished to see her. Her eyes prickled and she blinked them rapidly. She couldn't afford to cry about this, not when it would do no good and would only reveal weakness in front of a man she despised with all her heart. He had all but admitted that he chose to pursue that murder because her father was the suspect.

She swallowed her tears and wondered what would become of her and her family.

SEVENTEEN

LUCIAN KNEW HE should have written to Sylvester earlier, before the auction, but there were other things needing his attention. He and Alaric had rushed back to the prison that day, only to find both Desmond and the prisoner dead, their throats slit. None of the guards had seen or heard anything and the wards were untouched.

He and Alaric had both questioned each guard individually till they finally found the one responsible for letting an assassin in. He had distracted his partner while the assassin slipped in behind his back. The guard admitted to what he did, and that he was paid a hefty sum by someone who was masked and hooded and didn't speak, using written parchments to communicate.

The parchments self-destroyed, so they had nothing.

It had taken a couple of days to arrange his trial, and by then, the auction was over, and Alaric had bought Hamin and his family, to everyone's chagrin but Lucian's. He knew Alaric would never harm them, but Bertram was not so easily convinced. His mother had forbidden him from buying them since Keylin had refused to marry him before the trial. Bertram had asked Lucian to buy them on his behalf, but Lucian hadn't been able to, for more reasons than one.

Today was the first time he had time to breathe, and he had dashed off a letter to Sylvester before going to office. He and Alaric had to meet the King, to discuss the spy. Lucian grew afraid at the thought that someone high in the Echelon was selling out Castrial to her enemies. Lucian had to find out who it was. After all, it was his job.

Alaric was already in the waiting room outside the King's office when Lucian was ushered in by a guard. Royal guards stood close to the walls, the windows closed, and curtains drawn.

It was to be that kind of meeting then.

"You're late," Alaric observed neutrally, but his gaze was cold and remote. It hurt more than Lucian cared to admit, but he pushed it away and sat down on a chair.

"Had to send word to Sylvester," Lucian said, hanging his head and lacing his hands behind it. "He might be on his way already, but at least he can be at ease now."

"At ease?" Alaric said, his voice strange, and Lucian resisted the urge to look at him, determinedly looking down at the rich rug that carpeted the floor. There were designs on it, forests and valleys and mountains. His feet rested on a valley.

"Yes," he said. "Sylvester knows better than anyone that yours is the safest place for them."

"Even though I hate Lord Giles?"

Lucian looked at him then, dropping his hands and straightening.

"So what? He's a hateful man. That doesn't mean you will mistreat him. You think I don't know how you punished the soldiers who roughed him up in prison?"

Alaric's face was pale as he stared at Lucian.

"How do you know that?"

Lucian smirked.

"I'm the Blade of Castrial," he said with as much pomposity as he could muster, dropping his voice and making it rough.

Alaric snorted, and Lucian grinned at him. It was easy in moments like these to forget that he and Alaric were no longer friends, that Alaric was still angry at him, that Lucian had failed him.

"What did your mother say?" he asked before the droplet could be lost.

"She understands." Alaric frowned. "She asked for you. Said you hadn't been to see her since I returned."

Lucian swallowed, looked away.

"I wasn't sure I would be welcome."

"Whatever I may feel for you, you're always welcome to visit my mother," Alaric said. "It makes her happy, and that matters to me."

Whatever I may feel for you.

Lucian's heart seemed to want to leap out of his chest and splatter at Alaric's feet. He couldn't look at Alaric, not after what he just said. He told himself Alaric was justified in hating him. Alaric didn't have all the information. That wasn't his fault, but it was hard not to feel bitter.

But as always, they had more important things to do.

Astra came from inside the office. "His Majesty will see you now," she said.

They both rose to their feet and as they passed her, Astra asked Alaric in a low voice, "Are you all right?"

"I'm fine," Alaric said, a softness to his tone that Lucian had rarely heard.

Jealousy reared its head, clawing at him, and he ruthlessly suppressed it. Alaric was his own person and he and Lucian had never been anything but friends in the first place. Lucian had no claim on him, no reason to be jealous.

The King sat behind his desk, which was free of clutter today. The windows to the office were closed and orbs of magic lit the place brighter than day.

Lucian and Alaric both bowed.

"Your subject greets Your Majesty."

"Sit down, both of you," the King said, waving to the chairs in front of him. "No need for formalities today. As soon as Astra joins us, we shall begin."

Astra came inside a droplet later, closing the door, and casting a privacy spell that would prevent eavesdropping, both magical and physical. She sat down next to Alaric.

"So, Astra has already given me an overview of what happened. I appreciate that you have managed to keep the guard's arrest a secret so far, but do you think it will serve?"

"We can only try, Your Majesty," Lucian said. "The only thing that's certain is that we have a spy, someone high in The Echelon, but we have no clues to their identity. We can only speculate."

"And what are your speculations?" the King asked.

Lucian and Alaric exchanged a glance. "We both have our own thoughts on the matter," Alaric said.

"I would like to hear you both," the King responded.

"Lord Sartian, the Minister of Works," Lucian said. "On the surface, he's the perfect official and does his work diligently and has never been known to skim anything from the funds for public works. Every single coin is accounted for, and all accounts are perfect."

"But?" the King prompted.

"The man lives austerely, but his son is another matter," Lucian said. "He's a frequent visitor to brothels and gaming parlours, spends far more than any man can afford on his father's salary. He doesn't have an independent income that we know of, and Lord Sartian's estates are not sufficient to support such extravagance."

"You think the son may be spying on the father?" the King asked.

"That's my belief."

"And you, Alaric? What do you feel?"

"Being new here and to the post of Shield, I am not too familiar with many ministers, Your Majesty. But the minister of finance, Lord Girone elicits my suspicion. He throws lavish parties, spends money like water, far in excess of what his estate and job can provide. Audits of his office have turned up no proof of any embezzlement."

"Two ministers, both experienced and high in the Echelon, both privy to state secrets, and both who have been serving Castrial for farials." The King sighed. "A mistake would be devastating. If they are loyal, we will be destroying them and their families for nothing."

"We understand that," Lucian said. "We would like to collaborate on this, Your Majesty. To investigate both ministers in secret."

"And you, Astra?" the King asked, his gaze swivelling to her. "You handled the Shield's office for five farials. Have you any insights?"

"The Minister of War," she said. "Lord Fitzroy. He's the son of Serenian refugees. Though he has a family, nearly everything he earns goes to helping the Serenian refugees in Castrial. On the surface, it's noble, but we have long suspected all Serenian refugees aren't actually refugees."

"His title has been granted to him by me," the King said slowly. "He had made a lot of contributions during the last war."

"Which was with Garaner, not Sarian," Alaric said quietly. "Your Majesty, let's investigate him as well. In this matter... We can't afford to overlook anyone who looks suspicious."

"It must not be a witch-hunt," the King said sternly. "I will not have my ministers harassed. Do you understand?"

"All investigations will be held discreetly, and we will not move against anyone till we have solid evidence," Lucian said.

"Then, let us decide so," the King said. "I wish you success. Till we find the spy, we cannot be easy in our mind."

"We will not let you down," Lucian said, rising and bowing to the King.

The King dismissed them with a wave and Astra took off her spell so they could leave. As soon as the doors opened, the guards outside filed in, taking their places next to the walls of the office.

The King didn't trust even the royal guards, except Astra. Lucian didn't blame him, but his worries were intensifying.

EIGHTEEN

ALARIC ENTERED HIS house and knew immediately that Lucian was there. It was like a seventh sense, that knowledge. He walked towards his mother's sitting room, knowing that he would find Lucian there.

Lucian was sitting next to his mother on the couch, both of them smiling. Lucian's face was half turned away from Alaric that he could see only the sweep of his jaw, the curve of his cheek, the dimple that appeared only when he smiled.

The sitting room was fragrant with incense and the bouquet of flowers that sat on the table. All of his mother's favourite blooms, blue wild soniers, yellow heart flowers, purple soul blooms, red fiery breaths, orange follies. The sparkle from their magic and the fragrance both filled the large room. The windows were open to the gardens where the plants were not yet in bloom.

"Alaric," his mother said, her eyes full of joy as she smiled at him. "You're home."

Lucian turned his head, the smile still on his face, but there was something almost like wariness in his eyes.

"You said I could come visit," he said softly.

"I did, and I meant it." Alaric didn't frown. What did Lucian think he was going to do? "You two catch up. I've work to do."

He turned and left, going to his own chambers. Once inside, he leaned against the door, closing his eyes and trying to breathe normally. He had never expected it to hurt so much to see Lucian here, in his house.

This was not the house he was familiar with; there were no memories here. It was something the King had granted him on his return, an estate away from the city. He and his mother had made it a home, a refuge for him after the farials of hell he'd been through.

He'd never known how terrible it would feel to have Lucian here. It was even worse than having Lord Giles and his family here.

Did Lucian visit them too? Or did he only visit Alaric's mayi?

A knock on his door had him startle and blink before he turned to the door. His eyes were blurry and his cheeks wet and he hastily wiped his face before opening the door. His mother stood there, eyes troubled as she looked at him.

"Mayi," he said, attempting to smile. "Something wrong?"

"Do you hate it so much, having Lucian here?" she asked.

Alaric couldn't reply, because the truth was, he didn't know what he felt. He didn't want to analyse his feelings right now.

"I don't hate it," he said after a droplet. "I just... I can't pretend like everything's normal, Mayi. I work with him, and I can do that, but anything beyond that... I don't know that I'm able."

She frowned, looking up at him. "Alaric," she said softly. "Do you really believe Lucian betrayed you?"

Alaric felt as if someone had punched the breath out of his chest. Even now, a part of him believed there had to be another explanation, that Lucian couldn't have done it. But if that was so, why didn't Lucian say anything to him?

Besides, that letter was written by Lucian, the letter that still was in Alaric's pocket, torn pieces held together by glue and magic, which seemed to Alaric to be a metaphor for his own heart which was held together by very few things.

One of them was the immense love he had for the woman whose careworn face looked at him with such anxiety and care that only a mother was capable of.

Alaric didn't want to break her heart any more than it already was.

"I don't know," he said finally. "I want to believe he didn't, but he... he wrote to me, Mayi... It was him..."

Alaric had never asked Lucian to lie for him, to say anything. If Lucian hadn't offered, he would have looked harder for evidence to prove his innocence. As it was, he trusted Lucian too much.

"Ask him," she said quietly. "Ask him, my child. Before it's too late to mend things."

"There's nothing to mend," Alaric said at last. "If he did... I don't know that I can forgive him... And if he didn't... How can he forgive me?"

"That's up to him, isn't it?" she asked. "Don't make his

decisions for him."

It wasn't that simple. He could never tell his mother the things he had done while he was an exile, the blood on his hands. But he was fairly certain that Lucian knew. After all, he was the Blade of Castrial. If he knew, then how could things go back to what they were again? How could Lucian ever feel the same as he once did?

Besides, Lucian and he both had other things to worry about now. Castrial's safety, the identity of the spy, all those things took prominence. Everything else was irrelevant.

"I'm not ready yet," he said finally.

His mother sighed and embraced him, and he hugged her back.

"It's all right," she whispered. "Take your own time. You have to do what's best for you. I just hate seeing you both hurt. It will be fine."

Alaric wished that things were that simple.

NINETEEN

THE CARRIAGE MOVED smoothly through the streets and Lucian stared out, eyes moving over the familiar sights without registering any. He had gone to see Bertram and hadn't been able to leave for a while.

Lucian hadn't expected Bertram to be so worried. But he couldn't expect Betram to understand why Keylin was safe in

Alaric's house.

Lucian didn't think it was for him to tell Bertram that ancient history. He knew very well that Alaric wouldn't hurt Keylin, but that confidence didn't extend to her father. Alaric wouldn't physically harm the man, but Lucian knew the barbed tongue of his old friend well.

Old friend.

It hurt to call Alaric that. To reduce him to just a friend when once…

But what else had they been? Just because they had sex a few times didn't make them anything. Back then, they had both treated it as just a diversion. After all, Lucian was a noble and nobles were expected to marry whoever could give them children, so they could continue their lines.

Not that Lucian had ever cared. He wasn't the last of his line. He and the rest of his family might be estranged, but he wasn't the one with the title and the responsibility to carry on his father's name and line.

Alaric hadn't cared either, but their positions in the Echelon meant that their lives weren't their own, nor their hearts.

Not that hearts were ever involved, except on Lucian's part, and even then, he had been too afraid to reveal it. He wished once again that he had refused to do the King's bidding. Which was impossible. Garret was a good King and just, but that didn't mean he would appreciate insubordination. Lucian was the Blade of Castrial, and he couldn't refuse to obey his liege.

But Alaric didn't know Lucian had had no choice back then. He had trusted him, and Lucian had let him down, left him with no defence and no time to find any evidence to clear his name. Now, there was a chasm between him and Alaric, one which he didn't know how to bridge.

But he could put Betram's mind at ease. He had sent a message to Alaric, asking permission to meet him at home. Going there to visit Calla was one thing, but Lucian didn't dare to go there to meet Alaric, not unless Alaric let him.

"Any messages for me?" Lucian asked Garth as he opened the door for him. The butler shook his head.

"None, sir, but there's a visitor. I put him in the study."

Lucian frowned at that. If Garth put him in the study, that meant it was someone from the Echelon and that they were there on official matters. His heart racing, he walked towards the door, and hoped there was no bad news waiting. He didn't think his heart could take any more. He was already hanging in by a frayed thread, and he feared what he might find inside.

Except–

The man inside turned to face him as he opened the door, and it was only a lifetime of training that made Lucian not stop on his tracks or his knees buckle. Even then, once he stepped inside and closed the door, he had to lean against it, his own pulse drumming in his ears, and his own breathing a harsh grate.

"Lucian," Alaric spoke, voice distant, formal.

Lucian could count on the fingers of one hand the number of times he and Alaric had been alone since Alaric's return. Every other time they had met, it had either been in court or in His Majesty's presence or in public. Even in their offices, there had been others. Usually, even when they talked to each other, they avoided each other's eyes, except on the rare occasion when they didn't and even then, they had always turned their gazes away quickly.

Now, their eyes met each other's and neither of them turned their gaze away.

It troubled Lucian that he couldn't read Alaric's expression. His gaze was cold, the kind he would have given to any stranger, and Lucian's heart was already battered enough that it hurt beyond anything to meet those eyes.

"Alaric," he said, everything else gone out of his head, this first time they had been alone in five farials in Lucian's home, in his study, where Alaric had once been as much at home as Lucian himself was.

"You asked to meet me," Alaric said, his tone frosty. "I assume it's to do with your former fiancé's family."

There was something almost scornful in the way Alaric's mouth twisted when he spoke the last words, and it reminded Lucian of how Dew had almost the same mannerism when she spoke of something she didn't like.

Dew.

It was like a bucket of cold water was dropped on him, reminding him that neither of them was what they once were, that Lucian had asked to meet with Alaric not to catch up or reminisce, but to–

To what? Request? Beg? Lucian had his share of pride, but this was Alaric, and–

For Dew's sake, for her family's sake, for Bertram's sake, Lucian was ready to bend his knees if needed be.

Except the words would not come, they remained firmly stuck in his mind, refusing to spill forth into sounds. If delaying the inevitable was the price for keeping Alaric's trenchant gaze upon him for a few more moments, Lucian would gladly pay it.

His eyes drank in the sight of the man he had never stopped missing even for a droplet. Alaric was still dressed in his uniform, the blue coat fitting him well, though he had lost weight. Lines of silver threaded his hair, and Lucian's heart ached at the sign of Alaric's suffering. There was a lean look to his face, his chiselled features standing out even more. His dark amber eyes stared at Lucian stonily.

"Are you not well?" Alaric asked, in that same frosty tone,

though he took a couple of steps towards Lucian. "You've been leaning on that door since you came in."

"I'm okay," Lucian said, but didn't move. He wasn't sure he wouldn't crumple to the floor without the solidity of the door behind him. "Just a little dizziness. It will pass."

"You look pale," Alaric said. "You should sit down. I will ring for Garth."

"No, I'm fine," Lucian muttered. "No need to bother Garth."

"Are you sure?" Alaric asked, and he was right in front of Lucian so close their fronts were but a hairsbreadth apart.

Lucian stared into the eyes of the man who he had once called friend, and whose trust he had betrayed. Lucian might not have been directly responsible, but he held himself responsible for Alaric's disgrace and fall, if only because he had failed to defend him to the King. Nothing he said or did was ever going to make up for five lost farials.

"Alaric," he said. "I need a favour from you."

"A favour." There was a pronounced sneer in Alaric's tone and expression now. "The Blade of Castrial wants a favour from me. The bastard who was exiled till recently. Sure. You may ask. Since I'm here, I'm at least obligated to listen."

"It's on behalf of a friend," he said. "Bertram, the Count of Sartho."

"I know who Bertram is," Alaric said, with barely concealed contempt.

"He was engaged to Keylin," Lucian said. "He wants to buy her from you."

"She won't go," Alaric said dismissively. "Even if I am willing to let her go, I am not willing to release her parents, and she won't go without them."

Lucian closed his eyes briefly.

"Of course," he murmured, opening them. "I suppose you

wouldn't consider releasing them to me either."

"You assume right." Alaric moved back into the room, turning his back on Lucian. "Is this why you wanted to meet me?"

"Why else?" Lucian muttered.

"I don't know." Alaric's tone had changed, still even, but with an undercurrent of something. "I was perhaps hoping you wanted to apologise for the wrong you did me."

Lucian swallowed. "Would an apology make any difference?" he asked. "Will you consider forgiving me if I apologised?"

Alaric laughed, and it was a bitter sound as he turned away from Lucian, his shoulders rigid, and back straight.

"I might have," he said. "Once, even when I was in exile, I might have, but now–" He turned to face Lucian, and his eyes were blazing. "Now, my lord, the Blade of Castrial. Now, even if you begged me on your knees, I would not forgive you. I hate you more than you can comprehend, and I will see you brought down as I saw your former fiancé's family." His lips twisted. "Condolences, by the way."

If it was possible, Lucian would have taken a step back, but the solid door behind him was a barrier.

"Thank you," he said, striving to keep his voice even and failing miserably. "And in that case, apologies are meaningless, aren't they?"

"Yes," Alaric said. "But it would have given me great satisfaction to see the Blade of Castrial beg for my forgiveness." He bowed. "I will take my leave then, my Lord. See you in court."

Lucian swallowed but didn't move.

"Alaric," he said. "There's nothing I can say that can ever make up for what happened. But I'm sorry and there hasn't been a day where I didn't regret my role in your exile."

"Your role," Alaric said flatly. "Is that what you call it now? I guess I was the fool in expecting more. Get out of my way, Lucian.

I need to leave."

Lucian stepped away from the door, and with every last bit of his training, kept himself upright as Alaric walked out. Once the door to the study closed behind him, Lucian crumpled to the floor, his whole body shaking uncontrollably as tears sprang free.

TWENTY

ALARIC HAD TO lean against the closed door for a droplet to catch his breath. It had taken more out of him than he had imagined. He had thought he could do this, meet Lucian here, and be distant and polite, and–

He should have known how impossible that would be. The study had looked exactly the same as it had five farials ago. Lucian, on the other hand—

They had met so many time since his return, but Alaric hadn't noticed till today how changed Lucian looked. He had noticed before how gaunt Lucian had become, the shadows under his eyes, the lines on his face, and the smattering of grey in his hair.

Oh, Alaric knew he bore the signs too, not of age, but of suffering. Exile had not been an easy life, but Alaric was used to hardship, had been since he was a boy. The kindness of Lucian's elder brother may have helped set him on the path to rise above his circumstances, but that didn't mean Alaric had forgotten his origins.

It shocked Alaric how much worse Lucian looked than the brief glimpses he had caught of him previously. Lucian looked like a man waiting for death. It had taken everything in Alaric not to rush to Lucian and ask him what he had been doing to himself.

Once, he would have, and chided the other man, and—

Once Lucian would not have looked at him with nothing but anguish in his gaze. Lucian had always been so full of joy and laughter, but now he looked at Alaric with only pain and pleading. Alaric didn't know how to deal with it. If he wasn't still in love with Lucian, perhaps he would have, but as it was, he didn't know what to do.

They had grown apart, in more ways than one, and Alaric's heart couldn't take any more betrayal, any more hurt, and so he had attempted to wall it up.

"Sir?"

Garth's soft voice recalled him to the present, and the cold wood at his back reminded him that he was standing with his back to Lucian's study door. It must look very odd to anyone, but Garth had known him since he was a boy.

"How long has he been like that?" he asked, keeping his voice low.

Garth looked troubled.

"Since you were exiled, sir," he said, his voice equally low. "For a while, he had regained something of his old self when he was engaged to Miss Dew, but then–" Garth shrugged.

Alaric didn't wince, but it was a near thing. He had seen Dew a couple of times before his exile, and she had struck him as someone who was good and kind. She had not been patronising to him as many others were, but genuinely kind. He wished he had had a chance to know her, to tell her the truth. But that was gone, and he had lost his chance to know Dew.

There was still Keylin, who was as much a spoiled brat as he could have expected. Alaric knew Bertram but wondered if the Count was serious about Keylin now. Lucian seemed to believe it, and despite being friends with Lucian since childhood, he and Bertram had never crossed paths since Bertram had been abroad for most of his life. So, Alaric wasn't sure just how much stock he could put in Lucian's words about Bertram.

"Take care of him," Alaric said quietly as he straightened.

There was understanding in Garth's eyes.

"The two of you should talk," he said quietly.

Alaric could not make a proper response, so he nodded at Garth and walked to the front door. A footman opened the door, and Alaric stepped outside, still feeling discombobulated. His carriage was waiting, fortunately, and he climbed in.

"Home," he said quietly.

Home where the ex-lord Giles and his family awaited. Alaric didn't know all of them. There was Hamin Giles, his wife, their daughter, their nephew, and his wife's sister. The King could have sentenced Giles to death and exiled the rest.

He should perhaps think of the man as Hamin now since he was no longer Lord Giles. That title had been stripped from him, and even if he was pardoned someday, he wouldn't be able to regain it.

At least he was alive, and so was his family. Not executed or exiled, but only enslaved.

Exile might sound a better fate than slavery, but Alaric had been there, and he knew that exile was often a euphemism for lifelong incarceration in a place away from home. He had been lucky to be sent there a free man, which enabled him to live without being imprisoned, but not everyone was so lucky.

And women, well–

Exile meant prostitution for them, and those that refused died faster. Slavery was sometimes as bad, but not always.

Not always.

Perhaps he should have let Lucian have them, but Alaric had his orders. Even if he didn't, he couldn't, because the King was right. Castrial still had some antiquated notions about women and their role in society, Keylin would invariably be a subject of talk, but as long as she was under his roof, he had the means to end that talk.

He was also petty enough to want Hamin and his family to suffer, at least a little bit, to realise that the world wasn't as they thought, that their station didn't give them immunity from the consequences of their actions. Perhaps Alaric also wanted them to know that they couldn't have everything they wanted just because they wanted it.

So, he wouldn't let Lucian have them or Bertram or anyone who may coddle them and treat them like the nobility they no longer were. Not even if he was free to let them go.

Hamin's family is not responsible for what he is.

Perhaps not, but Keylin had been all too ready to defend her father when he was bringing them home. From the way she had raged at him, he was ready to wager that they had taken it for granted, their own nobility, that a noble wouldn't do something bad without good reason.

Good reason, bah!

Alaric was so sick of the hypocrisy of the nobles who had once looked down on him and now tried to smarm up to him.

The carriage wound its way between other vehicles, through the familiar streets of Fastan, between the well-known buildings, lights glimmering inside and on the streets, the paved wide streets letting it move smoothly. Soon, they reached the outskirts. Buildings tapered away to trees and open plains, but the road was as smooth here as it was in the city.

Travers gave the horses their head, and spoke softly, but audible, even over the sound of hooves, the spell on the carriage ensuring that.

"How did it go?"

"As bad as I'd expected," Alaric replied. "I shouldn't have gone there. I thought... I don't know what I thought..."

"I'm sorry," Travers murmured. "I was hoping you could resolve your differences."

"Why does everyone expect that?" Alaric demanded, almost angry now.

Bad enough that he couldn't stop thinking of Lucian, that he still cared, wanted, loved. But to have everyone around him hoping that the two of them could go back to being what they once were, which–

What were they?

They had been friends once.

Lovers if they could be called that, though Alaric still held that sex did not equate to love, and their sex had always been about release and passion rather than emotion.

But whatever they were, they couldn't go back to it, not even be friends again, because Lucian had betrayed every last vestige of Alaric's trust, had trampled on his heart, and Alaric couldn't allow him to do that again.

"Because you are the Shield of Castrial, and he is the Blade," Travers said calmly. "And it is in the best interest of everyone in Castrial to have the two of you work together rather than against each other."

"You know that neither of us will allow our personal feelings to affect our working relationship," Alaric said rather stiffly this time. "We are both committed to Castrial and her well-being, and nothing would change that."

He was a bit offended that Travers would think it would.

"If you say so," Travers said drily. "But hasn't it occurred to your brilliant mind that a working relationship is better when both parties don't hate each other?"

Alaric made no answer, just started out of the window, frowning. Travers had a point, but Alaric wasn't ready to accept it. A working relationship. That was all he had with Lucian now. But Travers was wrong too. He and Lucian didn't hate each other. It might have been better if they did; it wouldn't have hurt so much. That he still loved Lucian was what hurt, and though Lucian hadn't said it, it was evident that he still cared for Alaric, that he would do anything to change how things were between them.

He still betrayed me.

It was still Lucian, who knew everything about him, who could have done incalculable damage to Alaric's reputation had he chosen, who had risked his life to lie to the king back then. Could Alaric blame him for not extending the lie enough to protect him?

But if Lucian hadn't assured him he would lie, Alaric would have looked for another way to protect himself, to find any evidence... As it was, once Lucian's first lie was believed, there was absolutely no way for Alaric to extricate himself without outing Lucian's lie. Not even to save himself would he have risked Lucian's life. Not then, not now.

But Lucian had still lied to the king for Alaric.

Alaric struggled to reconcile the dichotomy of Lucian's actions, the obvious guilt he saw on the other's face and the words he had spoken, as if–

As if he hadn't been the one to betray Alaric.

Alaric sighed even as his heart leapt at that thought.

What if his mother was right? What if Lucian hadn't done it?

The letter in his pocket even now, gave the lie to that thought. It was naught but a fantasy to believe Lucian was innocent, but Alaric indulged it till he reached home.

TWENTY ONE

LUCIAN STRODE THROUGH the hallways of the palace, one of the King's personal servants showing him the way. Lucian never failed to be amazed by the ingenuity of the King's senior mages who cast illusions so real that existing corridors and rooms looked completely different. Lucian had visited the King so many times by now, but every time it seemed like he was following a different route to the man's office. To some, it might seem unduly paranoid, but Lucian knew it was necessary. During the last war with Garaner, there had been assassins sent to Castrial to take down the King, and they had been foiled both by the efficiency and ingenuity of the royal guards and mages respectively.

Today, however, it seemed that he was not going to the office, but to the royal study. The royal study was a personal space, and the King rarely conducted business there, let alone have meetings. It was where he spent his spare time, when he could find any, reading something for the fun of it, or painting, which used to be one of his hobbies back when they were students.

Lucian relaxed almost unconsciously. It seemed that he was about to see Garret, not the King. A part of him wondered why. Was this about Sarian or the spy?

In the last war, Sarian had refused to take part, leaving Garaner to face Castrial alone. Garaner had been overconfident, which had helped Castrial. Still, the war had dragged on for farials and had ended only when key persons in the Garanerian army and government were assassinated by unknowns.

Lucian believed it was one of their spies in Garaner, though he didn't know their identity. He had asked their head in Garaner, but Sylvester had told him that it was an independent operative whose identity couldn't be disclosed. Lucian read it to mean that it was someone Sylvester wanted to protect.

Lucian had taken part in the war, which had also afforded him an opportunity to look for Alaric. He had failed to find him, and since many of the prison camps were unguarded due to the war, prisoners escaping to Garaner or Sarian was a common occurrence. He had thought Alaric might have escaped. His magic signature had been masked so Lucian couldn't track him.

He had kept looking all the same, going to every border town and village in all three kingdoms, and failing to find the man he sought. Even after the war had ended, Lucian had kept going back, kept searching, to no avail.

And now, he didn't need to search anymore because Alaric was back. Lucian wondered how the King had found him but then it was only to be expected. Though Lucian was the Blade, he was still subservient to the King, and all the spies reported directly to the King whenever it was deemed necessary. The King could by-pass Lucian and issue orders to them, and though Lucian was their head, he had never been a spy, never had field experience, and so was not as good as them at finding anyone or doing things that they did.

The latest report had come to him, and while he was almost certain that the King would have received one too, he had sent the report with his notes to the King as was expected of him.

But if it was about Sarian, why was the King meeting him in the study?

He put it out of his mind for now. No doubt, he would know soon.

Astra was guarding the door, and he nodded at her. She inclined her head in acknowledgement, but there was no sign of recognition in her eyes or a smile. It had been the same since her retrieval from Sarian three farials ago. She had gone missing at the beginning of the war and was found only after two farials. Human traffickers had taken her, and Lucian had read the report Sylvester had placed on his desk after her rescue. Other than Sylvester and Astra herself, Lucian and the King were the only two people in the world who knew what she had suffered for two farials.

It had changed her so much that she refused to acknowledge anyone who had known her before. Lucian had known her only because she and Dew had gone to school together. He had never met her before her kidnapping, but from what Dew told him, she had been a serious person who was very passionate about music, painting, and books.

The woman she was now, the Captain of the Royal Guards, was a very efficient machine. Lucian had seen her on the training grounds where she utterly destroyed soldiers twice her size and experience. It wasn't war that had left its mark on her, as it did on Lucian, but the mark was there, nevertheless.

The door to the study was opened by a manservant who announced Lucian and gestured him to go inside. Lucian entered the study and looked around. He had never been in here, and it didn't match his expectations.

It was a far simpler room than he would have imagined. The only furniture was a reading desk with a couple of chairs and books piled on top. Various paintings adorned the wall, and Lucian recognised the scrawled signature at the bottom of each. All of these were from their student days and Garret no longer signed the same.

Garret was standing at one of the large windows that opened to a garden. A tree's branches were at eye level, and hung heavy with fruits, with insects buzzing around. A bubble of magic encased the window, protecting Garret while allowing him to enjoy the view and the fresh air.

"Lucian," Garret spoke without turning around. "Come, stand by me."

"Your Majesty," Lucian said as he stood next to Garret.

"None of that now," Garret said. "Call me Garret."

"It wouldn't be appropriate," Lucian said quietly.

Garret gave him an amused glance. "You'll only be obeying your King's orders."

Lucian bowed. "I know, but it still wouldn't be appropriate."

"You used not to be so stuffy," Garret said, smiling as he turned back to the window.

Lucian chuckled. "I was not the Blade of Castrial then, and you were not my King."

Silence fell and after a droplet, Garret asked. "How's Alaric? Have you two made up yet?"

"It's not that easy," Lucian said, his heart aching. But he schooled his features to neutrality. "He's angry and I can't blame him."

"You haven't told him the truth yet, have you?" the King asked. "That I forced you to do what you did, to write that letter to him."

Lucian swallowed past the lump in his throat. "He's the Shield of Castrial. It wouldn't be good for him to know that particular truth."

"Always so loyal," Garret murmured, but there was something sad and resigned in his voice. "In the end, I have to use that loyalty for my own ends."

Lucian had never asked what ends were served by lying to Alaric, by turning him against Lucian, but he knew Garret and had trusted him. The King wouldn't have done it if there wasn't a need for it. Lucian might not have seen it, but that didn't mean there was no reason.

Now he knew why, and he could understand why it was necessary. It was either him or Alaric since no one else had the same training, and it just happened to be Alaric.

"I'm at Your Majesty's service," Lucian said. "My life belongs to you and Castrial. You're not using me."

Garret looked at him. "Have you made any progress on finding the spy?"

"We're investigating, Your Majesty, but we haven't been able to find anything yet."

The King nodded as if he had expected it. "I have a plan to deal with Sarian and to find the spy," he said. "But once again, I would have to wrong you, Lucian."

Lucian shrugged. "Your Majesty has the entirety of Castrial

and its people to think of, to protect. Whatever your plans, I will follow them."

Garret nodded again.

"So be it. We have a few spies in Sarian, but Wayan was our best. None of the others come close, but they're good people, Lucian, who try their best."

"And?" Lucian asked, heart sinking, knowing what the King was going to say.

"I fear they've been compromised by this spy," the King said. "I've issued an order for all of our people in Sarian to return home, but I don't know if it will reach them in time."

"If we pull them all out, we'll be blind, and we cannot afford to be, especially now," Lucian said.

"Their lives are important too, Lucian," Garret said. "There are a few who couldn't have been compromised yet, who are attached to the staff at our embassy. But as you know, embassy staff are always watched with more than ordinary attention. None of them are in a position to gain us any but the most basic of information, and more importantly, I cannot use any of them to flush out the traitor in our midst."

"And you have a plan to do that?" Lucian asked.

The King looked sombre as he inclined his head in agreement.

"My plan is a bit more elaborate than that. If it works, we may never have to fear Sarian again. But for my plan to work properly, I need you and Alaric to make up," he said. "Even accounting for the fact that I cannot have my Blade and my Shield at odds with each other, I hate that I had to cause this rift."

"I cannot tell Alaric the truth," Lucian said.

What could he say anyway? It could do incalculable damage to Castrial if Lucian couldn't find the right words.

"I know. When the time comes, I'll do that myself. In the meantime, try to get him to at least acknowledge your existence."

Lucian chuckled. Alaric had spent a few meetings pretending that Lucian didn't exist.

"I'll try," he said.

He didn't think it would be that difficult. Alaric wouldn't be pretending to ignore him so hard if Lucian still didn't have a place in his heart.

But Lucian wanted more. He wanted Alaric's trust back, and he knew that was a tall order. Whatever Garret wanted with them didn't matter. For Lucian, Alaric was the most important person in his life.

But even so, Castrial and her safety always came first.

TWENTY TWO

ALARIC STARED AT the clothes laid out on his bed with distaste. The blue tunic, black pants and the dark blue coat all looked expensive and so completely unlike anything he liked to wear. They did resemble his uniform, but the material was different. But if he was going to attend a party at a noble's house, he had to dress the part.

As much as he wished he didn't have to go to this party, he had no choice. Not even though it was not an official one. It was being hosted by Lord Sartian, and the man had personally invited him. Lord Sartian's daughter was getting engaged to the son of one of the few other nobles who Alaric admired.

Despite all their suspicions, Lord Sartian was also one of the few nobles who Alaric respected, mainly because he had never abused his status or position as the Minister of Works. He could have enriched himself easily, but he hadn't, and he had kept a hawk eye on his subordinates to ensure that the money allotted for development of roads and waterways as well as other infrastructure went towards that and not to line anyone's pockets. Alaric admired that integrity.

Which made it all the more ironic that his son was suspected of being a spy, of selling state secrets to the enemy for money. Alaric wished it wasn't so, but till they could find a source for the young man's extravagant spending habits, he would remain under suspicion. It was a pity that Lord Sartian hadn't paid as much attention to his family as he did to his job, or they wouldn't be in this situation now.

Grimacing, he began to dress, thankful that the clothes were not so tight he needed someone's help to get into them. They fit him well, and as he looked at himself in the mirror, he looked very much like the nobles he despised.

This was a job, he reminded himself. He was not going there to enjoy himself, but to investigate the source of Lenil Sartian's unlimited income.

Investigating the man on an occasion such as this was perhaps not right, but he couldn't really worry about all that right now.

For appearances' sake, he had picked out a present already, and he hoped he would be able to leave quickly, despite the investigation. He wasn't used to parties and had attended very few, even after his installation as the Shield of Castrial. Before, he had always attended parties with Lucian, both of them leaving as soon as it was polite to.

Those days were past now, however, and he had to be by himself today.

A knock on the door and Donald entered.

"Miss Keylin wants to talk to you," Donald said as Alaric turned to him, adjusting his coat. It was not his uniform, but it was the same colour.

Blue had always been Lucian's favourite colour.

Alaric pushed the thought from his mind, and he glanced at the door that separated his bedroom from Keylin's. It was locked from her side, and she had the key.

Alaric had made Keylin his personal slave so she could have more freedom than ordinary slaves. But it also meant she had to be near him, and hence the room next to his, with the connecting door. Giving her the key was to put her mind at ease since she didn't know who Alaric was to her yet.

There were times Alaric longed to tell her that truth, but he had to stay his words. What could he say anyway, especially since he was her master?

"She's waiting for you in the library," Donald added, bringing an end to his ruminations.

Alaric checked the time on the small device in his pocket. He was early, and Lord Sartian's house was only a few streets away. There was plenty of time yet before the party would officially begin.

He walked to the library, and entered, surprised to find Keylin dressed in a muted yellow gown which looked like one of her old dresses. It was not a fashionable gown, though the colour suited her warm bronze complexion.

"You want to go somewhere?" he asked.

"I wanted to ask if you would take me with you," she said, her colour high, but gaze steady. "I asked Donald, and he said that personal slaves can be taken to such events."

Alaric stared at her. "And you think I will take you to an event where you are likely to run into people who knew you before? Who may bully you now that you're a slave?"

Keylin nodded.

"Why?" Alaric asked. "If it's to see your former fiancé, I can ask him to visit you here. You don't have to expose yourself to the world's censure."

He could imagine what that would be like, and his fists curled inside his pockets. If someone said something about Keylin, Alaric didn't think he'd be able to control himself.

Keylin's eyes widened. "I... I just want to go... Only once, if that's all it takes. Yes, I want to see Bertram, but that isn't the only reason. Marcia, Lord Sartian's daughter, is a friend." She paused. "Was a friend, and I promised her that I wouldn't miss her engagement or wedding."

Alaric looked at the beseeching expression on her face and couldn't bring himself to say no.

"All right," he said. "But you're going to wear something suitable. Don't go in that. I know that your clothes were brought here. There has to be something there that's better suited."

Keylin looked surprised. "Yes, but–"

Her hand crept to her neck where it was, the slave collar. It wasn't a real collar, but a magical tattoo that would stay for as long as one was a slave. It had a spell that bound the slave to their master, which made them unable to harm their masters except in self-defence, and to obey their reasonable orders. It couldn't be removed by force or magic, but it could be made invisible to all but the master.

Alaric walked up to her, and touched the collar, focussing his magic. He wouldn't know if it worked since it was still visible to him.

"Look in the mirror," he said, taking his hand away. "Can you see it?"

Keylin walked up to the only mirror in the library, which was beside a bookshelf and behind a reading chair. Her hand went to her neck again, eyes wide as she turned to him.

"It's gone!"

"It's not gone," he said. "But only I'll be able to see it now. Now, go change your dress and join me in the front room. We don't want to be late."

She smiled at him before hurrying outside. Alaric shook his head. He was likely to regret this decision, but how could he have said no to her?

Once, Alaric had thought her merely a spoiled brat, a noble with nothing in her head. Even when he knew what she was to him, he had thought that, but that was before he got to know her.

It bothered him more than he could say that she, her mother, her aunt, and her cousin were all slaves because of an archaic law and Hamin's actions. There was nothing he could do about Hamin Giles and his deeds, but the law was not immutable.

As long as His Majesty agreed, the laws would change, and Keylin wouldn't have to be a slave for long.

In the meantime, he hoped everything would go well tonight.

TWENTY THREE

LUCIAN COULDN'T KEEP his eyes off Alaric. No matter where he was, his eyes were drawn to that tall figure. He tried not to look, to focus his attention elsewhere, but to no avail. He had watched Alaric lead Bertram and Keylin out of the hall and come back alone. Now he moved among the others, seemingly unconscious of Lucian's gaze as he was to the many other gazes and whispers that followed him.

Most of the gazes were speculative, but Lucian had no doubt that his own was different. Seeing Alaric here, so soon again after their earlier meeting was evoking a lot of different emotions in him. Memories surging up, and with it, desire, love, self-loathing, guilt, shame.

He should be leaving the ballroom and going into the house, try to find out something on Lenil Sartian, but right now, he couldn't think of anything. The room was suffocating, and Lucian turned away, seeking a way out of it. He made his way into an antechamber, and walked to the window, opening it and sticking his head out, gulping in lungfuls of air.

"You might fall off," a voice spoke, the voice of the man Lucian had been staring at all evening.

Lucian yelped, and nearly fell off, but caught himself in time and turned to see Alaric standing inside the room, his back to the closed door.

"Alaric," he said, his voice coming out breathless.

"Lucian," Alaric spoke, his voice even. "Mind telling me why you have been staring at me all evening? Have you forgotten we have work to do?"

Under any other circumstances, Lucian would have lied, or brushed it off, or even denied it. But his heart was still racing, and he couldn't stop the words that slipped past his lips.

"I couldn't help it. I've missed you. You've changed, but not so much... I just... It's been so long."

"We met each other last griel," Alaric said drily. "We've been seeing each other every day at court."

"You know what I mean," Lucian said, moving towards Alaric.

"Do I?" Alaric asked, not moving from where he stood.

"Alaric," Lucian said as he stopped, right in front of the other man. One more step would bring them chest to chest. "Alaric, it has been farials since I saw you like this."

"Like what?" Alaric asked, as if he was determined to make things difficult for Lucian. "I'm afraid I don't get you."

"In an informal setting," Lucian said. "Where I could just look at you and not worry about anything."

Where I could dream of taking you home later and making love to you.

Alaric's eyes held his.

"Five farials, twenty griels and sixteen days since we last had sex, if that's what you mean." He paused, adding with deliberate casualness that would have deceived anyone except Lucian. "Five farials, twenty griels and three days since we saw each other before my return."

Lucian's breath hitched. "Alaric..."

"Is that all you can say?" Alaric demanded, his voice harsh. "Five farials I suffered, and you have nothing more to say to me?"

"What do you want me to say?" Lucian asked.

"What should I tell you?" Alaric asked, bitterness palpable in his tone. "Is it too much for me to even hope for a proper apology from the great Blade of Castrial? An explanation? Without me having to ask for it? I was in abyss, Lucian, and now you stand there, refusing to speak, and you expect me to believe that you care? That you missed me?"

"What good would another apology do?" Lucian asked, his heart hammering as he tried to parse Alaric's words.

It sounded as if Alaric suspected the truth, even though he wasn't sure. But Lucian couldn't tell him, not before the King did. For Castrial's sake, the truth had to stay inside his heart.

"What I did was unforgiveable, and I dare not ask for it. I regret what I did, and I have regretted it even when I thought you were guilty, but my regret serves no purpose... It doesn't help ease any part of what you went through, and no amount of apologies can make up for what I did."

"You're right," Alaric said, his eyes boring into Lucian's. "They don't. But at least an expression of that would have made me feel like you care, would have made me inclined to... Perhaps it's best this way."

"Alaric..."

"Stop it!" Alaric growled. "Stop saying my name like I mean something! Stop looking at me like you care!"

"I do," Lucian said. "Whatever I did, however I wronged you, doesn't mean that I don't care for you!"

Alaric turned as if to leave, and Lucian caught his arm and spun him around. Alaric knocked off his hand and pushed him away. "Don't touch me!"

They stared at each other, Alaric's eyes full of anger and something else, something so intensely familiar that Lucian couldn't stop himself from stepping forward and reaching out. Alaric's hand caught his shoulder and slammed him on to the wall next to the door.

"Do you never listen?" he demanded. "Why do you keep pushing?"

Lucian leaned forward to press his lips to Alaric's, and the other man stiffened for a droplet before kissing back. It was not like how they had kissed before. It was rough and harsh and full of need, and a lot of pent-up emotions. Lucian's hand fisted on Alaric's shoulders, afraid Alaric would pull away.

Alaric didn't, pulling Lucian even closer, his hand on the back of Lucian's neck almost vice like. He had forgotten this, Lucian realised. Forgotten the shape of Alaric's lips, the taste of Alaric's mouth, the feel of his hard body under his hands. Lucian's roaming hands had found the fastenings of Alaric's tunic and had started to loosen them. He needed to feel Alaric's skin, to touch its warmth. He needed it like he had not needed anything in his life.

Alaric's grip gentled, as did his lips, and Lucian licked into the other man's mouth eliciting a reaction as Alaric's grip around his middle tightened.

Alaric was the one who broke the kiss, but Lucian wouldn't let him move away.

"We can't," Alaric said, but he looked and sounded every bit as wrecked as Lucian felt.

"We can," Lucian said. "Alaric, please."

Alaric shook his head. "It's not enough," he whispered. "We can't because it won't change a thing, and I... I can't anymore, Lucian. I can't..."

Lucian let him go, and watched as Alaric fastened his tunic again and took a comb from his pocket to wrangle his hair back in place. He checked himself on the mirror on one corner and held out the comb to Lucian without a word. Lucian took the comb almost mechanically and started putting his hair in order, his thoughts churning and his heart aching so much that he wanted to rub his chest. Lucian felt shattered, as if his heart was only a bloody mess inside his chest.

Of course, hearts didn't really shatter. It only felt like they did.

"Oh, for!" Alaric said before grabbing the comb from his hand. "Don't look like someone has stabbed you in the heart. We still have work to do, remember? Pull yourself together!"

He walked out, his stride as steady as ever, and Lucian stared after him, his vision blurring.

Pull himself together. As if it was that easy. But Alaric was right. They had work to do.

TWENTY FOUR

ALARIC WALKED TOWARDS the room where he had left Keylin with Bertram. He had managed to slip away to Lord Sartian's office but hadn't found anything. The only other place where something could be was Lenil Sartian's bedroom, and Alaric wasn't going to go poking around there. Lucian was better suited for that.

So, now he was ready to go home. After Keylin had met her friend, she had wanted to have a private word with Bertram, and he had found a room where he had left them alone. He was wondering if he should have, but it was too late for worries now. He knocked and waited for the door to open.

Both Bertram and Keylin looked dishevelled, but both were fully dressed, and Alaric hoped that they had at least taken precautions.

"We're leaving," he told Keylin. He nodded to Bertram. "Be seeing you later, Lord Sartho."

"What happened?" Keylin asked as he led her through a corridor and down a flight of stairs to the entrance where his carriage was. "You look ready for murder."

"I hate events," he said.

She remained silent, and he was grateful. Not that she could have said anything that could make him angrier or more upset. Still, he was afraid of lashing out, especially when his anger wasn't directed at her.

"Thank you," she said once they were inside the carriage. "I am grateful."

"You're easily pleased," he said. "If you had sex with him, I hope you at least took precautions."

She blushed and muttered something incoherent.

"Did you or did you not?" he asked.

"No," she said. "Precautions, I mean, not sex... It didn't occur to either of us, and I wasn't... I didn't... Oh fuck you!"

He sighed and pinched his nose.

"Are you likely to get pregnant?"

Her face paled, and she seemed to think for a droplet.

"I should be safe," she said finally.

"I'll ask my mother for a contraceptive spell she learned while a slave," he said. "She said it can prevent pregnancy if cast before or within two days of sex, but after that, it's efficacy goes down."

Keylin bit her lip.

"Thank you," she said again. "I never thought of it, because... I... I didn't plan on doing it... and before... I... We always took precautions."

"It's all right," he said. "I get it. You got carried away. But I'm not having people point their fingers at you if I can stop it."

"Afraid it will tarnish your reputation?" she asked, frowning.

"I was thinking of the child," Alaric said.

He knew what it meant to be born to a slave, to have that pointed out as if he was to blame, as if it was some moral failing on his part to have been born that way... He never wanted anyone to go through that, least of all a child born to Keylin.

He had never spoken of those things to anyone except Lucian. Lucian...

His lips tingled, and a part of him was even disappointed that they hadn't gone further, that he didn't get to touch or taste Lucian more.

He clamped the lid tight on that line of thought and focussed on Keylin's pale face.

"I was a child born of a slave," he said, wanting her to know. "And people pointed fingers at her and me till my master felt compelled to free me, though my father never acknowledged me. I made friends with a child from a noble family accidentally, and he took me home, and his older brother took pity on me, and educated me alongside his younger brother. He freed my mother, found her a job, and a place to live. When I completed my education and came of age, they recommended me to a minor position in His Majesty's government. And when I was falsely accused five farials ago, everyone who had till then treated me like an equal, were suddenly remembering that I was but the bastard son of a former slave."

Keylin was even paler now.

"And your father?" she asked.

Alaric shrugged.

"He never cared, so why should I?" he asked.

It was something that had stung once, but it was more on his mother's behalf than his own.

Now, all he had was anger towards the man who had fathered him; he'd never had any great expectations, but the younger him had been disappointed all the same.

The him of now… Well, he had learned the hard way not to have expectations of anyone.

Keylin looked thoughtful, but didn't say anything more, and Alaric was grateful. He was half afraid she might recall some of it, but of course, she wasn't even born back then. Alaric had her contract which had her age, and she had been born only after his mother had been freed, so by the time she grew old enough, people had moved on to other scandals.

"Who was it that helped you?" she asked after a few moments.

"Wayan," he said, and it hurt even now, to speak of him. Wayan's loss had devastated both of them, but Alaric had hidden his own because he wanted to comfort Lucian. "Lucian's older brother."

"Then you and Lucian…"

She looked at him, surprise on her face.

"We were friends," he said, though there was something tight around his chest, and it felt like he couldn't breathe. Friends didn't even begin to describe what he and Lucian were.

Alaric could still taste Lucian's mouth, still feel him in his arms. Lucian's taste hadn't changed, his lips still felt the same, and Alaric had not realised just how often he had remembered and missed Lucian and everything about him.

"Was there evidence against you?" she asked.

"The evidence against me was largely circumstantial," he said quietly. "But I couldn't prove my whereabouts at the time of the crime. The crime was also committed with a weapon that could have been in my possession, and I couldn't account for its whereabouts since it was stolen from me. The combination of all that was... damning."

Alaric paused, looking outside. Why was he even telling her this? But it seemed like he couldn't stop now.

"The murder of someone as prominent as Lord Hark was bound to create an uproar. I was his second, and His Majesty was already considering me to his post. It must have seemed to everyone that I couldn't wait for Lord Hark to be removed and decided to kill him myself."

"I heard Lucian said you were with him that night," she said.

"We were used to spending the nights in each other's houses," he said calmly. "It was no big deal. It was pointed out that I could have crept out of the house in the night without Lucian's knowledge."

"Could you have?" she asked, and her eyes held something, almost an understanding, that he hated.

Alaric shrugged. "Why not?" he asked.

She bit her lip. "If Lucian was ready to go that far, he might have said you were together in the night so you could have been saved," she said.

"It's a capital crime to lie to the king," Alaric said calmly. "I couldn't have asked him to do that."

Lucian had offered and then changed his mind, leaving Alaric in the lurch. Did that even count as a betrayal? Alaric's mind was numb from thinking too much.

"But you might have died!" she cried.

"There wasn't enough evidence to condemn me outright," he said. "And someone pleaded with His Majesty on my behalf. The

King had always been a fair judge. The evidence so far was inconclusive, but I was the only suspect and hence he had to punish me."

Alaric had never presumed on the fact that the King and he had once studied together. He had known him when the King was merely Garret. At that time, no one had expected him to succeed to his father's office, not when the previous King had a younger brother who was very much alive.

Garret's uncle had declined the throne after the previous King's death, making Garret the King. But despite their prior acquaintance, the King had taken his decision impartially.

"So, he exiled you, but now... Now, your name has been cleared."

"Someone found more evidence which led to the real killer," Alaric said.

He still didn't know who it was, but he knew he would like to find out.

"I don't know who, and His Majesty refused to tell me, only that it was a frame up. But he felt that he had wronged me, and hence he gave me the position he had once planned to give me, a title, an estate, gold, and an official apology."

Keylin said nothing for a while, just looking at him.

"Do you hate Lucian?" she asked finally.

It was a question Alaric had expected, and he looked away for a droplet, because talking of Lucian was always difficult, not least because of the way his heart behaved.

"We grew up together, and though he did condemn me, he also took care of my mother when I was in exile. I can never trust him again, or be friends with him, but I don't hate him." He fixed her with a stare. "Everything I told you today, I hope you'll keep to yourself. Don't tell even your fiancé."

Because Lucian did lie for him, and he wouldn't even tell

Keylin that, and he couldn't risk anyone suspecting it.

"I won't tell anyone," she said. "You can trust me, Alaric."

Warmth bloomed inside him at how she had called him by name instead of any honorifics. It felt right, and though she didn't know it yet, she was among the few people who had the right to use his name. Someday, he would be able to tell her.

TWENTY FIVE

LUCIAN READ THE report twice before rubbing his eyes and rotating his neck. It was late, and he should be heading home. The report would wait.

He had been unable to find anything in Lenil Sartian's room and Alaric hadn't found anything in Lord Sartian's office. As of now, the source of Lenil's income stayed a mystery. The spies they had planted in Lord Girone's and Lord Fitzroy's houses had turned up nothing either. Which meant their investigation was making no progress.

Lucian frowned before stretching his arms and sighing. The general populace remained ignorant, but to him and to the King, it had been clear for a while that Sarian was gearing up for war. Sylvester's report had confirmed it as well.

Worry lodged like a spike in his mind that Sylvester wasn't home yet. But Lucian couldn't afford to be distracted by other matters now. The report was on the latest influx of refugees from Sarian to Castrial.

There had always been Serenians seeking refuge in Castrial, but of late, their numbers had doubled. Lucian had no doubt that at least some of them were spies, planted by the Serenian royalty.

It was too much work to separate the wheat from the chaff, though Lucian's staff were working overtime to ensure that the spies were identified and observed. Not everything came to Lucian, though, which was good. No matter how good he was, he wouldn't be able to do everything. But he had good people under him, who he trusted, who had Castrial's wellbeing and safety at heart.

Except, someone was selling them out, and while Lucian was ready to vouch for everyone on his staff, it meant little. Till now, they had no idea of the nature of the information leaked. The identities of most of the spies in Sarian were known to the Minister of War and the Minister of Finance. The Minister of Works should have had no access to it, but confidentiality meant little to most noble officials when it came to others of their kind.

All three men were still suspect, and Lucian didn't like it one bit.

The Minister of Education, the Minister of Agriculture and Trade, and the Minister of Magic were the only ones who were high enough and free of suspicion, other than Lucian, Alaric, and

Astra. The three women who held the positions of Ministers had all been appointed by Garret in his attempt to give women more role in the officialdom and the Echelon. It had caused a lot of uproar when it was first done, and many had resigned their posts in protest, but the King had hired more women to replace them. In the end, it was the fear that they would be entirely replaced by women that had made the rest stay put.

Could that be a possible motive? Other than money? The Minister of Works had supported the King, but the other two had been staunchly against it. For someone whose origins was in a kingdom ruled by women, Lord Fitzroy had been especially vocal in his objections. But then, the ruler of Sarian was not the kind of person anyone wanted to be in charge of anything, so perhaps Lord Fitzroy's objections made some sense.

For better or for worse, Lucian had agreed to the King's plan. It was a good one, even if a bit extreme, but Lucian recognised the need for it. There were a lot of variables even now, but he hoped that he would be able to improvise and adapt as the situation demanded. For now, no one else was in the know, and they had both agreed that it had to be that way. If at some point, the truth had to be revealed to anyone, it would be done. Lucian was under no illusions as to what it would cost him, but he was ready to pay the price.

For Castrial, for her safety, no price was too high.

He got up from his chair, took his coat which he had hung at its back, and put it on. Next, he took the report he was attempting to read, one about some of the refugees in Sarian, and put it in the inside pocket of his coat. He would go through it at home. Not like he had anything better to do.

His stomach grumbled as he made his way down to where his carriage awaited, the emblem of the Blade of Castrial emblazoned on its side. It was easily recognisable, and while Lucian would have liked to be less visible, he acknowledged the reasons for it. The work of the Blade of Castrial was in shadows, but the man had to be in the light, for everyone in Castrial to see and weigh.

Davies touched the edge of his cap as Lucian approached.

"A quiet night, my lord Blade," he said.

Lucian put a hand inside his pocket and conjured a dagger. He and Davies had a code which sounded like inane chatter to anyone else. Davies' words meant there was someone in the carriage, waiting for Lucian.

"To be sure. I hope you were able to entertain yourself."

"Tolerably well, my Lord. The stars are bright and the sky cloudless."

Lucian's shoulders relaxed, though he didn't remove his hand from his pocket or release the dagger gripped inside it. Whoever was waiting was not an enemy, but Lucian didn't want to be careless.

"Let's hope we have a quiet journey," he said as Davies opened the door and Lucian climbed aboard.

A shadowy figure was inside, and Lucian didn't acknowledge their presence till the coach started moving. He cast a privacy spell and conjured an orb of light to illuminate the gloomy interior.

"Your highness," he said, concealing his surprise as he bowed from his seated position. "What brings you here?"

Prince Geran, the only uncle, and heir to the King, scowled at Lucian.

"You knew I was here," he said, almost accusingly.

"I would make a poor Blade if I did not. What is it you wish of me?"

"I wish you would talk to my nephew," he said. "I've been trying for days without success."

"About?" Lucian lifted his brows.

"His marriage," the prince snapped. "Garret's what, pushing

forty now? It's time he started thinking of getting married and producing heirs."

"His Majesty is going to be thirty eight this farial," Lucian said equitably. "He's aware of his duties to Castrial very much. But he's also busy with matters of state and he cannot consider marriage while Castrial still remains beset by enemies."

"Something or the other is always there," the prince said dismissively. "Castrial having enemies and Garret remaining celibate has no correlation. Just say you won't talk to him about and be done with it instead of all this hogwash."

"As his uncle, you're the only person who could broach this subject without it being seen as a gross impertinence," Lucian said calmly. "I'm afraid that His Majesty and I are not on such terms that I could ask him something so personal."

"There's nothing in a King's life that's purely personal," the prince countered. "You're the Blade of Castrial. This is a matter of Castrial's stability. Talk to him."

Lucian pinched the bridge of his nose. What the old man said did have a modicum of truth. A war with Sarian would again put Garret at risk from assassins, and if something should happen to him, without an heir in place, Castrial could plunge into anarchy, to be taken advantage by her rapacious neighbours.

He had no illusions as to why the prince had approached him. The man had no desire to step into his nephew's shoes any more than he had wanted to step into his brother's. In the absence of Garret's children or wife, the throne would pass to him if something were to happen to Garret.

"I'll try and broach the subject in tomorrow's court," Lucian said. "In the meantime, should I ask my coachman to take you back to the palace?"

"Just drop me here," the prince said. "My coach is following us. You just need to keep me company till it arrives."

Lucian bowed again, suppressing an inward eyeroll.

TWENTY SIX

THE RAIN FELL heavily, and Alaric leaned forward from the balcony, allowing the stray drop to fall on to his face and hands. His hands gripped the railing tight, and he wished that he could lose himself in the rain as he used to as a boy. Standing here now, his mind was full of worries, thoughts, and as always, he allowed them free rein. There were some things that he could think of only in the privacy of his bedroom, his balcony, in the pouring rain.

Alaric was worried about Lucian, though he would never tell the man that to his face. Or express it to anyone who knew Lucian. But he was concerned. Lucian was working too hard, not sleeping and eating enough as was evident from his appearance. Alaric sensed the magic that concealed the dark circles under his eyes, but he had always been able to see through Lucian's little tricks. The illusion was impeccable, but Alaric was certain about what it was concealing. Lucian was fairly predictable, if one knew him, and Alaric did.

Perhaps that was why his betrayal hurt so much, because the Lucian Alaric knew would never have done it.

Alaric could guess at the source of Lucian's worries. The spy and the war that was almost certainly upon them. Alaric had been co-ordinating with the three ministers he was investigating and a few others to repair roads, inns, and arranging provisions.

While Alaric was relieved that he was not going to have to do the things he did the last time, he was worried. Castrial still hadn't recovered from the effects of the last war. External appearances belied how desperately short of money they were.

Even if the nobles had to bear the burden of additional taxes, there was the issue of food, as the Minister for Agriculture never ceased to remind them. There had been floods two farials running followed by a drought, and though the harvests this farial was good, there was only enough to feed the populace, with not much surplus for armies.

King Garret would never dream of taking food from the mouths of his people to provision his soldiers, but he also couldn't not provision his soldiers. Which meant that food had to be imported, and with both Sarian and Garaner at odds with Castrial, that meant turning to the kingdoms beyond the northern border, across the ocean.

Castrial's coastline had always given her an advantage when it came to trade, but ever since the last war, even trade had started suffering. It was beginning to pick up only now, but Alaric knew that they simply didn't have enough money to get sufficient food to provision their armies. The border patrols were provisioned with what they had imported, but a war would mean more people in the frontlines, less people to produce, more farms having to lay fallow, less things to trade.

One thing Alaric was certain of was that King Garret would never be the cause for a war. He would do everything he could to avoid it, but with Garaner impatient for revenge and Sarian wanting Castrial's land, they had little choice.

If he had to do what he did during the last war, assassinate key personnel in Garaner or Sarian, Alaric would gladly do it. For Castrial and her people, it was worth it, no matter that it still gave him nightmares, that he woke up at night and could still hear screams in his head and smell their blood. At times when he looked at his hands, he was surprised to see no blood on them.

What would Lucian say if he knew?

What would his mother say?

What would Keylin or Bertram say?

It surprised him that their opinions mattered. Not as much as his mother's or Lucian's perhaps, but they did.

He was equally worried about Sylvester, who hadn't yet arrived in Castrial, though he should have. Was he even safe? Especially if he was suspected of being a spy? Sylvester was part of the ambassador's staff, a simple clerk for appearances, but he was their most efficient and effective spy, and Alaric couldn't but help be worried for the man's safety.

Though the King had exempted Sylvester from being enslaved, he had demanded the man to stay on for two more farials as a spy, if not in Garaner, somewhere else. Lucian had objected and the

King hadn't been pleased, to say the least. Alaric had wanted to object but knew that it was pointless. At least, Keylin's brother wouldn't be a slave now. That was the best that could be hoped for.

A knock at his bedroom door brought him out of his reverie and he turned to look over his shoulders to see Donald entering, looking apologetic.

"Your mother wishes to see you, my lord."

Alaric frowned. It wasn't always that she asked for him. He visited her frequently enough that she had almost never had to. He had seen her for breakfast today and had gone to her as soon as he reached home from work. She should have retired for the night now. Why had she asked for him?

He didn't allow his worries to show as he nodded at Donald and smiled.

"I'll go to her as soon as I'm dressed. Thank you, Donald. You should head to bed."

"I will once your lordship and my lady have," Donald said calmly.

Alaric didn't expostulate further. From experience he knew that it was of no use. Donald would only do what he wanted in some matters, even though he obeyed Alaric implicitly in anything related to his work.

Alaric dressed quickly and walked out the door to his mother's quarters. It was at the east wing of the house, which she had picked out herself. Her bedroom had south-facing windows and a patio that led to the garden. The former Lord Giles wasn't allowed to come near that place, though the rest of the compound was free to him. It was a restriction that Alaric himself had imposed.

His mother was in her sitting room with Keylin's mother and aunt in the room, sitting on a sofa near to the one she was sitting on. She got along well with those two, and what surprised Alaric was the warm affection in their eyes whenever they were with her. It was not feigned either. Alaric had spied and deceived enough to recognise falsehoods and prevarication when he saw it.

"Mother."

He went to her, smiling. She put out her hands for him to take and nodded at the seat next to her. Alaric took his seat, and surveyed the room, a habit carried over from his espionage days. His mother's sitting room looked the same as ever, the flowering plants and vines lending an air of beauty and grace while the muted walls and minimal furniture made it look light and spacious. Magical orbs of light floated near the ceiling, overshadowing the candles in the large candelabra. His mother loved using her magic to create light.

"Alaric," his mother said. "Estella has a request for you."

Alaric looked at Keylin's mother, quirking an interrogatory brow.

"It's about my son," she said, looking nervous. "If he has heard of what happened... He is likely to come home, and I... I fear that he..."

"That he'd be made a slave?" Alaric questioned. Honestly, he was surprised it had taken her this long to ask him this. "Don't worry. His Majesty has exempted Sylvester from enslavement."

"I have a letter for him," Keylin's aunt spoke. "Can you send it for me?"

Alaric held out his hand, and she placed a small envelope in his hands. It was unsealed, and Alaric used his magic to seal it.

"I will send it tomorrow," he promised, and the woman nodded.

Sitting next to each other, the resemblance between the two women was noticeable. They both had the same oval face that Keylin inherited, the same amber eyes, and the same upturned nose. Keylin didn't have that. They looked like two noblewomen, even dressed in the uniforms of his household.

"We'll not keep you up then, Calla," Keylin's mother said as she rose, and her sister followed suit. "Good night, Calla. Good night, my lord."

Once they were gone, Alaric looked at his mother. "They don't know, do they?"

"Estella does, though she may act like she doesn't," his mother said quietly. "Elda... I don't think she knows. The scandal was hushed up every quickly back then... and anyway, Hamin's name never came up."

Alaric nodded, frowning.

"Do you believe I was looking for revenge?" he asked.

It was something he had never asked her before, not daring to, fearing her response.

His mother touched his cheek.

"I brought you up, I know you. I'm sure you did this to protect them. Let anyone else think what they will."

Relief swept through him.

"Alaric," his mother said softly. "You should talk to Lucian. Clear the air."

Alaric looked down.

"It's not that simple," he said through a suddenly tight throat.

"Alaric," she murmured. "There's always an explanation, and the obvious needn't always be the truth. You love him. Don't lose him."

Alaric didn't look at her.

"It's not my choice alone," he said finally.

All he wanted was for Lucian tell him the truth. How could they move forward without even that?

TWENTY SEVEN

LUCIAN LOOKED AT himself in the mirror. He looked the same as ever. To anyone not familiar with him, there was nothing wrong with his appearance. But Lucian didn't think anyone who knew him well would be fooled. The shadows under his eyes, and the way his clothes were slightly loose on his frame all pointed to his mental state of late.

But fortunately, he was not going anywhere this evening. He would just sit and read a book. He should ask his tailor to come one of these days and adjust his clothes. There were spells that could do that, but Lucian was not familiar with those. Alaric was good with those, but Lucian could hardly ask him.

Alaric.

Lucian turned away from the mirror, not wanting to face himself, or the pain he was sure to be reflected in his own eyes.

After everything, it still hurt to think of Alaric. Lucian ached for him, longed for him, but he knew very well that Alaric wouldn't want that. No matter what they once were, no matter what he felt now, he had failed Alaric. He had accepted Alaric's guilt, and even his hiding that piece of evidence was indication that he thought Alaric guilty. And that—

How could Lucian ask Alaric's forgiveness for that?

As he left his room, and walked towards his study, he was intercepted by Garth.

"You have a visitor, my lord," he said in a low voice. "Fortunately, I opened the door. None of the others have seen him. He's in the library."

The library was hardly a place for a visitor, and Lucian frowned.

"Why are you being so mysterious?"

"You'll know," Garth said, and while Lucian was not happy with how enigmatic Garth was being, he didn't question the man.

Garth had been his manservant when he still lived in his father's house, and he had left his father's service and a well-paid job to come with Lucian when he set up his own establishment, thanks to an inheritance left by his maternal grandfather. Garth knew him as well as anyone did and had been more his family than the people he shared blood with. He was someone Lucian trusted implicitly and without reservations.

The choice of library and the meaning of Garth's words became clear once Lucian entered the room and closed the door. The wards kept prying eyes and ears out. The library and the study were the only rooms in the house to have such wards.

The visitor turned to face him, pulling off his hood, to reveal a familiar face, slightly haggard now, with more than a day's growth of stubble on his face and purpling bruises under his eyes. There was weariness in the brown eyes, and the smile that appeared on his face did nothing to dispel the overall impression of someone at the end of his tether.

"Sylvester!" Lucian gaped at the man. "You're here."

Relief flooded him, the tightly wound ball of anxiety in his gut loosening slightly.

Sylvester nodded. "I came straight here as you asked. It has been an interesting journey."

Lucian sighed. "Sit down. You look like you're dying. Have been using too much magic?"

Sylvester shook his head. "No. It would have been the fastest way to travel, but I couldn't do that with Lord Baldir himself escorting me." He sat down on an armchair next to the fire and held out his hands to it. "Someone tried to kill me on the way, which slowed us down some, or I would have been here earlier."

"What?" Lucian's hands clenched into fists. "Who?"

"A Serenian spy. I wasn't the only target."

Lucian sat on the other armchair, facing Sylvester. "Lord Baldir?"

Sylvester nodded. "Needless to say, Garaner is not happy with Sarian. I've tried to make some overtures, but I don't think I made much headway. We're on our own this war, but so is Sarian."

Lucian ran a hand through his head. "Small mercies," he said. "What do you need right now?"

"I could do with some food and rest. I wanted to go to Alaric's but I'm not familiar with that part of the country."

"No, I guess not," Lucian said. "I'll ask Garth to bring you something to eat. Do you want to rest tomorrow or go see them?"

Sylvester looked at the fire, his outstretched fingers trembling slightly.

"I'd like to go see them." He looked at Lucian, eyes worried. "How are they, Lucian?"

"I haven't met them more than a couple of times. Keylin is well according to Bertram who has seen her more often. She has reported that the others are well too. Did you think Alaric was going to mistreat them?"

Lucian kept his tone neutral, but he was offended on Alaric's behalf. If even Sylvester thought that, who would trust Alaric?

"No," Sylvester shook his head. "I knew he wouldn't... I just... I want to meet him, Lucian. I know it's perhaps too late, that I should have.... Never mind all that now. I want to meet him, and talk to him, know what he wants."

"I think he wants to protect them," Lucian said. "This was the only way he could have done it."

"Perhaps," Sylvester said. "But I am not convinced that he wouldn't mistreat my father."

"He wouldn't," Lucian said. "I know him, Sylvester. He would never take advantage of his power over them."

"What if he has changed? Have you any idea what it is like to be exiled? The toll it takes? It changes people, Lucian. You can't tell me that he's the same now as he was five farials ago."

"I know he's not the same," Lucian said, his chest so tight that he felt breathless. "But I trust him, Sylvester. I don't think that a person can change that fundamentally."

"I want to believe that but allow me to make my own judgement on the matter. What are you afraid of? I was exempted from punishment, so it's not like he's going to arrest me."

Lucian sighed. That was not what he was afraid of. It was that Alaric may deny them entry, that he may simply refuse to see Lucian.

A knock on the door alerted Lucian. His magic twinged as the wards were alerted. He went to the door and opened it. Garth was outside, looking apologetic.

"Your brother is here, sir," he said. "He insists he has to meet you."

Lucian sighed again. "Bring him here, Garth, and have a message sent to Alaric that I would like to meet him as early as possible. Also, bring some food for Sylvester and have a bedroom made ready, and take his luggage there." He turned to Sylvester once Garth had left. "I can give you three griels. After that it's up to His Majesty. I want to send you to Sarian or Ihweith, but he may disagree."

Sylvester smiled at him, despite the weariness on his face.

"Three griels is more than generous, Lucian. Can you arrange an appointment with His Majesty for me?."

Lucian smiled. "Of course. I can also accompany you if you wish." He glanced at the open door, as the sound of footsteps was heard.

"What does he want?" Sylvester whispered. "I thought you were estranged from all your siblings."

"Perce has been making some overtures since our father's death," Lucian murmured. "He's probably here because Danae has got engaged to Patrice."

"Bertram's cousin?" Sylvester looked surprised but he didn't raise his voice. "I wouldn't have thought he would catch your sister's eye."

"I don't know if she has any feelings for him," Lucian said quietly. "She probably thinks it's a good match because Patrice has a docile personality and would defer to her."

"Patrice is not that docile, but yes, he is no match for her in a battle of wills." Sylvester nodded. "He hates confrontations and prefers his comfort, so I can see him give way just to keep his peace."

Before Lucian could reply, Percival was at the door, followed by Garth who closed the door once Percival was inside. Percival gaped at Sylvester.

"Sylvester?" he asked and turned to look at Lucian. "You didn't tell me you were expecting him!"

"He wasn't," Sylvester said. "I dropped in without notice. How are you, Percival?"

"I'm fine, but... What are you doing here?" Percival sounded and looked unusually agitated. "Why are you here?"

"I am here legally, don't worry," Sylvester said. "I'll leave you two alone. I need to beg Garth for some food and a bath and a room to rest."

"One would think Garth is the head of this house." Lucian grinned. "But yes, you should rest."

Once he was alone with his brother, Lucian smiled at him. "You look well, Perce. I don't see why you're so worried about Sylvester being here, though."

"Weren't you?" Percival threw himself down on the chair Sylvester had vacated. "I know he was exempted from punishment, but that doesn't mean it's not dangerous for him."

"I didn't even know the two of you were friends."

"We aren't," Percival muttered. "We were classmates, if you must know, but he was always aloof from everyone else."

"I keep forgetting that the two of you are older than me," Lucian said blandly, earning an angry glance from Percival, though it changed to an amused one almost immediately.

"A dig at my age? Seriously?"

Lucian chuckled. "What brings you here, Perce?"

"Can't I visit my little brother?" Percival asked.

"You never bothered when Father was alive," Lucian said. "So, forgive me for being sceptical."

Percival leaned forward, a frown on his face.

"You know what Father was like. He would never have let me hear the end of it if he learned of it. Say what you will of Danae, she lets me do what I want and is not nearly half as judgemental as Father."

"Perhaps," Lucian said. "So, this is just a social call?"

"How are you doing, Lucian?" Percival asked. "I haven't seen you since Alaric came back. Is he giving you a hard time?"

Lucian had almost forgotten that his siblings knew how close he and Alaric had been. None of them would think that the past hadn't created its impact on them.

"We only meet for work," Lucian said. "We don't interact much outside."

Percival said nothing, just gazed at him.

"What do you want me to say, Perce?" Lucian asked. "You can't expect things to be as they were, and Alaric... Have I even the right to ask his forgiveness?"

Percival said nothing, but the understanding in his eyes was too much for Lucian to bear, and he turned away.

"I'm sorry if I re-opened old wounds," Percival said, his tone gentle. "That's not why I came. It's Danae... She wants to meet you, Lucian. She's rather afraid to come here without an invitation."

"You came," Lucian said, turning to face his brother again.

Percival shrugged. "It's different for me. She... She feels guilty for never having tried to change Father's mind, for never having spoken up for you... She feels guilty for stepping into Wayan's shoes, even."

Lucian shook his head. Wayan had been the oldest, but he had always taken care of Lucian, had shielded him from their father's anger and coldness. Danae, the second oldest had not. After Wayan's death, Lucian had grown even more distant from his siblings, but he was nevertheless happy whenever Percival reached out.

"Tell her she's welcome to call on me," he said. "But I will not enter that house again, Perce. I can't."

It held too many memories, and most of it bad, that Lucian couldn't trust himself not to be triggered if he went back there.

Percival nodded. "I'll tell her," he said, adding. "She has changed a lot of things in the house, you know. It looks nothing like how it did during Father's time."

Lucian felt a rush of gratitude, and he smiled at his brother, though he said nothing more.

TWENTY EIGHT

ALARIC STARED AS Garth led Sylvester and Lucian into his office. It was evening, the open windows let in a breeze as well as cast a patch of fading sunlight on the carpet in front of his desk. He rose, the report he was going through forgotten, as he rounded his desk.

"I'll give you two some privacy," Lucian said softly as he

withdrew from the room, leaving Alaric staring at Sylvester, his insides churning with disbelief, shock and something he could not name.

"Sylvester," he said.

Under any other circumstances, Alaric would have been happy to see Lucian go, but right now, he needed him here.

"Alaric," Sylvester said, looking cautious. "You look well."

Alaric didn't know what to say.

"You look tired," he said, his heart aching for some reason as he took in the shadows under Sylvester's eyes, and the strain on his brow. "Sit down, Sylvester, or you might fall down."

"I'm sorry," Sylvester said, but he did sink into one of the chairs. "Alaric, I don't even know what to say… Everything you suffered these five farials… I should have at least tried to make things easier for you."

Alaric stared at him. "That's not what I expected you to say," he said.

Sylvester had saved his life, had ensured that he would only be exiled and not executed, and as for everything else, well, they had a war to win, and Alaric really couldn't blame the other man.

Lucian had looked for him, even though Alaric had hidden himself away so well that he couldn't find him. Lucian had never stopped looking, though.

He didn't know why he was thinking of Lucian right now.

"You don't owe me anything," he added.

"We both know that's not true," Sylvester said, drumming his fingers on the table. He looked completely exhausted, no surprise after everything he had been through. "I just feel like I'm here only when I need something from you… Can I visit them?"

Alaric nodded. "Who do you want to see first?"

"My father, if that's all right with you," Sylvester said.

Alaric nodded again. "He's outside," he said. "He prefers it that way. Follow me."

They walked in step, and Alaric saw Sylvester's eyes stray towards him more than once.

"Something on my face?" he asked.

Sylvester stopped.

"I lied," he said. "You don't look well, Alaric. You don't look good. You look awful. What have you been doing to yourself?"

Alaric wanted to say it was none of Sylvester's business, but he didn't.

"You don't look so great yourself," he said, attempting to sound light.

Sylvester chuckled. "At least mine is due to unavoidable causes," he said. "I'm so sorry, Alaric."

"You keep saying it as if it was your fault or there was something you could have done," Alaric said. "No one could have done anything back then. And you helped, as much as you could... Without you... You are the only reason I'm still here and had a chance to prove my innocence, so stop apologising to me."

"I talked to Lucian," Sylvester said. "He was... He was really torn back then, Alaric."

"I know," Alaric said. He did, but that didn't make things any easier. "Shall we go, Sylvester?"

Sylvester nodded, still looking troubled. Alaric wished he knew how to assuage Sylvester's guilt, but there were no more words that he could say that could help. He hoped Sylvester knew Alaric meant every word he already spoke.

He took Sylvester to a sitting room and sent for Hamin and Estella. He left once the two came, telling Sylvester to come find him in the office when he was done.

He ran into Keylin on his way back.

"I heard Sylvester was here," she said, looking both worried and glad. "Is he here?"

"He's meeting your parents," he said, steering her back to the house. "He'll come see you later. I already gave him permission."

"But he–" She paused and frowned. "Is it safe for him?"

"He was exempted from punishment and anyway, he had been let go from his post, so he had nowhere to go," Alaric said smoothly.

Sylvester's family didn't know what he was, what he did, and Alaric wasn't going to be the one to betray that secret. Even if Sylvester had to leave Garaner under a cloud of suspicion, his family was not going to learn of it.

Keylin still looked troubled, so Alaric added, "He's perfectly safe. His Majesty has already offered him another assignment in another embassy, and he has to stay for two more farials. Provided his service remains as unblemished as it had been the last eight farials, he would be allowed to leave with no risks of being a slave."

"Makes me wish I had joined the army or the diplomatic staff back then," Keylin muttered. "Not that you're a bad master, but–"

"A slave is a slave," Alaric said, understanding. He would be the last person to feel upset at someone who wanted freedom. "Why didn't you? And your cousin as well?"

"Father," she said briefly. "He believed that being a soldier or a clerk is beneath us. Nothing lower than a general's or an ambassador's rank would have been acceptable to him. In the end, Dew, Benji and I gave in to his wishes by not pursuing any careers he thought unsuitable. Syl did not. I'm glad he didn't."

Alaric said nothing. His dislike of Hamin Giles grew the more he heard of him. The man was a fool, but it was none of Alaric's business.

"You could always leave," he said quietly. "Bertram would marry you, slave or no, no matter how his mother feels about it. As his wife, His Majesty would grant you your freedom."

"You don't know how tempting that is," Keylin murmured.

"But I... I can't." She smiled at him, though it was tremulous. "Thank you, though. For being so kind. You always allow everyone to meet us... You don't have to."

They stepped into the living room and Alaric paused.

"Perhaps," he said. "But I've nothing to gain from not allowing it. Stay here. I'll send your cousin and aunt here as well. Your brother will come to you soon."

Alaric went into his study, forgetting for the droplet that Lucian was there. He was sitting on his usual chair, chin on his hand, and staring at the dark fireplace. It wasn't cold enough to have a fire during the day. Alaric stopped, allowing himself to look at the other man for a droplet, his treacherous heart leaping and behaving as though it wanted to exit Alaric's body and lay itself at Lucian's feet.

"Lucian," he said, not wanting to leave.

Lucian started, and turned his face to him, hand dropping. He rose to his feet.

"Alaric. You need anything? Should I leave?"

"Stay," Alaric said. "Is he staying with you?"

There was no need to specify. They both knew who he meant. Lucian nodded. "He'll be fine."

"I know," Alaric said. "Thank you."

"He's my friend," Lucian said. "Alaric... Can we talk?"

Alaric both wanted it and didn't.

"Would it do any good?" he asked.

Lucian sighed.

"I wronged you... I should have... Will you ever forgive me?"

Alaric felt his chest tighten.

"I don't know that I can," he said.

Lucian nodded, a look of resignation on his face.

"I know," he said, sounding weary beyond anything Alaric had ever seen. "I shouldn't have done any of the things I did. I don't know what to do now, how to make up for it."

"I don't know either," Alaric muttered. Was it even possible?

Lucian looked even more devastated than ever, his shoulders sagging, and head bowing, but not before Alaric had seen the abject misery on his face. It hurt, much more than he would have anticipated, to see that expression.

Alaric took a step forward.

"Lucian, I..."

Lucian shook his head.

"Don't you dare apologise," he said. "We... I was the one who broke us... You have nothing to apologise for, Alaric... I wish things could have been different...but I... I know you can never trust me again... And I don't know what to do..."

"Start over," Alaric heard himself say, his voice strange even to his own ears. "Can we?"

Lucian stared at him, and Alaric's heart raced even faster.

"I don't want to start over as just friends," Lucian said quietly.

"You were engaged to Dew," Alaric reminded him, another barb in his heart. "What else can we start over as now?"

Lucian's eyes dropped.

"I want more," he said. "I ... Dew and I... It wasn't the same, and I never stopped loving you."

Alaric knew it. Lucian had looked for him, even when he was engaged to Dew. But Alaric hadn't wanted to see him back then. Even after five farials, he hadn't, and if his name hadn't been cleared, and the King's personal envoy hadn't approached him with a message written by the man himself, he would never have returned either.

"It's too late for that," Alaric said quietly. "If we cannot even be friends, what hope have we of anything else?"

Lucian's face was pale as he lifted his eyes to look at him.

"I cannot pretend that I am content with friendship when I

want more," he said. "And it would be unfair to you for me to... To even express myself when you don't feel the same."

"Don't be such a child, Lucian," Alaric said quietly. "What I am suggesting is the best I can do... I don't want to lose you, but I can't accept anything more right now."

Lucian stared at him. "Right now," he said.

Alaric nodded, heart pounding, and was rewarded with a blinding smile. Alaric had forgotten the effect Lucian's bright smiles had on his heart, but he was happy to see it all the same. He had missed it, missed seeing Lucian happy, smiling, cheerful.

"All right then," Lucian said, his expression tender. "Let's start over."

Alaric again nodded, wondering if he was allowing his feelings to override his reason, but his heart didn't care, basking in the expression on Lucian's face and the brightness of his smile.

TWENTY NINE

LUCIAN FROWNED AS he looked at the King from across the board of the game they were playing. This had become a new routine now, the King asking for him every evening, and they ended up playing late into the night.

The game was called Castles and Forests, one that Lucian had started playing as a child. Each player had to conquer as many castles belonging to the other player as they could and use the forests to trap the other. Lucian had considered himself a fair player, but Garret was on a league all his own. Lucian had been trounced every night so far.

"I heard Sylvester is back," Garret said. "And that he visited his family."

Lucian didn't know why, but his hand stilled, hovering over his piece, carved in the likeness of a lion, which was about to pounce on one of Garret's castles. His heart started hammering as he looked up and saw that Garret's attention seemed to be riveted on the game. Lucian swallowed, lowered his eyes, and touched his piece, activating the magic which made it pounce on the castle, claiming it. Today's game had been the closest with Lucian matching Garret's number of castles claimed, and right now, he was ahead for the first time in forever.

"He's staying with me," Lucian said. "And he wants to meet you."

Garret moved his own piece closer to one of Lucian's castles.

"Alaric has submitted a proposal for my consideration."

Lucian moved a forest between the piece and the castle. "Oh?"

"To amend the current law about enslaving the families of convicts," Garret said, tapping his chin as he seemed to consider the board. "Provided there's someone in the family currently not a slave and has rendered meritorious service to Castrial."

Lucian was afraid to even hope, the last time still fresh in his mind. He had protested when Garret had insisted that Sylvester had to stay on for two more farials, but Garret had been angry.

"And?" he asked. "Are you considering it, Your Majesty?"

Garret sighed and leaned back. "The game is yours today, Lucian. Well played." He rose and walked to the window while Lucian started putting away the pieces. "I've asked him to prepare a list of people who will benefit from the law, and the list of the masters."

"I see," Lucian said.

He wanted to press, but he knew that angering the King would serve no purpose.

"I didn't expect Alaric to be so soft," the King said unexpectedly. "I had always thought him harder than this, but he is really very kind, too compassionate for his own good."

Lucian swallowed again as he got up to place the board and the small box with the pieces on its shelf. His body wanted to stretch, but that would be inappropriate here. He knew what the King was talking about, and he wished he didn't.

"Alaric has always been so," he said finally. "He's always been kind and compassionate. I'm glad to know that exile hasn't snuffed it out."

A part of him was still rejoicing that Alaric had been willing to give him another chance. Start over, he had said, but he hadn't rejected Lucian's feelings, which gave him hope.

"Exile..." the King murmured. "I'm inclined to favourably consider his amendment," he added. "If I could do away with slavery altogether, I would... It's always been one of our most unfair laws. But the nobility would be up in arms if I even proposed it, and now, more than ever, we need their support."

"Because of the war that's coming," Lucian said quietly.

The King nodded, his face sombre.

"Many of them have the resources we need, and unless I'm planning to do away with the titles and appropriate everything in Castrial's name, I can't afford to alienate them."

"Why don't you?" Lucian heard himself ask, and he himself was surprised at his temerity.

Garret looked amused.

"Wasn't your father a noble?" he asked. "Isn't your sister one?"

Lucian looked down, feeling his face burn.

"Yes," he admitted. "But that doesn't mean I support their order or everything they do. They seem to believe they're entitled to things the ordinary citizens aren't... If not for the law that you have the right to demand their resources and money in times of war, they would hoard everything to themselves."

"They still try," Garret said, his brows furrowed, as he crossed his arms. "They claim they don't have anything, and if anyone but Alaric is the Shield, I fear they would have got away with it too." He paused. "But as to why I don't take away their wealth and privileges at sword point, the truth is I can't. I would need armies to quell the rebellion such a decision would bring, and most of our generals and officers belong to the ranks of nobles. Even so, Alaric has been putting the fear of gods into the hearts of the nobles, so they will support me in this war with everything they have. That's something."

Lucian was not surprised. If any one man could be trusted not to fall for the nobility's tricks to hoard their supplies, their money, and their food, it was Alaric.

"Alaric is loyal and diligent," he said.

"That he is," Garret said. "Not that different from you in that respect. There are a few like that, and they're the ones I can depend on in trying times." He smiled, and it was amused. "As long as I can trust you all not to pester me to get married."

Lucian chuckled.

"Your uncle is afraid that he will have to become King if Your Majesty doesn't get married and produce heirs."

Garret grimaced.

"I'm not interested in a political marriage," he said. "And I've yet to meet a woman who holds my interest like that." He paused. "Or man, for that matter."

Lucian suppressed a smile.

"Marrying a man won't solve the problem of heirs," he

pointed out.

"Adoption has always been an option for royals when there is no direct heir," Garret countered. "I can always go that route if I don't meet someone for whom I can feel something more than the most tepid of feelings."

Lucian nodded.

"Have you anyone in mind?"

"To adopt, you mean?" Garret asked. "Not yet. But I don't think there's any hurry. As of now, there are no threats to my life, and I'm certain that Garaner and Sarian wouldn't try to harm me this time."

Lucian frowned.

"You mean?"

"The last time, we showed them the way," Garret said. "I fear they may do the same to us this time. Assassinate key officials, and the war is as good as won."

Lucian's mouth was dry. He didn't need Garret to spell it out for him, but as Blade, he would be on top of any kill list, and as Shield, so would Alaric be.

"Ask Sylvester to come and meet me tomorrow morning," Garret said, turning away from Lucian. "You should go home and rest. We need to put our plan in action soon."

Lucian bowed to the King's back. "Yes, Your Majesty."

THIRTY

ALARIC BOWED TO the King. "Your Majesty."

"Have a seat, Alaric," the King said, his attention on the document he was perusing. "Let me finish this."

Alaric sat down on the chair next to the desk, his eyes moving across the room, taking in every detail. He had been in this room countless number of times, and yet, he couldn't help but look around. The single window on the left was enchanted to show a different part of the garden every time. The other walls were covered with maps of Castrial and her neighbours and the continent of Gorahin.

Alaric found his eyes straying to the map of Garaner and from there to Sarian.

Castrial's location and their access to the coast was what attracted Garaner and Sarian to them. The other side of the continent bordering both of those nations was an arid plain before ending in a mountain range beyond which lay the ocean. Impossible to have ports there, so both Sarian and Garaner had to depend on Castrial's ports to trade with the kingdoms across the ocean, paying her levies and taxes. It was a situation they had always chafed at, no matter how reasonable the tariffs were.

Garaner had a coastline, but it was adjoining the Kraken Bay where sea monsters dwelt, and the volcano called Moon's Vengeance occasionally spewed its fire over that area too. Too many ships had sunk in those waters before Garaner had given up on attempting to build a harbour.

Castrial also had a bridge connecting it to Ihweith, which gave them access to the rest of the peninsula of Ulwia.

"Some people have too much time on their hands," the King remarked as he laid aside the document he was going through. "Now, what does my Shield want of me?"

Alaric felt a smile tug at his lips.

"The list you asked for is ready," he said. "I have deployed extra guards around the houses of key officials, but they will be in disguise and out of sight. There are also similar guards in and around the areas where the Serenians live."

The King nodded as he accepted the list.

"This is the full list of slaves who would be freed if your new proposal is accepted," he said. "And the list of their masters."

Alaric nodded. "Yes, Your Majesty."

The King looked at the list, a frown on his face.

"Are there any in this who should be free urgently?"

Alaric understood why the King asked it. Slaves who belonged to abusive households would be more vulnerable and any delay in implementation of the law would cause more danger to them.

"I've put the names in that order, Your Majesty."

The King's eyes scanned the list, lingering at the very end.

"You've put Hamin Giles' family at the very end."

Alaric nodded again.

"Their situation is not urgent," he said. "They're safer with me than by themselves at this time. A Serenian spy has already attempted to assassinate Sylvester, and we can't be certain that his family won't be a target."

"I know you hate having slaves," the King said quietly. "Are you sure you don't want to bump them up the list?"

Alaric swallowed and looked down.

"I know it's not ideal, Your Majesty," he said. "But there are people in that list who are suffering as we speak. I cannot in good conscience ask you to let them be to ease my mind about owning the former Lord Giles' family."

"Alaric," the King said. "Look at me."

Alaric obeyed, and his chest tightened at the compassion and understanding in the King's eyes.

"You're suffering too," the King said gently. "And you've suffered more in the service of Castrial than any man, and unjustly too... And I won't have any of my people suffer unnecessarily for a droplet longer than they need to." He placed the list on the table.

"I've asked the Vice Minister of Law to meet me today, to draft an amendment to the existing law. In the meantime, I shall dispatch royal guards to the residences where the slaves in dire need live with orders to take them into royal service till the new law is passed."

Alaric bowed, his heart full of gratitude. "Thank you, Your Majesty."

"No need to thank me. It was an unjust law and needs changes. I hope this is only the start." He paused. "Lucian came out strongly in support of this amendment when I asked him."

Alaric said nothing, but warmth unfurled inside him. He and Lucian might still have a long way to go, but there were things about each other they still knew, that they could still trust.

"Sylvester came to see you?" the King asked.

"He came to visit his family," Alaric said.

The King's gaze held too much understanding. "Are you not part of it?"

Alaric looked away for a droplet, unable to form a response.

"Have you and Lucian reconciled yet?"

Alaric's eyes met the King's, and he hid his surprise at the question. He sensed it was not merely a wish for the Blade and Shield to get along behind it. That compelled him to be honest.

"I wouldn't say we have," he said. "But we are going to try."

They had agreed to start over, true, but that was hardly a reconciliation. More like a compromise.

The King's expression turned thoughtful as he regarded Alaric, and Alaric wanted to look away, but the King's eyes held his. The King's face softened before a look of resolution replaced it.

"Alaric," the King said, looking away from his face. "Do you remember our school days?"

Alaric was startled by the question, and he was sure it showed on his face. "Your Majesty?"

"You were one of the kindest people I knew then," the King said, looking contemplative. "You would never speak a harsh word to anyone who didn't deserve it, you never allowed younger and weaker children to be bullied, and you were always ready to help even though you had so little."

Alaric was touched that the King remembered it, but he couldn't understand where he was going with it.

"I used to be envious of your friendship with Lucian, the bond you two shared. I had no siblings, and my position necessitated me to keep my distance from almost everyone... Even if I didn't know then that I would be King, I was still a royal and couldn't make friends." He paused. "When I became King and appointed Lucian as the Blade and decided to make you the Shield, I believed I was doing what was best for Castrial. And yet, when an opportunity arose, I sacrificed you without a second thought."

"Your Majesty," Alaric said quietly. "You did what you could. You could have had me executed, but instead you only had me exiled. Sylvester and you saved my life, and I can't forget that."

"We didn't," the King said, once again, meeting his eyes squarely. "Or at least, I didn't. Sylvester didn't know the whole story. I used him the same way I used you. I knew back then that you were innocent, but I needed an assassin in Garaner, one who was desperate to redeem himself, one with the training and education of a noble, whose magic was strong, and whose loyalty unquestionable." He paused. "Lucian told me you were lovers, that you spent the night together and when the royal guards started investigating, I commanded him to keep quiet, to write that letter to you."

Alaric stared at the King, unable to speak, to–

"Why?" But he knew why, the King had already told him.

The King's eyes stayed on his, resolution and regret both shining in them.

"Because we were facing war, and I needed my Blade at hand more than my Shield."

Shield. For a droplet, Alaric couldn't breathe.

"You mean if it wasn't me, it would have been Lucian?"

"I had so few choices," the King said calmly. "You, Lucian, Sylvester, Hyacinth... I needed Lucian and Sylvester where they were, and Hyacinth had just had a baby... So it had to be you."

Alaric didn't know who Hyacinth was, but he was suddenly glad it was him.

"Then why does Lucian blame himself?" he asked, even as he knew.

"He blames himself for putting Castrial before you, for obeying me," the King said, his lips quirking. "Insolence, but I understand it. He knows now why I used you, and I had asked him not to tell you the truth."

Alaric wanted to punch the man in front of him, even if it would get him killed.

"Five farials of my life," he said. "My trust in Lucian, our friendship..." His heart...

"I would apologise," the King said. "But that would mean little. I won't lie, Alaric. I don't regret it."

"The war has been over for at least a farial now," he heard himself say. "Why didn't you send for me earlier?"

The King looked away.

"Because I didn't want you to guess the truth and you might have if your name was so conveniently cleared just as soon as the war was over." He paused. "The only regret I have is in lying to you, Alaric. If I had asked you back then, you would have done it willingly."

Alaric's breath punched out of his chest, but he nodded.

"I would have."

"I was younger and more foolish then," the King said. "I am not that any longer. Thank you for your service, Alaric. Castrial and I owe you a debt we can never repay."

Alaric shook his head. He was angry, but he also understood.

A king had to make choices like this. He had to think of everyone in Castrial.

"It was my honour to serve," he said. He swallowed and looked at the man in front of him. Angry as he was, he understood. Besides, Garret didn't need to tell him anything. "I swore myself to your service, Your Majesty, and it's up to you to decide what use to put me to. There's no need for regrets and recriminations."

The King looked devastated, but he nodded. "Thank you, Alaric."

Alaric was itching to leave, however, because he needed to see Lucian now, to apologise to him. What hurt the most right now was the realisation of how much he had wronged Lucian, all the harsh words he had spoken to the other coming to the fore of his mind.

THIRTY ONE

SYLVESTER KNELT, HEAD BOWED, his chest so tight it was suffocating him.

"Your Majesty."

"Rise, Sylvester. No need for all these formalities."

Sylvester rose but kept his eyes downcast. They were in the King's study, and there were no guards in the room. It spoke of trust and eased Sylvester's mind somewhat.

"Lucian has suggested I send you to Sarian," the King said.

"He told me," Sylvester said. "Your Majesty disagrees?"

"I haven't thought about it much, to be truthful," the King said. "Come, join me for a game, Sylvester. I remember you used to be good at games."

Sylvester shuffled closer obediently and took his seat from across the King, staring at the board in front of him. It was not Castles and Forests, as he had expected, but the Kraken and the Fire. It originated in Garaner, and players had to get their ships across the Bay of Kraken on the board without being devoured by the Kraken or caught by the spewing fire of Moon's Vengeance.

The pieces were magic as was the board, with a very real replica of the Bay of Kraken, the Kraken itself, and the volcano on the board. The fire it spewed was very real too, and players used shields to protect themselves. Accidents had been known to happen, resulting in fires.

"I didn't realise Your Majesty liked this game," Sylvester remarked as he studied the board.

"It's something to pass the time. Besides, I find it quite intriguing. The magic is nothing short of genius, and the skills needed are useful."

The King made the first move, expertly guiding his ship past the volcano and the kraken, but just as he appeared safe, a tentacle swept the ship into the waters.

The King chuckled and sat back. "That was anti-climactic," he said.

Sylvester moved his ship to the bay, but his ship immediately caught fire from the volcano's eruption

"There goes a perfectly good ship," he said.

"Do you want to go to Sarian or Ihweith?" the King asked as he manoeuvred his ship successfully past the dangers.

"I am willing to go wherever Your Majesty needs me," Sylvester replied as he watched the King expertly move another ship into the ocean beyond danger.

"That's not what I asked."

"Ihweith is not a hostile nation," Sylvester said carefully, eyes on the board as the King's next ship caught fire.

He managed to guide his own ship to the open ocean this time.

"There would be little for me to do."

Sylvester's next ship was swallowed whole by the kraken.

"Do you think it was harsh of me to demand that you stay as a spy for two more farials?"

The King's ship was smashed to pieces by a tentacle.

"My life belongs to Castrial and you; it's my duty to do what you ask, for however long you deem fit."

Sylvester's ship caught fire.

"I heard you were attacked by a Serenian assassin," the King said. "How do you feel now?"

"I was injured, yes, but I'm fine now." Sylvester lifted his eyes to meet the King's for a droplet. "I'm fit for duty, Your Majesty."

"That's not what I asked," the King said, his voice as sharp as his gaze and Sylvester had to wrench his eyes away, looking down at the board.

"I'm really fine," he said, his voice feeble.

"I have a plan to meet Sarian's threat," the King said as his ship once again found safety.

Sylvester's hand stilled and he looked up. "And what do you need me to do?"

The King looked at him, sitting back. "Something you might hate."

Sylvester swallowed. "If it would help Castrial, I am ready to do anything. Your Majesty knows this."

The King nodded. "You're not going to Sarian or Ihweith, at

least not yet. I need you here in Castrial." He paused. "I'd sent you a message asking you to identify the Serenian spies here the day you arrived. Have you done so?"

Sylvester extracted a scroll from within his tunic and presented it to the King, head bowed. The King took it, unfurled it, and started to read.

The kraken on the board let out a mighty belch just as the volcano erupted once more and Sylvester found a smile tugging his mouth despite the severity of the situation.

The King's three ships bobbed on the ocean, next to Sylvester's one, all of them looking pitifully small.

THIRTY TWO

LUCIAN WAS SURPRISED to see Alaric at his office. It was late, and he was alone here. The others had already left, but Lucian had been held up with some reports. Rhen had offered to stay, but Lucian had sent him home.

"Alaric," he said. "What happened?"

Alaric looked– wretched was the only word Lucian could

think of.

"Lucian," Alaric whispered. "Can you ever forgive me?"

Lucian stared at him, not understanding for a droplet, before his brain caught up.

"His Majesty told you," he said.

Alaric nodded. "He did," he said.

"There's nothing to forgive," Lucian said. "You didn't know, and... I did write that letter."

Alaric swallowed. "Lucian..."

Lucian shook his head as he rose, rounded his desk and reached Alaric. "There's nothing to forgive," he repeated. "I just..."

Alaric kissed him, and Lucian felt as if everything that was coiled tightly inside him had unspooled, leaving him weightless. He had missed this more than he could say, the feel of Alaric in his arms, the taste of him. Lucian held him so tight, not wanting to have even a sliver of distance between them. He wanted to crawl inside Alaric, for Alaric to be under his skin, to have Alaric in his breath, his veins, every space inside him.

The need for air made them pull their lips away from each other's and Alaric smiled at him.

"Come home," he said softly. "I'll wait."

"I won't get anything done if you're here," Lucian murmured. "Give me a droplet, and we'll leave."

Alaric smiled at him, warm, full of affection, the smile that he once always had for Lucian, and which Lucian had missed more than he could say.

THIRTY THREE

WHEN LUCIAN AND Sylvester were announced by his butler, Bertram was in his study.

"Lucian, Sylvester!" he said, as he rose from his chair and rounded his desk to greet them. "What brings you here? And when did you reach Fastan, Sylvester?"

"A few days ago," Sylvester said. "I take it you haven't seen

Keylin yet."

"You went to visit her?"

Bertram was surprised. Not that Sylvester would have visited, but that he must have gone to Alaric to do so.

Sylvester gave him an exasperated look.

"Of course, I did. What do you take me for?"

"I didn't mean it that way," Bertram said. "Just... Sylvester, you aren't in any trouble by being here, are you?"

He knew Sylvester was exempted from punishment, but he couldn't help but be worried.

"Relax, he's here legally," Lucian said. "Are you going to give us something to drink or are we to stay here parched all this while?"

"I'm sorry," Bertram said, ringing the bell. "I'll have something brought."

He was glad to see Sylvester, but despite Lucian's assurances he couldn't help being worried. What if someone tried to attack Sylvester? Of course, Castrial wasn't a lawless land, and if Sylvester was indeed here legally, then he wouldn't be harmed.

"How's Keylin?" he asked, once they all had glasses of fruit juice in their hands, and an array of light pastries on the table. "I haven't been able to see her for a while."

"I should punch you for not even trying to buy her," Sylvester said. "You seem perfectly content to let Alaric be her master while having an affair with her."

"You make it sound so sordid," Bertram said, taking a sip of his juice. It was cold and tangy and sweet and refreshing.

"It is, if you think about it," Lucian said. "Keylin isn't your betrothed anymore, or even a free woman. That you should go to her again and again with no concern for what the world may think of her, is a bit bad. Alaric may be kind and a good master, but the world will not see it that way."

Bertram stared at his friend, stricken, because it was true.

"You could have got her," Sylvester said. "Whatever the world said, it would be on you, and Alaric and Keylin would not be held at fault."

He could have, but he had wanted to placate the world's sensibilities, to appease his mother's anger, and he had not taken into account anyone else's situation. It was too late now, because Keylin wouldn't let him buy her now, but he had not tried to convince her either, had he?

He hadn't even tried to convince himself. He was happy with the state of things, that he could see her, be with her, and Alaric would let them. He had warned her to be careful, she had told him, and Bertram had thought that was all they had to worry about. But he had never thought of what it would mean to her, her reputation, and that of Alaric's.

After the brief period that he spent mingling with his high society peers after his return from Garaner, Bertram had been happy enough to do only the bare minimum to make sure he wasn't forgotten. He rarely attended frivolous parties anymore, and he was happy enough to attend to his estate and its needs, and to meet the few friends he had met. All the same, he should have paid more attention to how his actions would look, and how they would reflect on Alaric.

"Is there gossip already?" he asked, his voice low.

Lucian shrugged but made no answer.

"I'm surprised you don't know more than us," Sylvester said drily. "As if Alaric needs more worries right now."

Bertram knew that he was not used to how things were in Castrial since he essentially grew up in Garaner, but even so, he knew enough and should have been careful. But what bothered him right now was not that.

"Why do I get the feeling that the two of you are more worried about Alaric's reputation than Keylin's?" he asked.

"Because *his* matters more," Lucian said, his tone harsh, and Bertram flinched, from the words as much as the tone. How could Lucian say something like that? As if Keylin's reputation was of no matter? Lucian gentled his tone as he added, "He's the Shield of Castrial and can't afford a bad reputation. Even were he not, his reputation is the most at risk here. Keylin is not a free woman. None of her actions will affect her name, but all of it will affect Alaric, and he already has enough people looking down on him, calling him names behind his back, looking for stones to throw at him. Just because he doesn't care doesn't mean that the blows won't hurt."

"Alaric could say no," Bertram said. "He never had to give in to her or me. He can always stop us from seeing each other."

"Alaric won't do that," Lucian said quietly. "Not when Keylin's happiness is at stake. He would never stand in the way of that, not even if it affects his reputation."

Sylvester nodded along, and a pit formed at the bottom of Bertram's stomach.

"What do you mean he won't stand in the way of Keylin's happiness?" he demanded. "Is he in love with her?"

He was surprised at the flare of anger, of jealousy.

Lucian gave him an exasperated glance.

"Don't be an idiot," he said. "But I guess I have only myself to blame, if you misconstrued my words."

"What do you mean then?" Bertram asked.

A look passed between Sylvester and Lucian, and Sylvester sighed.

"I'll tell him. Leave, Lucian."

Lucian walked out without a word, and Sylvester looked at Bertram, sternness in every line of his face.

"There's something about Alaric that you don't know, that

Keylin too doesn't know. Lucian is the only one Alaric ever told. I know because... Well, you will know when I explain. Either way, I must have your word that you will not reveal this to anyone, not your mother, not your cousin, not Keylin. No one."

"Can I ask Alaric about it?" Bertram asked, wondering what it was that had both Sylvester and Lucian so protective.

Lucian, he could understand. The two of them had grown up together, been friends, best friends till that incident five farials ago that had caused this rift to form between them.

"If you want to, yes," Sylvester said. "But I want your word, Bertram, and more. I want a magically binding oath."

Bertram stared, mouth agape. Magically binding oaths were serious matters and not given or asked for lightly. And yet, here Sylvester was, asking him for one. Whatever he was about to tell him, was it that important? That secret?

"What if I don't want to know?" Bertram asked.

"Don't you?" Sylvester asked.

Bertram did, but–

"I do," he admitted. "But your asking for an oath like this tells me that you're doing this against your better judgement. That you don't have faith in my given word. Perhaps Lucian convinced you to do it, and perhaps Alaric's reputation is that important to you, but either way, you're not telling me this because you want me to know."

"Lucian is your friend, and he trusts you," Sylvester said.

"But you don't," Bertram said.

It stung for some reason. Sylvester would have been his brother-in-law. They had always got on well. Bertram had even considered the older man his friend.

"I don't know you," Sylvester said, sighing. "I remember you as a snotty toddler. You went abroad as a child. When I joined the ambassador's staff, you were still an adolescent and abroad... The only time we met before today was when I came on furlough three years ago for your engagement to Keylin. How can I trust you when I don't know you?"

"That's reasonable," Bertram allowed. "But the thing is, you don't trust me to know this, but you do trust me with Keylin's happiness? Does that even make sense? Or is it that you don't trust me at all, but trusts Keylin's judgement? But then, do you not trust Lucian's?"

Sylvester sighed again. "Alaric is my brother, and Keylin's," he said. "His mother was a slave, as you know. Her master allowed my father to have her in return for favours. When Alaric was born, my father and her master both refused to acknowledge him, but a test proved he was my father's... His master freed him while he was still an infant, though he had to stay in the household because his mother was not free."

Bertram stared as Sylvester stopped. He had never seen so much emotion in Sylvester, but then, as the man had said, he didn't know him. But Keylin did, and she had never talked of her brother as emotional.

"I'm sorry," Bertram said. "It can't have been easy for your family either."

"My mother and I are the only ones who know," Sylvester said quietly. "Dew was a baby when the scandal broke out, and Keylin wasn't born yet. Aunt Elda and Benji were not part of our household back then, so they don't know either. When I grew older and realised the implications of what my father did... The way he refused to acknowledge Alaric even then... I left home."

"And joined the ambassador's staff," Bertram muttered. Keylin only knew that there was a fight with their father, but not why.

"But if Alaric is her brother, then... Oh, he doesn't want anyone to know, does he?"

Sylvester shook his head. "He would announce it today if it would protect Keylin, but as long as my father refuses to acknowledge him, his situation is... not the same." Sylvester paused. "His former master wasn't as thick skinned as my father, and he left the capital to seclude himself to avoid the backlash from the scandal. He was forced to keep Alaric and his mother at the capital, however. That's why Alaric's situation is sensitive. And yet, he wouldn't do anything to cause Keylin even the slightest hurt. He would rather hurt himself."

"I see... I understand why... I promise, Sylvester. I won't tell anyone, and I... I won't do anything to cause harm to either of them. I won't implicate Alaric by my actions."

Something inside him broke at the thought of not being able to see Keylin again. But he couldn't be the one to hurt Alaric. He refused to be.

"I won't," he repeated.

It sounded like his heart breaking, but Bertram was a man of his word, and so he would keep this one even if it shattered his heart.

He almost hated Sylvester.

THIRTY FOUR

LUCIAN HAD TO know, and he didn't want to put it off.

Sylvester was quiet in the carriage, his expression brooding, as they returned from Betram's house.

"You didn't go to his house to berate him over Alaric or Keylin," Lucian said, with a knowledge born of experience dealing with people's secrets.

"Four of his free servants are Serenian spies," Sylvester said.

"Any in mine or Alaric's?"

Sylvester shook his head.

"No, which has me wondering what their purpose is in choosing Bertram."

"Because he has access to mine and Alaric's houses," Lucian muttered. "It is such a simple solution after all."

"Too simple," Sylvester said. "One of them has accompanied him on his visits to Alaric's house."

Lucian's breath caught. "Does Alaric know?"

"I haven't told him. He knows I'm a spy myself, but I don't want to involve him anymore than is necessary. He would never..."

Sylvester looked away, and it struck Lucian that he looked old. He was older than him, almost the same age as Danae, but the gap in their ages had never seemed so large as now. Percival had gone to school with Sylvester, but that was because Percival was a genius who had breezed through school in four farials.

"He won't to do anything," Lucian said quietly. "And he won't ask you to leave what you do."

"No, but he would never forgive either of us for letting me risk myself like this."

"You were already a spy when I took office, and very firmly entrenched," Lucian said tiredly. "There was little I could do."

"And yet you tried, the real reason you're out of favour with His Majesty of late." Sylvester regarded him gravely. "He means that much to you, doesn't he?"

Lucian didn't quibble. "Almost as much as Wayan meant to you. Perhaps more."

A flash of pain was on Sylvester's eyes. "Then you know."

"That he was your mentor? Yes. You could have told me when I asked you back then."

"It wasn't your father's fault," Sylvester said with a sigh, evading Lucian's query. "That he chose that road."

"Why do I not believe you?" Lucian asked. "Wayan was not deceptive... He had always been a terrible liar, and in the end... You tell me it's not on my father, but if not for my father, he would not have had the practice of lying and deception."

Sylvester's glance turned quizzical. "You blame yourself."

"He started lying to protect me," Lucian said, his heart aching so much that he wanted to rub his chest.

"He should never have had to, especially from your father," Sylvester said gently.

"Which is why I blame him as well," Lucian said. "I just... I wish I had known, I wish I had been able to talk him out of it..."

"You would not have been able to," Sylvester said. "And you won't be able to convince me either, Lucian. We both did it because of our belief, and our knowledge that we could make a difference. In his time, Wayan saved a lot of lives, and twice he singlehandedly prevented Sarian from declaring war on us. No one else may know it, but you should."

Lucian's vision blurred, and he blinked his eyes.

"I am too selfish to appreciate it when I had to lose my brother to it."

Sylvester looked away from him and swallowed.

"I'm more careful than Wayan, and much, much better at lying," he said.

"Should we leave the spies in Bertram's house in place?" Lucian asked.

Technically, it was his decision since he was the Blade, but he knew well the importance of Sylvester's knowledge and experience.

"I don't think His Majesty would like that," he said. "You will report them, won't you?"

Lucian's heart sank, but he nodded. "Yes," he said. "I need a few days, though. I'm busy with something else. Have we any new leads on the spy?"

"They haven't done anything new as far as I know," Sylvester said. "Astra is actively investigating, though secretly." He paused. "His Majesty told me about his plan, and he gave me a mission."

"Sylvester," Lucian said, not knowing what he wanted to say.

"He didn't tell me everything," Sylvester said. "But he told me what I need to do once he gives me the order."

Lucian knew the full plan, and he could guess Sylvester's role. "It could be dangerous," he said.

"I will be careful," Sylvester said. "But you know that Sarian is resolved to bring us to our knees this time."

Lucian knew it. "Hence this influx of spies."

"Exactly," Sylvester said. "Since Wayan's passing, we haven't had a good agent in Sarian, and the loss is felt keenly."

"We have good agents." Lucian defended his people. "You don't know everything, Sylvester."

Sylvester lifted his hands in a gesture of surrender.

"It wasn't meant to slander your people, Lucian. It's not the same, and you know it."

Lucian knew, though he had not been involved in official or political circles back then. It was farials after Wayan's death that he had been conferred the position of Blade of Castrial and had learned that his brother and Sylvester were both spies working for the King, who reported directly to the crown and to the Blade. No one knew it, except those two. It had been a shock, learning it for the first time.

Lucian had told no one, not even Alaric. He had grieved for his brother again, and he blamed his father for Wayan choosing to be a spy rather than inherit their father's mantle. Even now, it hurt to hear Wayan's name spoken, even if it was by Sylvester. Wayan had been Sylvester's mentor, he knew, and the two had become good friends.

"Were you lovers?" Lucian asked, because he had suspected and had never had the courage to ask.

Sylvester shook his head.

"No. Wayan was too dedicated to his work to care for anything else, and I never saw him that way either."

For some reason, it relieved Lucian. At least Sylvester didn't have to mourn the loss of a lover as well as friend.

"Alaric doesn't know," Lucian said. "I never told him."

Sylvester nodded.

"I know. You aren't the Blade for nothing. Not that Alaric shouldn't know, but it's safer to have less people in the know."

"I know I don't have to tell you this, but be careful out there, Sylvester."

Sylvester smiled at him. "Don't worry about me, Lucian. I'll be fine."

Lucian wanted to believe that, but he knew that anything more would come across as fussing. He cared for Sylvester, had done so for a large part of his life. He was Wayan's friend and Dew's brother, and that was reason enough. Since he had inherited the mantle of Blade, he had got to know Sylvester better, had come to consider him a friend as well. Yet, they both had their roles, their duties, and all Lucian could do was try his best to protect Sylvester and to keep his secret.

THIRTY FIVE

IT WAS NOT every day that the Shield had visitors, and hence Alaric was understandably surprised to see Sylvester waiting for him at his office. He looked tense, worried, but he also looked more like himself than ever. The gaunt look had disappeared, and the signs of exhaustion as well. There were no external signs of his injury. He had shaved too, his face as smooth as it ever was before.

He looked like a noble, albeit an anxious one.

"Sylvester," Alaric said as he closed the door to his office, casting a ward and a privacy spell. "What can I do for you?"

"I came to say goodbye," Sylvester said, fidgeting slightly, looking down, his hands in his pockets.

"You're leaving then," Alaric said. "New assignment?"

Sylvester nodded. "Yeah... I'll be leaving tomorrow morning. I wanted to see you before I left."

Alaric sat down on his chair and looked at Sylvester, his heart sinking.

"You're going to do something dangerous, aren't you?"

Sylvester looked at him, and spots of colour darkened his umber cheeks further.

"Not more or less than I have been doing before," he said.

"You mean you're going to get stabbed again?" Alaric asked, lifting a brow

Sylvester chuckled in response. "I certainly hope not."

Alaric sighed. "Sit down. I know you can't talk of it, but... Have you at least said goodbye to your family?"

Sylvester looked away, colour still high. "I was hoping you could do that for me," he mumbled.

"What?" Alaric stared at him, aghast. "No." He shook his head. "I'm not telling them anything. Your parents already lost one child. Keylin already lost one sibling. If you're going to get yourself killed, the least you can do is to tell them goodbye before you leave."

Sylvester sat down. "I don't know how to," he said quietly. "If they... They don't know what I do... I can tell them I've been reassigned, that I'll be leaving, but... I can't explain why... Lucian allowed me three griels to stay, but here I am leaving before even a griel is out... If they ask why, there is no explanation I can give."

Alaric sighed. "Haven't you ever lied to them?"

"I just get tired of it sometimes," Sylvester said, his voice low. "All the lies, the deceptions... Sometimes, it's too much..." He rubbed a hand across his face. "There aren't many people with whom I can be honest and even then, I have to keep things back."

"It's the nature of our work," Alaric said gently. "And it's only for two more farials. Lucian tried, you know, to get you to retire earlier. His Majesty was quite adamant, however."

"His Majesty has promised to let me leave this work once I finish this assignment," Sylvester said, but he looked bleak. "As happy as I am to be leaving it all behind, I can't but wonder if that's even possible."

"What do you mean?"

"Garaner already thinks I'm a spy. Sarian sent an assassin after me. Even if I stop, am I safe? Is my family safe?" Sylvester paused and his gaze sharpened, his voice growing so quiet that Alaric had to strain to hear it. "Are you safe?"

"I can take care of myself and any assassin that comes after me," Alaric said even more quietly. "You know that better than anyone. And no, no more apologies. I don't regret what I did."

No matter the nightmares, and the images he saw whenever he closed his eyes, he had no regrets. He had to make a statement, and he did, and it helped Castrial win a war. It kept everyone he loved safe.

"They call you the Red Shadow," Sylvester said. "The Garanerians. Lord Baldir is determined to kill you."

"Sounds personal."

"The previous Minister of War was his mentor, and he seems to have cared very much for him. He called him a truly kind man."

Alaric knew Sylvester was not trying to be cruel, but he couldn't help but flinch. A stricken look appeared on Sylvester's face.

"Forgive me," he said. "It was insensitive of me to bring it up."

"You were trying to warn me, to get me to take this threat seriously."

"Even so," Sylvester said, sighing. "Somehow I always end up hurting you."

"Sylvester, stop." Alaric leaned forward, his hands clasped on top of his desk. "You and I both have our roles to play, our own duties. You never did anything with an intent to hurt me. If I got hurt, that's not on you. I had choices too."

"We both know that's not true," Sylvester said quietly. "I volunteered, you know. To do what you did... His Majesty felt it was better for me to stay in the ambassador's office and gather intelligence."

"He was right," Alaric said lightly. "You might have made an excellent assassin, but I would have made a terrible spy."

Sylvester laughed, but there was something broken about it, and Alaric wanted to get up, cross the space between them, and hug him. He desisted, because no matter what he felt, Sylvester had never given any indication that he cared.

Guilt wasn't the same as love, something Alaric knew very well. He looked away, swallowing the words that threatened to spill out and composed his mind and schooled his features before looking at Sylvester again.

"I've proposed an amendment to the laws regarding punishing families of criminals," Alaric said. "That they be exempted if there are any members of the family who have made substantial contributions to Castrial."

Sylvester stared at him, eyes wide, mouth agape.

"What did His Majesty say?" he asked, voice almost hushed.

"That he would consider it favourably. He asked the Vice Minister of Law to draft a legislation."

There was no Minister of Law. The Vice Minister was a woman who His Majesty wanted to promote, but the male officials made so much fuss that it had to be put on hold. In the meantime, the Vice Minister continued to enjoy the perks due to a Minister and performed the duties as well but also enjoyed the immunity from certain acts due to her lower status in the Echelon.

Sooner or later, the other ministers would give way, but at the droplet, everyone had to think of the war.

Sylvester exhaled and his eyes were bright.

"Alaric," he said.

"Don't thank me," he said. "Besides, it wasn't all me. Lucian played a part too."

"Then I should thank him too."

Gratitude too, was not love, and Alaric only smiled and said nothing.

THIRTY SIX

SYLVESTER PAUSED OUTSIDE Alaric's house. He hadn't wanted to come, to see his parents, his sister, Benji who was as good as a brother, Aunt Elda who had been a more steadfast presence than his own mother... He didn't want to lie to them, to say goodbye.

Because if this mission went south, if Sylvester made the

smallest mistake, he would be dead, and this goodbye could be a final one. Not only that, but he would also have condemned Castrial and everyone he loved here to fall to Serenian swords.

It scared him more than the thought of his own death. Sylvester had been risking his life for Castrial for farials now. It didn't even need mentioning anymore. But never had the stakes been more than his life. Even when he was spying in Garaner, if he got caught, it was only his life on the line. But this time—

His Majesty's entire plan hinged on Sylvester doing this right, and that level of trust was frightening. Sylvester trusted his abilities, knew his own skills, but sometimes, his old insecurities peeked through. When, as a child, his father never had time for him, and later when he learned his father had another son from a woman not his mother, Sylvester had wondered if it was because he wasn't enough.

He shook off the thoughts and straightened his spine. No matter what, he had to see this through, and he owed his family a goodbye in case... Just in case, he failed.

A knock on the door brought the butler, Donald, to the door, who bowed to him.

"Lord Sylvester."

"I'm not a lord," Sylvester said. "I came to see my family."

"Please come inside, sir," Donald said. "My Lord Shield had informed me you would be coming to meet them. Miss Keylin is in the library. I believe your cousin is outside with your father, and the ladies are with Lord Shield's mother. I shall inform them you're here."

"If you can ask them to come to the library," Sylvester said. "I'll go meet Keylin, first."

"Follow me, sir," Donald said.

The man was every bit as wooden and correct as every butler Sylvester had ever met, but he knew Donald had never worked as one before Alaric hired him from a poor house. He had worked as a servant in the house of Alaric's former master, and Sylvester had to assume he must have been kind to him. Donald had probably seen how butlers were, however.

He hadn't paid much attention to the house the last time he was here. It wasn't large as mansions went, but it was homelike. The wooden floor was polished to a shine and the brick walls with their coating of paint was free of blemishes. Torches sat on brackets, idle while the house was lit almost exclusively by magical orbs. Windows had lace curtains and heavy drapes, both open at present.

It reminded Sylvester of his mother's house where he had spent a major part of his childhood. His father hadn't wanted him underfoot and he had been trammelled by groups of tutors and guards before his mother packed him off to her house where Aunt Elda had taken care of him. It was a house that held fond memories for him, and this place was similar in proportions and shape.

The library was a large room with floor to ceiling shelves and filled with books. Alaric had enjoyed books, Sylvester remembered. He wasn't interested in poetry or fiction but give him anything related to history, or philosophy, or science, and he would lap it up.

Was he still the same or had exile changed him? Sylvester remembered the first time he had come to visit his family here; he recalled Alaric telling him about the proposed new law, and he couldn't help but smile. Alaric was still the same man. Lucian had been absolutely right about that, and Sylvester was wrong to mistrust. He supposed it must have been his farials spent on spying that made him so cynical, so unable to trust, or believe that someone could retain their kindness and compassion after everything Alaric had been through.

Sylvester still had to try and put everything he felt for Alaric into words, but not right now.

THIRTY SEVEN

BERTRAM WAS GREETED by his mother's despondent face, a letter in her hands, as he entered his home that day, his cousin Evie with him. He noticed that his mother was dressed in her finest court gown, and a spike of worry lodged in his heart.

"Bertram," she said, giving him the letter. "His Majesty has summoned you and me to the court. Go and change quickly. The royal carriage will be here any minute."

"The royal– what? Mother, what are you talking about?"

He scanned the contents of the letter and was aware of the blood draining from his face. It was a very curt summons, and such never boded well.

"Quickly!" his mother said, pushing him, and she turned to Evie. "You need to leave, Evie. We don't have time right now."

"It's fine, Aunt," Evie said, though she looked worried. "I'll be back later. Bye."

Bertram saw the anxiety on her face as she left, and he walked quickly towards his room. His ceremonial court robes, a deep maroon paired with a white tunic and a pair of grey pants, all with the emblem of Castrial, a rising sun on an ocean with mountains on the background, was already laid out on the bed.

Bertram dressed quickly, his valet assisting him without words. His mind was in a whirl. What was it that necessitated the King to invite both him and his mother to the court? What could have happened? Bertram tried to wrack his brains and could come up with nothing.

He left his room, and to the front of the house, where he was soon joined by his mother. The royal carriage arrived soon after, and they both climbed inside, Bertram feeling suffocated, but not daring to complain. His mother had a handkerchief pressed to her mouth as if she was afraid of throwing up. Bertram felt queasy himself, but he schooled his features into one of calmness. He couldn't afford to show his anxiety.

Both of them stayed silent and the journey ended before Bertram was ready. They alighted at the palace, and Bertram followed a servant, his mother at his side. He was too nervous to notice anything, but it felt like only a blink of an eye before they were facing the King. The room they were shown to was large, and the King was seated behind a desk, scrolls stacked neatly to a side, and a quill and inkstand in the middle. It was likely His Majesty's office. The room was well lit, and sparsely furnished, but Bertram was not in a mood to notice anything but the man in front of them.

King Garret had on a simple brown tunic with golden embroidery on the neck and sleeves, and his crown was not on his head. His black hair was tied back, and a curl had escaped and hung down to his shoulder. Sharp grey eyes under winged brows regarded Bertram intensely. The full lips, straight nose and firm chin, added to his aura of majesty. It wasn't the first time Bertram was seeing the King, but it was the first time he was seeing him outside of court.

Bertram bowed low. "Your subject greets Your Majesty," he said, his throat dry.

"Your subject greets Your Majesty," his mother murmured.

"Lord Bertram, my lady," the King said, his voice cold. "I've summoned you because of a report I received. It appears as though you have Serenian spies in your household, Lord Bertram."

Bertram was startled. "Sp-spies?"

Cold sweat broke out on his body. He didn't know what to say. Was there anything he could say?

"Unfortunate," the King said. "You employ spies and need your King to tell you about them. Truly unfortunate."

Bertram knelt and bowed.

"Your Majesty," he said. "I dare not shirk my responsibility and am willing to accept any punishment you confer. It is a lapse on my part. I should have been more careful."

"Yes," the King said. "I'm glad you understand the gravity of the matter, and that you're ready to take responsibility." A pause. "I understand you're in charge of hiring, my lady. Have you anything to say?"

"No, Your Majesty," his mother said, her voice shaking. "I dare not evade my responsibility."

"I understand that you usually hire people only after checking their references," the King said. "How did such a lapse occur then?"

"I wasn't careful enough," his mother said humbly. "They must have forged their references, and I was not thorough enough in examining them."

A servant entered, and walked to the King, bowing and whispering something. The King sighed and nodded. The man left.

"It seems someone is here to plead for you," the King said.

Bertram was startled only for a droplet as Lucian entered the room and bowed.

"Your Majesty."

"Lucian." There was a definite touch of frost in the King's voice. "Are you here to beg me for your friends?"

Lucian knelt as well.

"If it pleases you, Your Majesty."

"It doesn't please me," the King said. "I don't like it when people who should know better make careless mistakes. Even a child knows that Sarian is our enemy, and yet, our nobles keep hiring Serenians, because they need to pay them less. Are our nobles so poor, Lucian? Is the difference in wages worth our secrets? Castrial's safety? Our security?"

"Your Majesty is wise," Lucian said. "And you are right. Our nobles shouldn't be hiring Serenians, but even if they are nobles, it is difficult for them to distinguish between a refugee and a spy, Your Majesty. Since we chose to grant asylum to these people, we cannot blame the nobles alone for the situation."

"Are you blaming *me*, Lucian?" The King's voice was mild, but Bertram heard the undercurrent of anger. "Is my policy to allow refugees asylum at fault here, or is it these people who will not do the bare minimum of due diligence while hiring?"

"Your Majesty cannot be at fault," Lucian said, steady and

calm, filling Bertram with admiration for his friend. If that anger was directed at him, he would be quaking, but Lucian seemed composed. "The fault is entirely ours. However, considering that this is a first offence, and the fact that Bertram is not privy to any state secrets, I beg you to be lenient."

The King's eyes kindled, and his voice turned even more icy.

"Lucian, you have already stretched my patience and goodwill to the limit!"

Lucian bowed his head. "I apologise, Your Majesty. I wouldn't dare to offend you."

"You wouldn't dare? And yet, here you kneel, wanting me to forgive someone you care for, despite their obvious mistake. Do not test my forbearance, Lucian."

"I dare not," Lucian said, bowing again.

Bertram was afraid suddenly, his throat dry. He wanted to tell Lucian to stop, to leave them to their fate and not to anger the King anymore, but he couldn't move or speak.

THIRTY EIGHT

LUCIAN KNEW HE was treading on thin ice, that the King was already angry, but he couldn't allow the King to punish Bertram for something that was not his fault. Lucian had an inkling of how the King came to know of the spies, but he could hardly blame that person. After all, that was his job, but he wished that Sylvester had warned him.

But then, he should have been the one to report it, and he hadn't, and obviously, Sylvester hadn't told the King that.

"Your Majesty," he said quietly. "Please."

The King stared at him, his eyes hard.

"Do you know what you're asking?" he asked.

Lucian did. How could he not? He knew there would be consequences, but he was ready to face them.

"I do," he said. "And I will accept whatever punishment Your Majesty may choose to bestow."

Bertram shot him a panicked glance, but Lucian didn't waver. He lowered his gaze and waited.

"Lucian, you!" There was wrath that was not feigned in the King's voice. "How dare you! Don't think I won't punish you!"

Lucian looked up, meeting the King's eyes, and for the first time, he appreciated how difficult this was for the man. The King had always seemed above all emotions, someone who made hard decisions without a second thought, but it had never occurred to Lucian that it affected the King just as much as it did any of them.

That the King was, when all was said and done, just a man too. He was called the representative of the divine, but it was evident that he was a helpless mortal as well, and that the hard decisions he made took their toll.

"Your Majesty," he said quietly. "I'm yours to command, and I will do everything in my power to serve you. How can I baulk from any punishment when I am at fault?"

"Leave," the King commanded, his wrathful gaze turned on Bertram and his mother. "I need a private word with Lucian."

Two guards appeared, who escorted Bertram and his mother out. Lucian stayed where he was, kneeling on the floor. The King made a gesture, and the remaining guards filed out and the windows and doors slammed shut. The man rose from where he sat and walked over to where Lucian was.

The King knelt in front of Lucian.

"Why must it be you?" he asked.

Lucian looked at him, this man to whom he had given his service and his loyalty.

"Who better?" he asked. "You know I'm best suited for this, other than Alaric... but I think Alaric has done enough for Castrial already, hasn't he?"

The King looked away.

"You're an idiot," he said, sounding tired.

"Aren't we all at one time or another?" Lucian asked, chuckling.

"Lucian, this is different; this has to be."

"I know, and I'm ready. Your Majesty, please don't doubt my ability or willingness to do this. It has to be me."

After all, they had made the plan, hadn't they? If it came to a war with Sarian, Lucian had to play his role.

The King sighed. "So be it, then. I trust you, Lucian."

"I shall not disappoint you," Lucian said quietly.

"You have, but then, that's my own fault," the King said. "You wouldn't be the man you are if you didn't do this. I just wish there was another way."

"If there was, you wouldn't be asking anyone to do this," Lucian said.

That was something he was certain of. Garret wouldn't sacrifice his people without need, and even that was done when the need was dire.

"I wish we lived in a world where this isn't needed," Garret said. "That we... That there is no war or spies or need for them."

Lucian said nothing, but he nodded. "I know," he said.

"Forgive me, Lucian," the King said softly.

"Your Majesty, I do this of my own free will. You don't owe me anything."

"I wish I could believe that," the King said, as he bowed to Lucian from his kneeling position. "I already owe you a debt I can never repay, and you keep adding to the tally."

Lucian caught the King by his shoulders. "For the sake of our former friendship, please don't say such things. We both do this for Castrial, for the people we love and want to protect."

That was something he believed in too, that whatever he did, whatever he regretted, ultimately, there wasn't another decision he could make.

"Sylvester will likely kill me for this," Garret said lightly.

"Sylvester more than anyone, will understand," Lucian said. "But I can't promise I won't kill him for dragging Bertram into this."

Garret chuckled. "You're loyal to your friends, but even more loyal to Castrial."

"You sound like that's regrettable," Lucian said.

"After everything you've lost, how can you not regret?" Garret asked. "Even I have regrets, though I shouldn't have. Lucian, I can never take these things for granted; the lives of my people matter, all of my people, and yet, I am forced to choose to send some into danger so others can live."

"In this matter, you shouldn't have regrets," Lucian said. "You're right that I have regrets, but I know myself, and even if I knew, I would still make the same choices." He paused. "It isn't that I approve of sacrificing the few to keep the many safe, but that is the best option for all of us."

Garret sighed. "In that case, I will accept your sacrifice, Lucian. Thank you."

"Your Majesty," Lucian said. "Am I not your official? Am I not the Blade of Castrial? Even if I didn't owe you my loyalty, I would do this for Castrial. This is my duty, what I owe Castrial. Just now, you spoke of sacrifices, but me doing what I can to keep Castrial and the people I care for safe is not a sacrifice. I have no regrets."

Garret nodded once and rose.

"Get up," he said, and Lucian got up as well, legs trembling slightly. "Since you made the offer, and I've accepted it, your friend and his mother will not be troubled over this. I shall also be setting Sylvester's family free soon. Except his father, unfortunately."

Lucian had expected it, but he still thanked him, which Garret waved away.

"It's the least I can do for you and him. Have you talked to Alaric yet?"

Lucian looked away, face burning. The King didn't know what Alaric meant to him, but Lucian had no doubt that he suspected. Garret had never asked anything outright, though. Till now.

"I trust Alaric with my life," Lucian said. "But I don't know if this is something I can actually tell him… Not yet."

Not ever. There were some things he had to keep secret, for Alaric's sake as well as his own.

"You don't want him involved," Garret said shrewdly.

Lucian nodded. "I don't, Your Majesty. I know it can't be avoided, but I'd rather he be kept in the dark for now. If a time comes that he has to know, I shall tell him."

Garret pressed his lips together.

"I used him once," he said. "And now I'm planning to do the same with you. Easy to say that you owe me your service and your lives, but I… I've tried not to be what my predecessors were… To no avail, since I must do these things, and use my people."

"If I know anything about Alaric, I know that he would not have regretted anything. What I regret is that he was never told the truth, was never given the choice."

"Was it ever a choice?" Garret asked, his voice quiet. "I wouldn't have let him say no, just as I cannot let you decline now."

"I don't regret this choice," Lucian said. "For Castrial, for you, for everyone I care for and want to protect, this is not even a choice for me, Your Majesty."

"In that case, good luck, Lucian. I hope you won't disappoint me."

"I hope the same," Lucian said, bowing. "I shall see Bertram home, and I will make other arrangements soon."

The King nodded, and Lucian left, going to find Bertram. The spies in his household were already under custody, and Lucian needed to interrogate them soon. But first, he had to make sure Bertram was sent home safely, with his mother.

Bertram looked relieved when Lucian told him he could go home, that the King might levy a fine for his carelessness, but that was all.

"Thank you," Bertram said, his hands clasping Lucian's tightly. "I know that it's you who have helped us, and I will never forget it, Lucian. I am grateful, and have no words to tell you how obliged I am."

"Between friends, there are no obligations," Lucian said. "Nor need for effusive gratitude. You would have done the same for me."

Bertram nodded.

"I would have," he said, but he also sounded a bit sheepish, and Lucian grinned at him, hiding his own despair.

It had been so easy to tell Garret that he would do what was needed, but Lucian doubted he was strong enough. But he had to be. He had already made the decision, and the only way out now was through.

THIRTY NINE

ALARIC WAS ALARMED when he heard of what had happened. Bertram was safe, but it was rumoured that the King had chosen to punish Lucian instead. Normally, Alaric was not used to giving credence to rumours, but this was about Lucian, and he couldn't let it go.

He went to see Bertram because he wasn't sure if Lucian would tell him the truth. Not out of any other reason than that Lucian wouldn't want him to worry, and Lucian had never liked it known when he did something for his friends, especially if it involved a sacrifice.

Bertram seemed happy to see him and took him to his study. Alaric could feel the thrum of magic in the room.

"Is it warded?" he asked. "Very powerful magic in this room."

Bertram nodded, looking both puzzled and delighted.

"Yes, but I didn't know it could be felt. No one else has ever said anything."

"It's something I can do," Alaric said. "I'm sure others won't be able to tell. Anyway, I came to see you because I heard some rumours."

"Lucian saved me and my mother," Bertram said. "That's the truth. But I don't know if His Majesty punished him. Lucian never said anything, and I didn't ask then, and now, if I ask, he will probably fob me off."

Alaric frowned.

"His Majesty is just," he said, swallowing his ire at how the King had used him once. "He wouldn't punish you for something that wasn't your fault, and I don't think he would punish Lucian either."

He had to remind himself that the King had told him the truth though he had no reason to, nothing to gain, only to lose. He had to believe it.

"I wish to believe the same," Bertram said. "But he was... He was really angry at Lucian, you know. I wish I had asked Lucian about it, but I didn't. I'm an idiot. I was so relieved that I was only to be fined that I never thought to ask Lucian what it cost him."

Alaric frowned again.

"Maybe nothing," he said. "Maybe Lucian was able to convince His Majesty that you were innocent in this."

Bertram nodded, looking relieved.

"That's what I believe too. If there was a punishment to Lucian, surely we would have known by now. I mean, it's not like something like that can be kept a secret."

"He's the Blade of Castrial," Alaric said. "His Majesty cannot punish him too openly because that would send a wrong message to the rest of the court, especially at this time when we're facing a war. There are enough people who hate him already, and the kingdom has enough enemy spies."

Bertram sighed. "Sometimes I wish Lucian could have stayed away from all this, and sometimes I wish I could have stayed away. That I had still remained abroad, but when the war with Garaner started... Well, as a patriotic son of Castrial, what could I have done but return home and do what I could to help?"

"Garaner expected an easy victory," Alaric said. "And they got a hard defeat. Now, Sarian is looking for a war. I just hope that they have better sense than Garaner."

"I don't even know why they bothered to plant spies in my house," Bertram muttered, almost petulantly. "I mean, I am a nonentity, I have no role at court, except a hereditary one. There's no reason why any spies should have been at my house."

"You're friends with Lucian and me both," Alaric said. That was the only reason he could think of. "I'm sure they've noticed it, and they probably believed that both of us might let slip something to you."

Bertram snorted. "Even for personal conversations, I prefer the study," he said, waving his hand to encompass the room they were in. "It's warded so heavily that no one would be able to get anything. But I suppose they wouldn't know that. I hope Lucian is able to get something useful from them."

Alaric smiled at Bertram.

"Lucian has been doing this for a while now. He will get the information we need."

Though torture was not something the law allowed, mind magic was another thing altogether. Alaric despised it, and he knew Lucian did too. To violate someone's mind was somehow worse than torturing them for information. Alaric couldn't even imagine the toll it took on Lucian to have to employ such methods.

But then, did Lucian have a choice in the matter? He was the Blade of Castrial, and a blade only had one purpose. It was for Alaric to be the Shield, to protect Castrial's citizens from dangers, to keep them safe, to enable them to sleep at night. Lucian had a different purpose, and Alaric couldn't really afford to judge him.

Perhaps that was why Alaric found himself directing Travers to Lucian's house in the evening. Because all Alaric could do right now was to be there, to be Lucian's safe space, to hold him, to let him break down if he needed to.

After all, Alaric was the Shield, wasn't he?

Who had been there for Lucian the last five farials? Had Dew been there for him? Had she held him and comforted him on days like this? Or had Lucian held himself back, afraid to let himself be a burden to the ones he loved? Had he buried his own pain, and pretended he was all right? Had Dew even known the cost of Lucian's job?

Was he jealous of a dead woman? And that too his own sister?

Alaric sighed. Jealousy was not something he had ever experienced, not even when he was a child. He had always known that there were things that were not meant for him, but he had never envied anyone who had them. As for Dew, he only wished that she hadn't died, that she was still here, that he had a chance to get to know her as he did Keylin.

As the carriage came to a stop, Travers spoke, "It's late, my lord. Is he expecting you?"

"It doesn't matter," Alaric said. "I'm here anyway. I need to see him."

"Do you want me to wait?" Travers asked.

"Come get me in the morning," Alaric said with a confidence he was far from feeling.

Lucian wouldn't kick him out anyway, so perhaps his confidence was not misplaced.

Garth opened the door, and he looked both happy and relieved.

"I'm glad you're here," he said. "He's been drinking steadily all evening. He won't say what's wrong, and he hasn't had anything to eat. He hasn't even changed his clothes after getting home, just locked himself in the library and started drinking."

Alaric concealed the alarm that the words awoke within him. Lucian was not given to excesses when he knew him, so this was truly concerning.

"Does he do this often?" he asked.

"Not often," Garth said. "The last time was when Miss Dew died...Before that, once during the war, and then when you..."

Alaric nodded, and made his way to the library, knocking.

"Lucian," he said. "Open the door. Let me in."

He was afraid that Lucian wouldn't, but there was the sound of a chair scraping, hurried footsteps, and the next droplet, the door was open, and Lucian stood there, hair dishevelled, and attire half open as if he started undressing and left it halfway.

"Alaric," he said.

Alaric took a step forward, and hugged Lucian, the scent of the spirits he had been imbibing filling his nostrils, but he didn't let go.

"I'm here," he said. "Lucian, I'm here."

Lucian's arms were tight around him, almost desperate. It relieved Alaric because as drunk as he was, Lucian had not taken complete leave of his senses.

"Alaric," he said. "Alaric... Alaric." His voice sounded strangled, and Lucian drew back his head, and peered at his face. "It's you... You're here... I thought you were gone... that I had lost you... Alaric, can you ever forgive me?"

Alaric saw the tears that trembled on the edge of Lucian's lashes, his own vision blurring.

"Lucian, talk to me."

"I dreamt I had betrayed you," Lucian whispered. "And I told myself that I had no choice... That I had to... Alaric, why did I do that? Why didn't I talk to you back then?"

Alaric stepped forward, the two of them still clinging to each other, and closed the door behind him, locking it. There were some conversations that needed privacy, and as much as he trusted Garth, this was something for him and Lucian alone.

"You didn't," he said. "It was a nightmare, Lucian, not real. You never betrayed me. You never would have."

"But I failed you..."

"You didn't." Alaric's throat was tight, but he had to force out the words. "I was the one who misunderstood you, who failed you... I should have known you were forced to do it... I should have trusted you more... I am the one who should ask your forgiveness."

Lucian shook his head. "No, no... You suffered... It was natural... I did write that letter... I too would have in your shoes... Are you here? Am I dreaming? I feel you shouldn't be here..."

"It doesn't matter," Alaric said. "Because I'm here, and I'm not leaving."

"They killed them all," Lucian whispered. "The spies... They somehow found the identity of one of our agents in Sarian, and they killed her and her family... She had a five farial old son and a nine farial old daughter, and even they were not spared. They killed them all, and set fire to her house afterwards... Alaric, what good am I?"

"Don't say that," Alaric said. "You didn't do it, and you weren't the source of the leak... It's not your fault, Lucian."

"They were all my people," Lucian said, his tone bitter. "I was supposed to keep them safe... To ensure their identities are not compromised... Bertram couldn't have known. There is no way those people would have died if someone in my office didn't leak the information."

Alaric was alarmed. A leak in Lucian's department was a serious issue. Was the spy they were seeking in the Blade's office, after all?

"Are you sure it was from your department?"

"There is only the palace and my department who knew her identity," Lucian said. "The leak could have come from anyone, but what do you think is more likely?"

"The timing is suspicious," Alaric conceded. "Sarian has been sabre-rattling for a while, but this indicates that perhaps they are closer to invading us than we expected. But Lucian, someone once bribed one of your guards. How do you know this isn't something similar? Besides, anything that the King knows is known to a great many people."

"I hate that we can't trust anyone," Lucian whispered. "That we have to go to war even when we only want peace."

Alaric hated wars. The last one was etched on to his memory like nothing else, and he hoped that he was wrong.

"It doesn't matter, anyway," Lucian muttered. "I already got reprimanded by His Majesty who has ordered me to vet everyone in the department with a fine-tooth comb. The royal guards will be doing the same to everyone in the palace with access to the information. Somehow, we need to find the spy."

Alaric wished he could say something more helpful, but all he could do was hold Lucian.

FORTY

SYLVESTER MOVED LIKE a shadow, stealthy and silent. The house that was his target lay shrouded in darkness, and Sylvester blended into it, his dark clothes providing enough camouflage. The front door was locked but not warded and a simple spell was all it took to open it.

He moved through the house silently, deftly avoiding furniture as if it was bright daylight. The house had a lot of furniture too, and Sylvester wondered how its inhabitants moved about during the day.

The ground floor had five rooms, all of which were empty, but Sylvester spent some time rifling through the drawers of the desk in the study. He riffled through the pages of a book he took from it, and inhaled sharply.

His Majesty was wise indeed, and right. While this book didn't give a clue as to who the spy in the Echelon was, it still gave enough to take care of a few immediate threats.

But what was more important was not these documents, but the one Sylvester had brought with him, the one in a code only a Serenian spy would know. Wayan had known that code and had taught their spies in Sarian. He had also taught Sylvester and because their spies were good at their jobs, Sarian had never discovered their code was compromised.

Placing the document on top of the desk, Sylvester retreated. The inhabitant of the house was a low level official in Sarian, but he was also a courier who carried reports for Serenian spies in Castrial to the Spymaster of Sarian. Sylvester had never seen Isolde, but had heard enough about her ruthless efficiency as well as her cruelty. He had no doubt that the letter he had planted would light a fire under her.

A fire that would burn Sarian down, hopefully.

Mission accomplished, he slipped out of the house, blending into the shadows. Using the portal stone on the chain around his neck, he opened a portal back to Castrial and stepped through. Portal stones were very rare and their use was strictly regulated. It was also something unknown to Sarian and Garaner who still used portals, which needed too much magic and drained any mage who cast it for griels.

Portal stones were better in that they didn't need as much

magic to create or activate. But they did have their issues too. While they allowed the user to transport themselves over great distances, they could be used by only one person at a time. The greater distance one travelled with it, the faster the magic in it drained away. The stone Sylvester carried had enough magic to take him to Sarian and back, and it would need to be charged with magic if it was to be used again.

It was the duty of royal battle mages to charge the portal stones, and Sylvester would have to leave his with them. This mission had taken less time than anticipated, but the more important mission was still waiting.

Sylvester was not an assassin, but he knew how to kill. He knew he could never be as efficient as Alaric, but he could be just as bloody.

He had a statement to make too.

But not just yet. Timing was everything. In a couple of days, everything would be ready.

FORTY ONE

LUCIAN WOKE UP in the small waves of dawn and was immediately aware that he wasn't alone in his bed. It worried him for just a droplet before memory returned. Alaric had come here last night and had comforted him. Lucian had been drunk, and Alaric had kept him company till both of them were roaring drunk. They had stumbled into bed together, fumbling for each other in the dark.

He closed his eyes. He couldn't recall everything, but he knew that they had sex. His body ached in a way that once knew intimately. It was more than pleasant, but he feared it wouldn't last.

He sighed and opened his eyes, looking at where Alaric was splayed on his front on the bed, still asleep. Neither of them had planned this, but it had happened. Lucian feared what it would do to the fledgeling friendship they had started to rekindle. Drunk sex seemed like a step back. The misunderstandings between them might have been cleared, but that didn't mean everything was back to how it once was. After all, neither of them was who they once had been.

Perhaps drunk sex wasn't something they should have done.

Lying back, he stared up at the ceiling. It had happened, and to be honest, he couldn't completely regret it. Not unless it cost him Alaric, and Lucian hoped that Alaric would take into account their inebriated state and not mind it. A part of him flinched at the thought. He didn't want Alaric to not just feel not bad. He wanted Alaric to be glad this had happened. A part of Lucian was glad, no matter what.

Alaric stirred, and Lucian tensed, but he just murmured something that sounded like Lucian's name before he was asleep again. Lucian wanted to move closer, to gather Alaric into his arms and hold tight, but he wasn't sure if it would be welcomed. If Alaric woke, what would he think?

Once, Lucian would have known. Once, he and Alaric hadn't even needed words. Once, Lucian had believed that he would never hurt Alaric.

In the end, his mistakes had cost both of them too much. If only he had not told the king everything or perhaps found some other evidence to prove Alaric's innocence. In the end, he had put

Alaric in a position where he could not prove his innocence without proving Lucian's lie and that was not something Alaric would ever do.

They had found the real culprit who had framed Alaric, a minor noble who had been jealous of Alaric and who had a grudge with Lord Hark. They would have found him sooner, but the war had happened, and they all had more important things in their mind.

If Lucian had found him sooner, Alaric would have suffered less.

"I'm sorry," he whispered, his throat tight. Alaric was still asleep, so Lucian had nothing to fear from baring his heart. "I'm so sorry, Alaric. I should have trusted you, should have believed you would find the truth, the real culprit... I should have found him sooner, ended your exile sooner... I'm sorry my inefficiency caused you more suffering..." He swallowed and allowed his fingers to graze the edge of Alaric's hand. "I'm not sorry about last night, though. I missed you... I never stopped... And I will always want you."

There were more words he wanted to say, but somehow, he was afraid. He had never confessed that he loved someone. With Dew, it had been respect and affection, and he was sure they would be able to make it work precisely because he hadn't wanted her. His relationship with her was one borne out of necessity rather than love, to help her out, and perhaps he was looking for something of Alaric in her.

He had always been in love with Alaric, even before he knew what it meant. It seemed to him that he couldn't remember a time when he hadn't felt this way about the man next to him. He might not have realised it till it was too late, but it was the truth.

I love you.

He didn't know if he would ever speak the words aloud, but

he would say it in his mind and be content for now.

His hand was seized by Alaric who pulled him closer and wrapped himself around him.

"Stop thinking so loud," he mumbled. "Need to sleep."

"Are you awake?" Lucian asked, the warmth of Alaric's body making him feel fuzzy.

"Trying not to be," Alaric yawned. "We don't have work yet, so sleep."

"So bossy," Lucian teased, but he closed his eyes and snuggled closer. "You're so warm."

"So are you," Alaric slurred, before his breathing evened and his limbs grew heavier.

It had always been like that with Alaric. He fell asleep very quickly when he did. Lucian closed his eyes as well and let himself slip back into sleep. It was full of vague dreams of people falling and running, and Lucian not being able to catch up to any of them. He heard a baby crying, and it turned into Alaric who walked away, and Wayan was holding Lucian back while Percival and Danae sat on chairs, watching them with unblinking eyes.

"Lucian."

A voice penetrated his foggy brain, and he woke up, groggy, to notice that he was still in his bed, the wave was considerably more advanced, and that Alaric was the one calling his name. Both of them were still in Lucian's bed, still naked, and Alaric was sitting up, his hand on Lucian's shoulder, and alarm on his face.

"Are you all right?"

"What happened?" Lucian asked, sitting up.

Alaric removed his hand, but the look of concern remained.

"You were whimpering in your sleep," he said. "Nightmares?"

"I suppose," Lucian said. "Weird dreams anyway."

Alaric said nothing as he put his arms around Lucian and drew him closer.

"Want to talk about them?"

Lucian shook his head and buried his face on Alaric's chest. Alaric smelled of sweat and something tangy and earthy and the soap he liked using.

"No," he said. "It's just senseless images anyway. I saw you as a baby. How weird is that?"

Alaric's body shook with laughter, and Lucian heard the amusement in his tone as he responded, "After last night, that was the last thing I would have expected."

Lucian lifted his head and drew back to see Alaric's face.

"I don't regret last night."

Alaric cupped Lucian's cheek.

"I don't either. I suppose it was bound to happen sooner or later."

"I want it to happen again," Lucian said. "But I know that we're starting over, and this is like not the best thing to help, but–"

Lucian saw the regret in Alaric's eyes, the pain. "I am the one who owes you an apology, Lucian. I am the one who misjudged you... Who couldn't trust... Who didn't see."

Lucian shook his head, adamant. No matter what Alaric thought, he was not in the wrong in hating Lucian. He hadn't known the truth, and the droplet he had known, he had come to Lucian, to apologise.

"I wrote that letter," he said. "I don't blame you for believing that. I wish I had fought against his decision harder back then."

"It wouldn't have made any difference," Alaric said, his lips twisting. "He needed me to be exiled, to..." He looked away. "To be his assassin in Garaner."

Lucian's breath punched out of his chest. He had suspected, though the King had never confirmed it. To hear it from Alaric...

"The assassination of the Garaner officials," he said. "It was you... I suspected... but I wasn't certain. Oh, Alaric... I'm so sorry."

Alaric looked away. "Sylvester recruited me," he said. "And I... I killed so many people, Lucian... I tell myself it was war, that I had to... but I..."

Lucian hugged him. "Oh, Alaric," he whispered again even as his heart ached for his friend, his lover, the man who held Lucian's heart and his happiness. "I'm so sorry. "

Alaric hugged him back.

"I don't regret last night," he whispered. "Whatever happened, I won't regret any night I get to be with you."

Lucian felt his tears slip free, tears for all the time they had lost, and for everything he knew was coming.

"Lucian," Alaric said softly as he pulled back, so they were facing each other, chests touching, and faces close enough to share air. "It's fine."

It wasn't, but it was the best they could both hope for at the droplet. Lucian felt a twinge for the betrayal Alaric was going to face again, but he had no choice.

Hopefully, Alaric would trust him now more than Lucian had trusted Alaric back then.

FORTY TWO

THE COURT THAT day went along expected lines, with both Lucian and Alaric giving their reports. There had not been a formal declaration of war by Sarian yet, but from every reports they had received, it was only a matter of time. Their armies were massing at the border, but what was more concerning was the news of movement from Garaner as well.

"At the rate they are moving, Sarian would be in a position to invade us within three months," Lucian said. "Garaner is also moving their forces, but it would take them longer, a farial at the least. Till now, we believed Garaner was staying out of the conflict, but at the droplet, we can't be certain of their intentions."

"Is Sarian likely to wait for a farial?" the King queried.

"In my opinion, no," Lucian said. "But Sarian may not invade us without any backup either. Queen Leshia is a careful woman. She will wait till the Garaner forces are of sufficient strength, I believe. Perhaps in another six months, we can expect an invasion from Sarian with Garaner committing whatever forces they had managed to move to the borders by then."

"But why must it take so long?" one of the nobles, a young man whose name Lucian couldn't recall asked. "It's only moving some soldiers, isn't it?"

"It's not just moving some soldiers," Lucian said patiently, suppressing the urge to eyeroll, though he saw the tightening of the King's mouth, showing he was displeased with the question. "Both Sarian and Garaner are taking pains to hide their troop movements from us, and therefore, it takes much longer than normal. Besides which, armies need be adequately provisioned, and as such, they must arrange for an unbroken supply line. All of this takes time."

"Your Majesty," the finance minister spoke, his face pinched with concern.

Lord Girone had been taking care of the finances of the empire for over twenty farials now, and despite being suspected of spying, they still had no evidence. The man was good at his job, and on the surface at least, seemed not to enrich himself from it.

"We cannot afford a war. Castrial still hasn't recovered from the last one. We need to find a way to sue for peace... If we wage this war, the ordinary citizens would be starving to death within a few griels."

"There can be no suing for peace, or treating with Sarian," Lucian said quietly. "I appreciate the concern you have for our people, Lord Girone. I share the same concern as does everyone else here, His Majesty included, but Sarian isn't looking for anything less than our total subjugation. We have already made all the overtures that we can and been rejected categorically. We're at this pass because Sarian isn't ready to treat with us. Unless we offer them our unconditional surrender and our heads on a pike, Sarian won't be satisfied."

There were murmurs, and more than one angry exclamation. The King cleared his throat, and the crowd fell silent.

His Majesty spoke. "We have reliable information on how Sarian treats its ordinary citizens. That there should be so many Serenian refugees flooding our kingdom even in times of peace speaks for the way in which they are treated. If it was only my life, I would gladly offer it to Sarian for a chance of peace, but I fear that the people of Castrial would fare no better under Sarian than during a war. If anything, their situation could be worse, and they would have no choice but to bear it for all eternity. I must beg your pardon, Lord Girone, but I don't see any other option but war ahead of us."

"Your Majesty," Lord Girone said smoothly. "I misspoke. I had no idea that things had come to such a pass and that all diplomatic avenues had already been exhausted. The people of Castrial are strong and proud, and we would bear any hardship than have our lives and pride trampled on by a foreign invader who doesn't know how to treat its people. Your Majesty's life is valuable to Castrial, and there can be no peace which involves your surrender or death."

"My life isn't worth the suffering of our people," the King refuted gently. "But if the cost of peace is more suffering for our people, then I can only hope that I can bring a war to a swift end and save our people as much suffering as possible."

They were just words. No matter how much Garret might want to, it was not in his power alone to conclude a war. If Sarian and Garaner were to ally, there would be no hope for Castrial, but Lucian held out hope that Garaner would stay out of the conflict as they had said they would. Lucian had contacted some of their agents there with instructions to sow as much chaos as possible. Garaner was better than Sarian at treating its people, and hence any internal strife would probably lead them to abandon war efforts.

Sarian on the other hand was ruled by someone who didn't care for anything but petty grudges and exhibiting their power. The present queen had been ruling for longer than Lucian had been alive, and he knew that she was waging this war to divert the attention of the nobles who considered that she had been in power too long. Her daughter was also getting impatient, not wanting to succeed to her mother's throne when her youth was past.

They needed someone in Sarian to fan all the banked flames, to ensure that the whole country went up in that blaze, and even the queen couldn't ignore such a conflagration. All her plans would have to be put on hold if so, and hopefully, Castrial would have enough time to get back on her feet so that the next time Sarian threatened them, they would be ready and strong enough to both care for her people and to resist the invader.

They had a person ready to leave for Sarian at a droplet's notice, with a cover story good enough to pass even the strictest scrutiny, and an ability to lie that was second to none. All it needed was His Majesty's word, and the plan would be in motion, the person on the way to Sarian, and Castrial's safety assured.

"Lucian," the King spoke. "I wish to have a private word with you. Stay behind once court is done."

Lucian bowed, trying not to hide his relief. The barely felt resignation on the King's face was enough evidence their plan would be set in motion soon. It was a long shot, but it was the best chance that Castrial had. A war was not a desirable option for either kingdom, and Lucian couldn't think of any other way short of assassinating the queen of Sarian to stop the war from happening. While that was not an option he would baulk at, they didn't have any spies in Sarian who were high enough in their hierarchy to carry it out.

The court dispersed slowly, with both Bertram and Alaric giving him concerned glances, but it was Danae who cornered him, to Lucian's surprise. His sister looked well, as majestic and beautiful as ever, her dress of a soft yellow complementing her warm golden skin tone.

"Lucian," she said. "I won't keep you long since His Majesty is waiting, but... Don't stay away, all right? Father is no more, and I... I don't want us to be estranged."

Lucian looked away, not wanting to make a scene, and trying not to lose it. Before he could respond, Alaric was at his side and placed a hand on Lucian's arm.

"His Majesty is waiting," he said gently. "Lord Faresk, please excuse us."

"How did you know?" Lucian asked as Alaric led him into one of the antechambers where a servant would come and get Lucian when His Majesty was ready to meet him.

"It was evident," Alaric said. "You looked like you wanted to punch her, and while I approve, I think that perhaps you should accept her overtures."

"You think?" Lucian asked, a bite to his voice. "Is that what you think?"

"Lucian," Alaric said softly. "Tell me it doesn't hurt, tell me you don't care, and I will never bring it up again. Yes, they were in the wrong, but if they are truly desirous of making amends, shouldn't you let them?"

Lucian looked away, because Alaric was right, damn him. Lucian still cared, despite how angry he was, and a part of him wanted his siblings to treat him well, and to be friends with them. He knew that it was not his position that had led Danae to approach him. That was one thing he knew about his sister.

"Why do you think they even mean it?" he asked, desperate for someone to reassure him.

"Because she came to you now, when we are on the brink of war, and when the danger to you is second only to the danger to His Majesty," Alaric said. "If she didn't care, she wouldn't have. She wants to mend fences because she fears it may be too late, and she has bent her pride. You just need to meet her halfway."

Lucian turned and pulled Alaric close, hugging him, burying his face in Alaric's neck, memorising the scent and feel of the man.

"We're all in danger," he said.

"None as much as you," Alaric said quietly.

Lucian heard the sincerity in his tone, and though he wanted to deny it, the words stuck in his throat, because damnit, Alaric was right. Lucian was the person most in danger next to His Majesty, but hopefully, with their plans in motion tonight, the danger would lessen.

He knew he would need to meet Danae, ask her to visit perhaps. Percival already did, and the only reason Lucian had denied entry to everyone except Astra, Alaric, and any messenger from the palace was because he had too much work and didn't want to be distracted by having to make small talk or reassure anyone.

The servant entered the room, and his expression showed no change as he saw them hugging.

"His Majesty will see you now, Lord Blade. Lord Shield, His Majesty wants to meet with you after he's finished his meeting with

Lord Blade. Please stay here."

Both of them moved apart, bowed, and Lucian followed the servant wishing he were back in that room, with Alaric's arms around him still. His heart fluttered in his chest like a caged bird as he thought of the future.

FORTY THREE

ALARIC PACED THE room as he waited. It was almost torture, having to wait while he didn't know what His Majesty and Lucian were discussing. He told himself that it was not his business, that he didn't need to know, that he would be told whatever he needed, but it was hard. Lucian was spreading himself too thin, and he was under so much stress that Alaric couldn't bear to be in the dark where he couldn't help Lucian.

What could I do even if I knew?

Officially, his powers were limited, and personally, well... Alaric would give his life for Lucian, but he knew that that wasn't what was needed. They both had their roles, their places in the Echelon, and there was little they could do now. All he could do was to be there for Lucian and hope that it would be enough.

It took nearly two waves before the servant came for him. Alaric didn't bother asking him about Lucian, certain that his friend would already have left. The palace wasn't the kind of place where they could wait for someone else. His heart was hammering as he followed the servant to His Majesty's private chambers and his private office.

He still remembered the first time he had done so, and the stiff formality of the occasion. Even knowing that it was Garret, Alaric hadn't known how to treat his old schoolmate as anything other than the King. He wondered if Lucian had felt the same confusion. The King had asked him to address him as Garret only twice. The first when he was exiled and the second when he was reinstated with honours and apology.

As for the last time, when Garret had freely admitted that he had used Alaric, that Lucian had never betrayed him, that Garret had lied... well, Alaric tried not to think of that too much. His life and self both belonged to Castrial and the King, after all. There was no need for Garret to feel guilty or to apologise to him. Not once, but twice.

Alaric was still young, despite his experiences, but even he knew how rare it was for a King to admit his mistake, to apologise to a subject. Yet, Garret had done it, and for that alone, Alaric would suffer everything he did twice over in his service. Loyalty like what Garret inspired was not easily won, and Alaric knew that everyone who served him felt the same. The King was simply different, not only from the other monarchs, but from his predecessors as well.

There were nobles who grumbled, who didn't like that he was changing things, that he allowed for nobles to be punished at par with commoners, who didn't allow them to cling to their births as justification for their actions, but the vast majority was not like that.

Garret looked tired as Alaric was led into his private office. Away from the court, out of the court dresses and the glamours that had been cast, he looked like a weary man who had been working too hard. Streaks of silver were visible in his black hair, and purple shadows under his eyes stood out like bruises. It was a look that Alaric was familiar with; his own, and Lucian's faces had similar shadows, similar lines of silver in their hair, and similar wrinkles on their faces.

"Your Majesty." He bowed.

"Alaric." The King smiled. "It's good to see you, friend."

Ah. So, it was that kind of meeting.

"You're working too hard, Your Majesty," he said, straightening.

"So are you," Garret said, pouring himself some water, and handing another goblet of water to Alaric. "I stopped drinking during the last war. I got addicted, couldn't function without it, and things got bad. Lucian forced me at sword point to throw out all the wine in the palace and had me quit cold. He stayed with me here to ensure I didn't drink again, had the royal physicians prescribe me medicines to help me get over, and used spells to help me through the withdrawal."

Alaric felt something in him warm.

"He was taking a risk," he observed.

"That he was. I think he was hoping at least in part that I would exile him." The King exhaled softly. "He regretted it, you know. What happened... He feels like he let you down, that he didn't argue enough... He doesn't know that it wouldn't have made any difference."

"Even now?" Alaric asked quietly.

"No," Garret sighed. "Now, he knows that there was nothing he or anyone could have done unless they could have produced the real murderer." He sighed again, more deeply this time. "Sometimes, it's hard for me to know what to do, to say. Sometimes I have to choose exigency over friendship, over everything."

"You're responsible for the safety of the entire Castrial, and all of its people," Alaric said. "Sometimes you have to make sacrifices of the ties of friendship."

"Or use them," Garret sounded bitter. "Alaric, sometimes I wish I had never been born a royal, that I had not chosen to be King, that I had told my uncle that I can't do this when my father died..."

"Would you have had any peace if you did that?" Alaric asked. "Even in school, you were concerned for the people and their welfare. You were born and bred to this position, and you would never have been happy if you just handed someone else the responsibility. Think of all the good you've done, Your Majesty. Do you really wish to step away?"

Garret sighed. "It's not so much that I wish to leave my position as that I hate some of the decisions that I have to take. You heard about the spies in Sarian?"

Alaric nodded; more than one spy had been killed in Sarian by now, but it was not classified information, and Alaric was the one who had to inform the families of those people who were still in Castrial.

"Today, I approved sending another person to Sarian as a spy," Garret said. "I might as well have had them put to death here itself."

"You're trying to fight a war with minimum of casualties," Alaric said. "We may all wish that such a situation was not necessary, but this war is not of our making."

"I know," Garret said, sounding weary. "And I've tried my best, and yet, they don't want anything other than my complete and unconditional surrender. By my I mean Castrial's." He rubbed his face. "Anyway, I didn't call you so I can indulge in self-pity, though I suppose that too... You and Lucian are the only ones with whom I feel safe doing that."

"Thank you," Alaric said, his voice quiet. He appreciated it, and he valued this trust that his King gave him.

"I called you about the law you proposed, the one we discussed the last time."

Alaric's heart started beating hard. "Yes?"

"It actually takes care of a problem I've been having," the King said. "The Vice Minister of Law has put up the draft for approval. The only modification is people convicted of treason and mass murder are excluded from its purview. I have approved it, Alaric. It will be announced next session of the court."

Alaric bowed, joy sparking through him.

"Thank you, Your Majesty," he said.

"Keep it between ourselves for now," the King said. "Let everyone know when it's announced. People are... unpredictable."

Alaric didn't know what it meant, but he was happy enough to keep it to himself for now. Keylin would know when the law was announced. There would be time enough for celebrations later.

FORTY FOUR

SYLVESTER cracked his neck as he rose from his bed. He was still staying with Lucian which seemed something he shouldn't be doing. He could have moved to his townhouse, but he didn't want to be alone. So, till his family gained their freedom, he would stay with Lucian. He could have stayed with Alaric, but he wasn't sure how to ask Alaric. It was easier with Lucian since he was more familiar with the man.

His body ached and he winced as he got up. He had gone to a brothel and had arrived late at Lucian's house. Garth had let him in with a disapproving stare, but Sylvester didn't care. Though he did have a pleasant night, he hadn't gone there for pleasure alone.

Fedri, the woman he had been with the night before, was one of the highest paid courtesans in Castrial. But more than that, she traded in information. While she projected an image of caring for nothing but money, she was choosey about the information she traded. Sylvester appreciated Fedri's patriotism almost as much as he did her body.

The information she had provided was interesting, to say the least. An indication that the time had come to put their plan in motion.

Sylvester cleaned his teeth and had a leisurely bath. The information could wait a bit. Sauntering downstairs, he encountered Lucian who gave a rather pointed glance at the mark on Sylvester's neck.

"Look who's talking," Sylvester whispered, waggling his eyebrows at Alaric who was coming from Lucian's room.

As he sat at the breakfast table, he wondered when Lucian and Alaric made up and how he had missed it. It certainly complicated things but was also good since it gave His Majesty's plan a better chance of working.

"You're back?" Alaric asked, brows furrowing.

"For now," Sylvester said. "I have one more task after which I can be home and be an idle nobleman."

"At my home, you mean," Lucian said drily.

Alaric grinned. "He won't be staying here for long," he said, and Sylvester and Lucian both stared at him.

"What?" Alaric asked as he started eating his porridge.

"His Majesty approved of the law?" Lucian asked, eyes wide.

Alaric nodded. "Don't let anyone else know. He asked me to keep it quiet for now."

"But you're telling us," Sylvester said.

"Because I trust you to keep it to yourself and it's not a state secret." Alaric started ladling more porridge into his bowl.

Sylvester cut some bread and poured himself a goblet of juice. "You're the second person I know who likes porridge."

"Who's the other one?" Alaric asked.

It was Lucian who replied. "Dew."

A shadow passed over Alaric's face, sadness and regret. "I wish I could have known her."

Sylvester swallowed past the lump in his throat. "She would have liked that."

Alaric swirled his spoon in his bowl. "Did she know?"

Sylvester shook his head. "I wanted to tell her so many times, but unlike me, she and Keylin were close to our father, and though they knew about his many affairs, I... I couldn't bring myself to tell them that he not only had another son, but that he refused to acknowledge him."

"I am past that," Alaric said quietly. "At least he didn't harm me."

"Sylvester," Lucian said. "You should tell him."

Sylvester went still, but a part of him wanted to tell Alaric, not for his gratitude, but because he wanted him to know that Sylvester cared.

"Tell me what?" Alaric asked, a look of inquiry on his face.

"I was the one who paid for your education in school," Sylvester said quietly. "I didn't think you would let me do anything, so I asked Wayan to do it... He didn't have an income in those days, and I did, but once he was left an inheritance, he refused to take anything from me. But till then, it was me."

Sylvester didn't know how to interpret the expression on

Alaric's face. He looked frozen, so still was he.

"You did that?" he asked, his voice strangled.

Sylvester nodded, trepidation filling him.

Alaric smiled, his face softening almost impossibly.

"Thank you," he said. "I wish I had known. I'd always wanted to get to know you, but by the time I grew old enough, you were already in Garaner."

"Do you want me to tell Keylin?" Sylvester asked. "She would want to know, Alaric."

Alaric looked down at his bowl, bit his lip, and raised his eyes. "Not yet, please. I would tell her myself, but not just yet."

Sylvester nodded, something within him melting. He still hadn't said everything he'd wanted to, but it was a start. He had resented his unknown brother once, before he had grown old enough to know what a scumbag his father was.

He was glad that neither he nor Alaric had become anything like the man who sired them.

FORTY FIVE

LUCIAN ROSE FROM his seat and straightened, cracking his spine and rotating his neck as he stretched. The office was empty at this time of the night. Once again, he had worked too late. He knew that both Garth and Alaric were worried about his late nights. The thought of Alaric made him smile. He and Alaric had been spending every night together these days as if they had to make up for the farials they had spent apart.

The thought of Alaric waiting for him made Lucian's steps lighter and springier. He hurried down the corridor and down the stairs. His carriage was waiting outside at its usual spot, and it was the only one in the street. Mornings, the street was full of carriages of all the others who worked here, the sidewalks full of vendors trying to sell their wares. Now, the makeshift shops were closed, the goods carted away, and the sidewalks empty.

"Sorry," Lucian said as he climbed into the carriage. "Time got away from me again. Thank you for waiting."

There were many who wouldn't have acknowledged it, since the man was paid to do it, but Lucian had never been of their ilk. The man was paid to drive him around, true, but even for the very handsome sum Lucian paid him, it didn't form part of Davies' duties to wait for his wayward employer so late into the night.

"It's fine, my lord Blade," Davies said, his rumbling voice calm as ever. "The roads are deserted, so we should make good time."

Lucian smiled and nodded, though Davies couldn't see it. Today, he hadn't brought anything with him. No work, nothing. Just him, and he sank back into the cushions and closed his eyes, a smile curving his mouth again as he thought of Alaric. Lucian knew that everything was not solved, that he and Alaric still needed to talk about many things, but for now, he was content to leave the future to take care of itself.

At present, he had other things to worry about. Like the war with Sarian, and the plan that he and the King had agreed upon. A part of Lucian quaked in dread at his own role in that, but he knew it was not something he would ever regret. Sarian was not a nation known for its benevolence. Castrial had its own faults, but they had never tried to invade another kingdom, never been an aggressor in any conflict they had been part of. Castrial treated its slaves better than Sarian did its free people.

The carriage slowed.

"My lord." Davies' voice came, thick with tension. "There's someone on the road. Someone hurt. Looks like an accident happened."

"Stop the carriage and see what aid we can give," Lucian said.

He leapt down from the carriage as soon as it stopped and saw what Davies must have. An overturned carriage by the side of the road, blood pooling on the road, dark and glittering under the moonlight. The streetlamp with its magical orb on top was snapped in half and lay with its broken top over the carriage.

A woman staggered to the road from behind the carriage, and what looked like a child lay on its side half in and half out of it.

"Help," she cried in broken Castilian. "Please... help."

A Serenian, judging by the accent. Lucian frowned. Did someone do this on purpose? Forced a Serenian carriage to overturn and left it here like this? Hate crimes always increased when there was threat of war in the air, and there were always a lot of Serenian refugees in Castrial. Alaric and his people worked very hard to keep peace, and yet, incidents like this happened. It was completely unacceptable.

"It's okay, Madam," Davies said. "We'll get you help. Never you fear."

"Please," the woman whispered, her voice breaking. "My child..."

Lucian moved towards the shape while Davies tried to comfort the woman. Bile rose to his throat as the stench of blood filled his nostrils. Anger flared deep within. He would find those responsible for it, no matter what it took.

Pain bloomed behind his head as something hit him from behind and Lucian fell on to his knees before toppling over, his vision blurring and darkening but not before he saw a pair of boots in front of him.

FORTY SIX

ALARIC WAS WOKEN in the middle of the night by Garth. He had fallen asleep in Lucian's library, waiting for the man to come home.

He was instantly awake on seeing Garth's face.
"What is it?" he asked.
Garth was pale, his lips trembling and eyes full of tears.

"He didn't come home, and the royal guards are here, looking for him... They... they say he left office last night and now he's... they say he's... He's turned traitor."

What?

Alaric rose, straightened his coat as best he could, a part of him still not able to understand what was happening as he walked out of the room and nearly bumped into Astra.

"Astra," he said. "What happened?"

She regarded him, her face impassive. "I think we better have this conversation in private, my lord Shield."

He nodded and turned towards Lucian's study. It was warded heavily, and he knew it was the most private room in the house. Astra looked around once she was there and he closed the door.

"Speak," he said.

"There was a secret mission to send a spy to Sarian, known only to my lord Blade and His Majesty," she said. "That spy is now dead. His Majesty suspects it's my lord Blade who has informed the Serenians of the plan, especially since he's missing since last night."

Alaric ran a hand through his hair and tugged at his collar. "I see. Is there any sign of foul play?"

"His carriage was found abandoned near the Serenian streets," she said. "His coachman's body was found inside."

Alaric's mouth went dry. Davies had been with Lucian for almost as long as Garth.

"Lucian wouldn't..." he said, his voice breaking.

"We all want to believe that," Astra said quietly. "If... If you can accompany me to the palace, my Lord Shield... His Majesty has asked for you."

Alaric nodded. He was still in yesterday's clothes, and he was certain he looked a mess, but one couldn't keep one's King waiting while one got oneself presentable.

"Lead the way," he said.

There had to be an explanation. There had to be. He wouldn't believe that Lucian would do anything like this. He was ready to stake everything on it.

FORTY SEVEN

SYLVESTER WANTED TO bite his nails and if he were anywhere except in the study of his monarch, he would have. Sylvester had always had to play a role, don a mask, but now, he was becoming himself again, as much as he was able to. But here, in the presence of his King, he couldn't afford that. He didn't want to think of why he was here, looking at his King who stood by the window, though it was dark out and the glass only reflected his face.

Garret's face showed his worry. His lips were pressed together, not in anger, and his usually ochre cheeks looked sallow. He held himself rigidly, as if he feared to relax. Sylvester found his eyes travelling over the man's frame, at the broad shoulders, the narrow waist. He looked down, face burning.

It wasn't the first time he found Garret attractive, but that was a dangerous road to go down. Sylvester didn't know when his devotion to the King became something personal, when Garret became a person more than a symbol, but he knew well enough that it wasn't to be encouraged.

The door to the study opened and Sylvester lifted his eyes, seeing Astra walk in, followed by a visibly dishevelled Alaric whose clothes were rumpled as if he had slept in them. Astra's expression became guarded on seeing him, closed off, which was strange. Was it because he was the one who had rescued her? Because he knew what she had been through?

Sylvester shrugged it off as Astra and Alaric both bowed to the King, who waved them off.

"Spare the formalities," he said. "Sit down, both of you. I take it Astra apprised you of the situation, Alaric?"

"Your Majesty," Alaric said as he knelt and bowed his head. "Lucian would never sell Castrial out."

"Alaric," the King said, sighing. "I'm aware. I do not believe Lucian is a spy, but what we speak of here is not to leave this room. The rest of the world should believe Lucian has turned traitor. Do you understand?"

Alaric frowned as he rose to his feet. "I understand what you're asking me," he said. "But I don't understand why, and I don't... Astra said that someone was killed that only you and Lucian knew of... so why do you believe he's not a spy?"

"If Lucian had been the Serenian spy we are searching for," Sylvester said. "The damage would have been much greater. Besides, I was the one who killed them."

Alaric stared.

"They were a spy," Sylvester said calmly. "One of my sources confirmed it. His Majesty had his suspicions too. But I assume the Serenians would be quite upset over his death."

Alaric sat down. "None of this is making any sense," he complained.

"He was planted by the Serenians and vetted by the Minister of War," Sylvester said. "Which means Lord Fitzroy is likely the spy we're looking for. His Majesty and Lucian made the plan which was known only to them and to the person being sent. His Majesty suspected Lord Fitzroy and had me investigate the spy he recommended. I discovered he was a Serenian agent, and I killed him. So now, the Serenians know we were on to their plan, and they have probably abducted Lucian."

"We have to find him, then," Alaric said.

"If the Serenians have taken him," Sylvester said, "that probably means he's in a Serenian prison somewhere. He may not even be in Castrial." He paused. "That means we have bigger problems than if Lucian is actually a spy. We all know that there are ways to make people talk, no matter how strong or capable they are."

The King looked thoughtful. His exhaustion seemed more pronounced now.

"Then we need to find him before he talks." He sighed and looked around the room. "Finding Lucian is the priority. Everything else can wait. Sylvester, you will be in charge of the Blade's office till Lucian returns. I shall draft a decree to that effect. Astra, you and Alaric are in charge of finding Lucian. Question whoever you want, but I want him found. Time is of the essence."

A deep breath. "If he's not in a condition to be saved, kill him." Another pause. "And no one outside of this room is to know anything. Whatever rumours and speculations there are, the three of you will keep your mouth shut."

Silence dropped and Alaric opened his mouth, but Sylvester was at his side, and he touched his shoulder. Alaric looked at him and Sylvester shook his head. Objections would serve no purpose but to antagonise the King. Finding Lucian in time was the only way out.

FORTY EIGHT

LUCIAN REGAINED CONSCIOUSNESS to find that his situation hasn't changed any. He was still in chains, and his whole body was aching from the torture that he had been subjected to. His mind and magic both felt sluggish from the drugs that were in his system. He had no idea how long it had been, but he was glad he was alone at the droplet.

As weak as he felt, at least he could feel his magic, unlike the previous times when he had regained consciousness and had panicked because he couldn't even feel his magic. His captors had taunted him with the drugs they had fed him which suppressed both his magic and sapped his strength and made him slow to understand things.

The most terrifying thing was that Lucian had no idea where he was or what these people wanted. They had tortured him, but they had also healed him, and they had not asked him anything, simply leaving him alone when they were done. They fed him, and they used magic to ensure that he was healthy.

He tried to use his magic and was relieved when it responded. It was weaker than usual, but it was enough to unlock the chains. Lucian fell on his knees, his legs trembling, and he sat like that, panting for breath. His body ached and he had some difficulty breathing. Healing was something he was good at, but he felt that his injuries were beyond his skills. He still tried to probe his body with his magic. There were internal injuries and broken ribs, as well as a fractured and poorly mended bone in his left leg.

Not good, he thought rather dazedly. He didn't know what these people wanted from him. From their accents, he knew they were Serenian, and that was not reassuring at all. This could very well be revenge for the actions he took against their spies. But how did Serenian agents break into Castrial and managed to capture him without any of them being aware of their activities?

Lucian tried to think of when he was taken, but it was difficult. He had been late at work that day and had left at some time after midnight. He remembered an overturned carriage on the road, a crying woman in torn and bloodied attire, and blood on the road. Davies had gone to help, and Lucian too had stepped down from the carriage. Something had hit his head from behind, and when he woke, he was in this room, chained to the wall.

Lucian tried to stand up, but his left leg wouldn't co-operate. It felt weak and wobbly, and Lucian wondered if the badly mended bone was on purpose to stop him from escaping. It was very likely, but he couldn't allow it to stop him. He sent a tendril of magic to strengthen his leg and managed to take a few steps to the door. His magic was not strong at the droplet, but he was sure that once the effects of the drugs passed, he would be back to normal again.

The door opened before he could try and unlock it, and a woman stood there, her gaze full of disdain. Lucian recognised the woman who had been crying for help.

"Oh, do you really think you can escape?" she asked, magic sparking at her fingertips. "It seems we must increase the dose of the drug if you could use your magic so soon."

Lucian tried to leap out of the way, but his bad leg gave way, and he fell down, groaning. Her spell sailed harmlessly over his head, but the next one hit him on the middle. He screamed as pain lanced through every single cell, and every part of him felt like it was on fire.

"You're not leaving here, you see," the woman said, her voice sounding like it was coming from inside his head, that even through his screaming and pain, he couldn't escape it. "We will see you dead for all that you did. And the agent you were planning to send to us? He's dead, so that little plot of yours is already foiled. Everyone in Castrial thinks you're a traitor, so what will you do even if you escape?"

The pain stopped, and Lucian lay on the floor, still twitching. He tried to parse the words she spoke, and all he could focus on was that he was believed to be a traitor and the assassin they were planning to send to Sarian had died. But that couldn't be right. That assassin was a spy. Why would the Serenians have killed him?

If they didn't, it meant that they were trying to manipulate Lucian. They didn't know who killed their spy, but they were trying to use his death to their advantage.

It meant that His Majesty's plan had a chance to succeed even now.

"Where am I?" he managed to ask. Was he in Sarian or in Castrial?

A kick to his ribs, and Lucian gasped.

"Hang him up," the woman ordered, and rough hands grabbed him.

Though Lucian attempted to struggle, it was futile. He was not yet strong, the drugs still working, and his captors were all stronger than him. He was back in the chains, but this time he was hanging from the ceiling, his hands above his head. It seemed like his arms were going to be wrenched out of their sockets, and he was unable to breathe.

"Give him a stool to stand on," the woman said. "We don't want him dying too soon."

The stool helped with the breathing, but little else. His arms hurt, and his ribs, and his bad leg was trembling so badly that he feared he would knock the stool over.

One of the men came with a vial of something that made him try and wriggle away. It was fear of losing his footing on the stool that made him still. The man used his magic to lift himself in the air and approached him. Lucian turned his head away, but someone else too lifted themselves up to reach him. Someone caught his jaw and forced him to open his mouth. The liquid in the vial was poured into his mouth, and someone clapped a hand on his mouth, and someone pinched his nose. Lucian swallowed reflexively, the liquid going down, burning like fire down his innards. Lucian sputtered and choked, and he heard the woman say something, but it sounded like he was underwater.

Lucian struggled against his bonds, but his limbs were sluggish now, and his magic was beyond his reach once again. He wanted to speak, but his throat wouldn't work. He tried to straighten his head, but it would only loll to a side.

"Sleep now," the woman's voice said, and Lucian felt a wave of darkness wash over him, taking him under.

A part of him thought that there was something important he needed to remember, but he couldn't struggle against the magic that pressed against his mind, and he gave up the unequal struggle, giving himself up to oblivion.

When he came to, it was dark, and he was lying on a bed. Lucian tried to move and found that both his hands and feet were bound to the frame of the bed. There was silence all around, and Lucian tried to see if he could free himself. His magic was again out of his reach, and his limited strength could only shake the chains, the sound loud in the silent darkness. He tensed, waiting for someone to come rushing in, but no one appeared.

Lucian tried to think, though it was so hard. He just wanted to close his eyes and sleep again, but he knew that he couldn't. He could only believe that his captors wanted nothing except revenge. They wanted to make him an outcast in Castrial, his reputation tarnished beyond repair while they kept him here and tortured him.

His eyes closed without conscious thought, and Lucian allowed his despair to overwhelm him. He just didn't know how he was going to escape. Everything looked hopeless. If he only knew where he was!

Perhaps the drug would wear off again, and he could escape then. That was all he had to hold on to.

FORTY NINE

ALARIC WAS FRANTIC as he looked at the buildings that stood on both sides of the street he was on. Lucian's magical signature had been in this area. It had appeared briefly and then was gone, like a flame that flickered before dying. Alaric didn't know where Lucian was, but all he knew was that he couldn't rush into every one of the buildings. If Lucian was being held captive, he didn't want to alert his captors. If he was hiding, Alaric didn't want to alert his people. He had led them here, all the same, because he was certain that Lucian was here against his will.

It was the area where most Serenian and Garanerian refugees were housed, and that made it all the more difficult to conduct a door to door search. If Lucian's magical signature hadn't appeared here, Alaric wouldn't have dared to come. It was a sensitive area, politically, and he had no wish to step on any toes or create any embarrassment for the King.

Yet, he had to do something, find Lucian if he was still alive, do what he could to clear his name. The King might know the truth, but it hurt Alaric that so many people thought Lucian a traitor.

"Lord Shield," one of his people spoke. "Where do we go?"

"Give me a droplet," Alaric said.

Lucian's magical signature was completely gone from his senses, but that didn't mean Alaric couldn't find him. The spell he was planning to use was draining and risky, but he didn't have another choice. He closed his eyes, and expanded his senses outward, and reached out his consciousness to the crevices in the buildings, to the insects and rodents within. It was a kind of possession, and done too long, it could scatter the consciousness of the user, and have it merge with the creature it was possessing.

Soon, he had eyes in every building, and it was difficult to focus on all the things that he was seeing at the same time. There was a man tied to a bed who looked familiar, and Alaric lifted his head and smelled blood, herbs, and something else. Something that was very faint, but familiar.

Lucian!

He withdrew his consciousness slowly, taking care to note the surroundings and the building, and soon, he was back in his body, all of him. He sagged, and one of his assistants supported him.

"Lord Shield?" Astra sounded concerned.

"He's in a building in the southwest corner, behind a tavern," Alaric said. "We don't want an incident. Have your cloaks up and hide your weapons. Don't speak unless you have to. The patrols in this area are mostly only to enforce curfews, and to ensure that the refugees aren't harmed. If anyone stops us, show your identification, but don't engage with the civilians."

"What if they don't let us search the building?" one of Astra's guards asked.

"They have to," Alaric said. He was exhausted so much that he felt his mind slipping. But he had to keep alert at least till they found Lucian. "It's the law. They're in Castrial now, and they have to co-operate with us. Just tell them we're looking for a criminal. Don't let them know that we're looking for Lord Blade at any costs."

Many people believed Lucian was guilty, and only by emphasising his title could Alaric ensure that his assistants would believe that Lucian was kept here under duress.

"Do you think they're holding him prisoner here?" Astra asked, her eyes reflecting the same fear that Alaric felt in his own heart.

"I believe so," Alaric said. "There is no way for his magical signature to flicker briefly like it did if he was here of his own free will."

He saw and ignored the exchange of sceptical glances between a couple of his people and the guards. It was only to be expected since most people believed that Lucian was a traitor. They might think that Lucian was here on his own, seeking refuge with the Serenians. Alaric didn't have time to disabuse them of their notions. Once they found Lucian, everyone would know the truth.

They went silently to their destination, and Alaric stopped in front of the tavern. They all pulled their hoods up and used magic and their cloaks to conceal their weapons and insignia while they walked inside. The tavern was nearly full, and the cacophony of noises hid their steps better than their own care. All the same, they moved silently between the tables ignoring the glances that didn't stay. Smells of alcohol and roasted meat wafted from the kitchen and the tables, reminding Alaric that he hadn't eaten all day. That coupled with the magic he used earlier had him feeling weak, but he managed to keep his steps steady.

Once outside the tavern through the back, he saw the building they had been looking for. Looming large and dark, it looked dilapidated with an air of having been abandoned.

"Let's go in quietly," Alaric said, trying the door, which opened silently as it wouldn't have, had the building been abandoned. Someone had oiled the hinges.

Foolish. If they intended to kidnap and stash people here, it would have been better to leave the door hinges unoiled so the creak would have warned them if someone entered. Amateur mistakes, but everything so far pointed to the fact that these people were professionals. It was a dichotomy that Alaric filed away in his mind, to be examined later. Right now, he had to find Lucian.

He and his people spread out once they were inside. It was Darla who found Lucian, and as soon as her magical message appeared, Alaric and the rest went to the cellar where she had found him.

Lucian was supine on a bed, unconscious, breathing laboured, and shivering. He was tied to it with chains, and Alaric felt the faint thrum of magic in them as well. Lucian's clothes were in tatters, and Alaric saw blood crusted on his body and soaked in the sheets, staining them brown.

"Fuck," Astra said, sounding enraged. "What have they done to him?"

"He has a fever," one of Alaric's people said, bending down

and examining him. "And many of his bones have been broken and mended, and his leg hasn't healed properly. We may have to break it again, to set it right."

Alaric didn't even feel any gratification in knowing that he was right about Lucian not being a traitor. Rage was boiling inside him at the people who had taken Lucian and treated him like this.

"Can he be moved?" he asked.

"With magic, yes," the one who had examined Lucian said. "He shouldn't be jolted. Where do we take him?"

"Let me get rid of these chains," Astra said, her hand hovering over them. The magic dissipated, and the chains broke apart like strings.

Alaric lifted Lucian on to his arms, careful not to jolt him, as he took a portal stone from his pocket. "Open a portal to my home, and get a healer," he ordered. Even the simple spell for activating the stone was beyond him, but he wouldn't let anyone else take Lucian.

Most houses were warded against portals, but Alaric and Lucian carried portal stones keyed to their houses. It was to escape in case of an emergency, but Lucian hadn't had his on him the night he was kidnapped. Alaric had found them at his home, inside his desk drawer.

Lucian's head lolled against his chest, and he whimpered, as if even that slight movement hurt. Alaric's chest ached as someone opened a portal for him to take Lucian through.

FIFTY

SYLVESTER WISHED HIS family would move to their mother's house. Staying with Bertram didn't feel comfortable. He knew the man didn't mind, that he was doing everything in his power to make them all welcome, but it was not the same as staying in Lucian's house.

There was always his townhouse, but till he could convince the rest of his family to move there, Sylvester didn't want to go live there alone. He didn't want to be alone anymore which was why he had stayed with Lucian.

He could no longer stay in Lucian's house was the thing, since Lucian was in Alaric's house now. The King had instructed Sylvester not to visit and had asked Alaric to ensure no one else did either. Sylvester wondered what the King had in mind, and it bothered him.

Bertram's house boasted of extensive gardens and Sylvester liked to stroll through them, trying to wrangle the thoughts in his head.

He could no longer pretend to be a minor official since he was in charge of the Blade's office and Bertram knew. Not that it was a secret since His Majesty had issued a decree to that effect and announced it in court. Though speculation and rumours ran riot about Lucian and his supposed treason, the King had refused to entertain any, saying that Lucian has been abducted and that the Shield and Captain of the Royal Guards were in charge of the investigation.

"You look so serious," Keylin said from behind, and Sylvester turned his head to smile at his sister.

Keylin was coming towards him, walking briskly, her long, cream dress sweeping the ground. Sylvester gave the hem of her gown a pointed look and Keylin shrugged.

"It has a dirt repellent spell on it, so it doesn't matter. I won't trip and fall, Syl."

He put an arm around her shoulder as she reached his side and smiled at her. "That's a good spell."

"Calla taught me," she said. "Did you know I never had much to do in Alaric's house? None of us did, except Dad."

"I can imagine," Sylvester said. "He's a good man."

"One of the best." She sounded troubled and Sylvester looked at her.

"What's eating you?"

"Aunt Elda... She said there are rumours about Alaric and me, and... People seem to pity Bertram and me, and Alaric... They make him sound like a villain... And she wanted me to not go see him again."

"When did you go to see him?"

"A day or so before... I wanted to see Lucian and Alaric too, but we were not allowed in. King's orders."

She sounded sulky and Sylvester chuckled. "We can't really break royal commands, you know."

"I know, but... Syl, do you think I ought not to see him too? Aunt Elda says if I go see him, people will say I was willing, but the fact is Alaric never did anything to me. How can I prove that?"

"Why do you have to?" Sylvester asked.

"Because it's wrong of people to say that and darken his reputation for no reason!"

Sylvester sighed. "How does Bertram feel about it?"

"He says he knows Alaric wouldn't have done anything dishonourable, that he agrees with me, but that isn't the point, Syl!"

Sylvester should have told her then, but he didn't, remembering Alaric saying that he would.

"I think you should do what you want," he said. "I've known Alaric almost as long as I've known Lucian, and I trust them both."

"It's not like Aunt Elda doesn't know the truth. She's so afraid of what it might do to my reputation and how it would affect Bertram and his reputation, but no one seems bothered about Alaric's reputation." Keylin looked angry. "Will I make it worse if I stay friends with him?"

Sylvester shook his head. "No. In fact, I think you'll make it better. You can ask Bertram to go with you and that will make it even better. Heck, I'll accompany you to his house whenever you want."

She smiled at him before leaning up to kiss his cheek. "You're the best, Syl."

He hugged her to him, holding her tight. "I'm glad everything worked out for you, Key."

She lifted her face and smiled at him again. "I'm too. I so feared they never might."

If only things would work out just as well for Castrial! Sylvester would be content with that.

FIFTY ONE

ALARIC HAD TO fight his impulse to hover as the healer examined Lucian. It was a royal physician who the King had sent.

"Well?" he asked, fists clenched at his sides as he fought the wish to rush to Lucian's side at every whimper of pain.

"He has some internal injuries that I have healed," the physician said, his face furrowed. "But his leg would have to be broken again for the bone to be set right, and even then, he might have a limp. There's some damage to the eye that's likely permanent, but shouldn't impair his vision in full. Other than that, let him rest."

Alaric exchanged a troubled glance with Astra who was the only other person in the room.

"I shall inform His Majesty," she said.

Lucian groaned, muttered, "Alaric."

Alaric moved to the bed, unable to stop himself. Was Lucian regaining consciousness? Astra had stopped as well, staring at Lucian.

The healer bent down. "My Lord Blade," he said. "How are you feeling?"

Lucian's gaze was hazy, but he muttered. "Where am I?"

"You're at my house," Alaric said. "You're safe now."

"Safe," Lucian murmured as he closed his eyes again. "How long has it been since I was taken?"

"A few days," Alaric said. "Don't worry about anything. We'll take care of everything. You just need to focus on getting better."

The physician handed a small bottle to Alaric, and a small pouch.

"Medicines," he said. "The instructions are also in the pouch. I will give you a droplet, but after that, I'll have to sedate him to break his leg. It really shouldn't be delayed any more."

Alaric nodded. "Let me explain to him. I'll call you."

As the physician left, Astra said, "I'll inform His Majesty–"

Lucian moved faster than Alaric expected from a man in his condition, his hand shooting out to grab the dagger at Alaric's belt before he plunged it into Alaric's chest. Alaric had started to move as well, stepping back and twisting his body away, that the blade made a glancing stab across his chest, but it was only a flesh wound. Alaric's hand came up to hold Lucian's.

"Lucian! It's me!"

Lucian seemed not to hear him, struggling against him, but then his eyes cleared and he stopped fighting. Astra hit him on the back of his neck, causing him to go limp.

"What's wrong with him?" she asked.

"Call the physician," Alaric said, as he laid Lucian down on the bed again. His chest stung and blood seeped through the wound, causing his tunic to stick to his body.

The physician came quickly, shocked noises escaping him as he cleaned and dressed Alaric's wound first. Afterwards, he examined Lucian again, his face becoming grave.

"My Lord Shield," he said softly. "It's... It's a curse... It's affecting his magic, and it will kill him soon."

"How soon?" Alaric heard himself ask, his voice too steady.

"I can't say, and I don't know what kind of curse it is... You need a specialist in magical maladies. I have a colleague who is discreet as well. I shall ask him to come. But in the meantime, let me take care of his leg."

Alaric nodded, as he watched the physician strap Lucian on to the bed, using magical restraints. Lucian's scream when the leg was broken made him wince and take hold of Lucian's hand, gripping it tight.

FIFTY TWO

LUCIAN SAT UP in his bed, propped up by pillows. That was all he had been able to do since he regained consciousness. His aches and pains were a faint throb, his injuries healed. Despite the best efforts by the healers, his badly healed leg could not be fully repaired, and he would always have a limp, and a dull ache at times.

It was fine. He was alive, and he was safe, and that was all that mattered. He knew that most people thought he was under house arrest in Alaric's house, and Alaric himself encouraged the rumours.

"It will give us time to come up with a plan to clear your name," he had told Lucian.

Lucian's eyes went towards the closed door of his room. Alaric hadn't been to see him yet today, and he missed him. Lucian's chest tightened with emotions he could not name. Alaric had trusted him, he had kept faith unlike Lucian who had almost betrayed their friendship. He swallowed and blinked to clear his blurry eyes. It happened too often these days.

It wasn't only due to emotions, he knew. The healers had told him that there had been some damage to his eyes. Though his vision was unimpaired, he would tear up from time to time. It was also something he had to deal with.

Lucian sighed and closed his eyes for a droplet. He and Alaric hadn't talked of anything serious yet. Alaric was waiting for Lucian to be better, and Lucian was too much of a coward to broach the subject. But he couldn't put it off any longer. He had to know. If Alaric should visit today, they needed to have a serious talk.

If Alaric visited.

Though he had visited nearly every day, and Lucian knew that he was exempt from court by the King's order as long as Lucian was under his roof, Lucian still feared that this might be the day when his friend decided that he had enough.

After all, Lucian had almost betrayed him once, and though Alaric appeared to have forgiven it, he couldn't have forgotten. Alaric seemed to think that he was the one in the wrong for believing Lucian had betrayed him, which was stupid. Lucian might not have caused everything that happened, but if he had been more capable, he would have found the real culprit sooner. That it took them all this time to find him was testament to Lucian's inefficiency. No matter how he spun it, he knew that he had hurt Alaric, though he didn't know the extent of that hurt. All he knew was that his own insides squirmed with guilt when he cast his mind to the past.

He had broken Alaric's faith, his trust, his heart, and their friendship, and while they were attempting to rebuild, Lucian wasn't sure if he deserved Alaric's forgiveness or his trust. That he had both seemed evident from how Alaric treated him, from his unquestioning faith in Lucian's innocence.

I wish I had been so brave.

But he had not been. He had been a coward, and Alaric had suffered.

Before Lucian's thoughts could spiral further, the door to his room opened, bringing the man he was thinking about into the room. Alaric stopped to close the door, and the gaze that rested on Lucian was sharp.

"How is the head?" he asked, moving to the side where his medicines sat.

Alaric mixed a powder into hot water and stirred it while Lucian watched, the familiarity of it making it seem as if his chest was being crushed, and his lungs seemed unable to take in air, and every word he had thought of leaving him. He swallowed hard, feeling like he had a large stone lodged in his throat.

"Not aching today," he said. "I feel much better today."

Alaric brought the medicine to him. "Take the medicine," he said. "It's hot, so blow on it before drinking."

Lucian did as instructed and drank it still hot, but it felt warm and not scalding hot.

"Can we talk?" he asked as he handed the empty bowl to Alaric.

A fleeting look of anxiety on Alaric's face, before he smiled.

"Sure," he said, putting the bowl back and striding towards

Lucian's bedside and sitting on the chair there. "What do you want to talk about?"

"What's been happening?" Lucian asked. "With the court, the war, Sarian, the accusations against me?"

Alaric frowned, but he didn't look away. "It's a mess," he said. "The murder of our proposed envoy has caused a lot of talk and paranoia. Since his identity was a secret known only to you and His Majesty, the evidence against you looks bleak. Though it can be proven that you were a prisoner at that time, the fact that we recovered you without resistance, that they left you there as if they knew we were coming, is not helpful to your cause."

Lucian digested it in silence, his brain agreeing with Alaric. Everything looked suspicious, but would his captors have left him there just to implicate him?

"What are you not telling me?" Lucian asked softly. "Alaric?"

Alaric's gaze turned away from him, a bad sign.

"What do you mean?"

"There's something you're hiding from me," Lucian said. "Please, Alaric, whatever it is, I need to know. Has His Majesty decided to execute me?"

Not that he could blame Garret. He was a King, and under the present circumstances, there was very little he could do. Laws were laws after all, and Garret had never been the kind of King to ignore them in favour of doing what he wanted.

"No!" Alaric exclaimed, his gaze swiftly rising to Lucian's face again, the horror in his eyes doing more than his words to convince Lucian. "What the fuck, Lucian! Would His Majesty do that, without even a trial?"

Lucian felt a lump in his throat again.

"You were exiled without a trial," he said.

Alaric looked away again.

"The King was not as certain of his position back then," he

said, his hands clasped on his lap, knuckles standing white. "If it went to trial, he may have had to execute me."

Lucian closed his eyes.

"Don't divert me," he said. "Tell me what you're hiding."

Alaric was silent, and Lucian opened his eyes and held out his hand which Alaric took without any pause. Lucian gripped it as tightly as he could.

"Alaric," he said, his head starting to ache again. "I need to know."

A knock on the door, and a low voice came through it.

"You have visitors, Lord Shield, and your mother welcomed them in, so I thought I'll come and tell you."

"Quite right," Alaric said with an apologetic glance at Lucian. "I've to go. I'll tell you everything when you're better, I promise. For now, you needn't worry."

He was gone, and Lucian closed his eyes and massaged his temples. He was exhausted still and hadn't tried getting out of bed yet. Perhaps Alaric was right in not telling him everything.

FIFTY THREE

"WHO IS IT, Donald?" Alaric asked his butler as they walked to the front room. "You know that visitors are not allowed here. Mayi knows too, and she wouldn't let anyone in."

"I may have prevaricated," Donald said. "He's in the library, sir. You will know when you see him why your mother couldn't have stopped him."

Alaric frowned, wondering what Donald meant. But he was curious as well. Stepping into the library, he stopped short.

"Your Highness," he said, bowing a beat too late.

Prince Geran, uncle to the King, and next in line for the throne, looked at him coldly, his glare ice and anger. Alaric wondered briefly what he had done to offend the prince but could come up with nothing. Prince Geran wasn't interested in the throne, and he had refused it when his brother had died, choosing to crown his young nephew instead. He kept himself away from court and country affairs both, so this visit was a surprise.

"I want to see Lucian," Prince Geran said, his voice frosty. "I don't care what excuses you and my nephew have for not allowing him visitors, but I wish to see him."

Alaric bowed again.

"Of course, if you have a written note of permission from His Majesty."

The prince's face suffused with colour, and his eyes flashed.

"Do you mean to say that you will not allow me to see him unless I go to my nephew over something so trivial?"

"His Majesty is the one who made the decision that no outsider is to be allowed to see Lord Blade. As such I am unable to take a decision with regards to allowing visitors, even one as important as Your Highness."

Alaric made sure to use Lucian's title so as not to offend the man before him. He understood where he was coming from. He was an old friend of Lucian's father, a connection the latter had flouted every now and then when he was alive. It was likely that Danae had put him up to this, and she had never cared much for Alaric. No doubt, she would have told the prince something disparaging about him to make the man so aggressively hostile from the outset.

"How is Garret going to know that you let me see him?" the

prince demanded, eyebrows contracting together. "I assure you that I mean him no harm. I just wish to reassure myself of his well-being so that his family may be at ease."

"I'm sorry," Alaric said. "I understand. I truly do, but I'm unable to help you in this. Without a written order from His Majesty, I cannot let any visitors into his presence. If it would put your mind at ease, I could produce the healer who is attending to him so that you may question him."

It was a matter of the visitor's safety as well. Alaric hadn't told Lucian about the curse inside him, a curse that had led him to attack Alaric when he had first regained consciousness. Lucian had been too weak to do any actual damage, but the knife he had used had still caused enough of an injury to scar. It was a vicious curse, a killing curse that would drain and kill Lucian if it was not fulfilled, but Alaric had no intention of allowing Lucian to hurt anyone else. They would find a solution to the curse later.

But he couldn't explain all that to this man, who, when all was said and done, was a total stranger to both him and Lucian. His Majesty had needed to be told, and they had taken the decision to isolate Lucian till they figured out a solution.

That solution seemed to be beyond them at the droplet, but still, Alaric had to stand guard, ensure that no one gained entry to his house or to Lucian.

"And if I were to walk in, you would no doubt stop me?" the prince asked, his face mottled with rage now.

As if on cue, the door opened, and two guards walked inside. Royal guards, Alaric was relieved to see, Astra, one of them.

"Your highness," Astra said, her voice such a welcome relief. "We are here to escort you back to the palace, on His Majesty's orders."

The prince stared at the guard who stared back, unaffected.

"I see," he grated out. "In that case, I bid you goodbye for now, my Lord Shield. Don't think this is over."

Alaric bowed, making no reply. He was used to making enemies. One more hardly counted. And this was for Lucian's sake. His friend would never forgive himself or Alaric if he ended up hurting someone he cared for. Apart from Alaric and the King, only the physician who had tended to Lucian, Astra, and Alaric's mother knew the truth. Alaric would have liked to tell Garth, but the King hadn't allowed it.

"I know that he's close to Lucian," the King had said. "But when even his family isn't allowed to know, I think it's not right to let his butler know the truth."

Alaric had bitten back the reply that Garth was more Lucian's family than the people he shared blood with. There were some prejudices that people couldn't even see themselves having, and no good had ever come of calling out a king. Besides, Garret was better than many kings, more open minded, and wiser than others. Of course, the only other rulers Alaric knew were the monarchs of Garaner. While they were not bad people, neither of them was half as good as Garret as rulers.

Garret had made Lucian the Blade, and Alaric the Shield, both actions that would have been unheard of even at the time of the previous monarch. Alaric was certain that the man who was just escorted out would never have made a decision like that. As such, Garret's unresolved prejudices weren't as much an issue as anyone else's. Besides, Garret always worked out his own issues. That was another thing Alaric could be certain of.

A knock on the door made him look up. Donald entered the room, opening the door but a sliver.

"The captain of the royal guards wants to see you, sir," he said.

"Let her in," Alaric said, wondering what it was about.

It was a relief to have Astra here, acting as the go between his house and the palace, her guards the messengers. Though he wasn't comfortable about letting her spend so much time here when the King needed protection. But Sylvester spent most of his time with the King these days, so Alaric supposed that was protection enough.

Astra entered, looking grave.

"The prince wasn't happy," she said. "He was making threats, and I fear he will go to His Majesty with this."

"I fear as much," Alaric confessed. No matter that the prince had been in the wrong, such a notion was incomprehensible to most royalty. "What do you think we should do?"

"Is there anything we can do?" she asked. "We can give the King our report, but in the end, it will come down to what His Majesty believes. Disrespecting a royal is a criminal offence."

"But not a capital one," Alaric said. "We could end up in trouble, for all that."

She shrugged. "So, I thought I'd go in person to give the King my report. Darla will be here in my place."

Alaric nodded.

"All right. I haven't prepared any report yet, but I'm going to wait till the King asks for one."

After all, he was not required to report every person who wanted to see Lucian. Astra's report would cover his role as well, and if the King asked for any explanation, Alaric would give it.

"Suit yourself," Astra said. "Just don't blame me if you end up exiled again."

Alaric grinned at her. "I'll take you down with me," he teased, and she smiled.

FIFTY FOUR

SYLVESTER LEANED BACK on his chair, a smile tugging at his lips as he watched his family. They were in Sylvester's townhouse while his mother's estate was being repaired and made ready. Sylvester had finally convinced them to move here even though it was smaller than the houses they were used to. Even so, everyone looked relaxed and in better spirits than he had seen them.

The dinner table was lively, despite Keylin and Bertram not being here, gone to attend a party. Benji was regaling everyone with a tale of his adventures with a magical vine which kept trying to strangle him while he was trying to rescue it from a parasitic plant that had grown near it.

"I could swear that Gloop Heart was laughing at me while the Nart Vine kept trying to kill me. How do you make a plant understand you're trying to save it?" Benji shook his head. "Stupid thing. See?"

He held out his arm, pushed his cuff back and sure enough, there were welts there, like rope marks.

"And finally, when I had managed to somehow almost free it, that Gloop Heart shot me!"

He showed his palm which had thick rashes.

"Ouch," Sylvester said, grinning. "Their acid could eat your flesh."

"Yeah, I had thick gloves and a coating of fen oil, but even so, this is the result. Last time I try to save a plant."

Before anyone could respond, there was a knock at the front door. Adion, Sylvester's butler went to open it and a droplet later, Keylin and Bertram were there, faces like thunder.

"You're back early." Sylvester saw the concern on his mother's face. "Everything all right?"

"No," Bertram said shortly as he sat down next to Sylvester. He was shaking.

Keylin took the seat next to her fiancé. "He punched someone."

"Lord Hathaway," Bertram said, almost a growl. "He dared insult Keylin and Alaric in my presence and hearing, knowing I was near."

Aunt Elda's face took on a resigned look. "I was afraid of this," she said. "I did warn you. The only thing we can do now–"

"I suggest you don't finish that sentence," Sylvester said, his voice icy. "Alaric is always welcome under any roof of mine or my family's. My sister will visit him if she wants to and so will I."

"Sylvester—" Aunt Elda began, her face furrowed and Benji looked confused.

"Sylvester is right," his mother said. "We should actually invite Alaric over some time. When he can, of course."

Sylvester smiled at her, grateful for the support, but then, she knew the truth about Alaric.

"Why do I get the feeling I'm missing something here?" Benji complained. "Mind you, I like Alaric. He is a good person, and he was very kind and understanding, but even so... Isn't this a bit extreme?"

"No!" Sylvester and his mother said together.

"He's family to me," Keylin declared, her colour high. "He treated me like a sister, a friend, and never once made me feel unsafe. I'm not going to repay him by cutting him out of my life."

"Well, I am not going to argue," Aunt Elda said. "I quite like Alaric, but the more we mix with him, the more people will talk. That's all I'm saying. You can't punch everyone, Bertram."

"Oh, can't I?" Bertram growled.

"I'll help him," Benji said. "No one talks shit about Keylin and gets away with it."

"Hear, hear," Sylvester said. "I agree completely and will join you in punching people who talk shit about anyone in our family."

Another knock at the door, but this time, it was loud and peremptory, like a soldier's knock. Sylvester rose from his chair, heart racing.

"I'll get it, Adion," he called as he hurried to the door.

Astra stood outside. "The King has sent for you," she said. "Immediately." She held out a ring with a portal stone. "Urgently."

Sylvester took the ring and transported himself to the King's study. Alaric was there and a droplet after his arrival, Astra joined them.

Once again, there were no guards in the study and the King was seated behind his desk, hands steepled in front of his face.

"Lucian is awake," Alaric said. "And he's started to guess everything is not well. I don't think he can be kept in the dark for much longer."

Sylvester frowned. "In the dark about what?"

The King looked at Alaric. "Tell him."

"Lucian has been cursed," Alaric said. "It makes him attack the people he cares for. The people he's loyal to. If he isn't allowed to do it, it will kill him. We have been able to suppress its effects, but that is killing him too."

Sylvester went cold. "And there is no cure? No counter curse?"

"If there is, only the Serenians have it," Alaric said. "So, in effect, we have to tell Lucian that he... He has to die... Because I don't think we can find a solution in time."

"How long does he have?" Sylvester asked, his chest tight.

"A griel at the most before his body breaks down," Alaric said.

The King sighed, rubbed his face and looked away. "Lucian is like a brother to me... One of my closest friends... I love him more than I do my family... But no one is more important than Castrial... Alaric, my instructions stand. Lucian is not allowed to know the truth, and he's not allowed to leave your house. No one is allowed to visit him. We can't risk Serenians trying to lure him with promises of a cure."

"So, you're condemning Lucian to die," Sylvester said, breathless.

"I'm choosing Castrial over Lucian," the King said. "I would do the same if it were me in Lucian's position."

Nothing more was said and only silence remained.

FIFTY FIVE

LUCIAN ALWAYS BELIEVED that he was a fool in many ways, as were most people. Yet, he was not a complete idiot. He was capable of logical thought and drawing his own inferences. Even when it was regarding something he didn't know much about, he was able to form his own opinions and conclusions based on what little he knew. For instance, he was certain that he was not locked in Alaric's house for no reason, that the headache he had every now and then was a natural reaction to everything that had happened to him.

Alaric might tell him everything was fine, but Lucian knew his own body and mind. There was something wrong beyond the eye watering, the limp and the headaches, something at the centre of his being. As if the very core of his magic was corrupted somehow. It was an intuition, and also an inference drawn from the many, many things that he had noticed about himself and about Alaric and their general situation.

It was clear that Alaric wouldn't tell him unless he asked out straight, so that was what Lucian planned to do today. If Alaric even visited him today. For the last three days, Alaric hadn't done so. Lucian's every need was met, and even his desire for news was fulfilled in the form of newspapers, but Alaric remained absent, something for which Lucian could find no reason either in the demeanour of Donald or in the papers. Donald had told him that Alaric was busy when he asked, but that was all. There had been no other explanation, and Alaric still hadn't come to him.

Lucian didn't know if he should be angry with Alaric for that.

He walked to the door, hesitating for a droplet. He hadn't left this room since he was brought here, but that didn't mean he couldn't. He wasn't a prisoner in his room, only in the house. He was allowed to leave the room. He had a feeling that he would find Alaric either in the study or in the library, and he wanted to meet him, to have a talk that they had postponed long enough.

Alaric was in the study, a stack of papers in front of him, reports, judging by the way he scowled as he read them. The door was open, which meant that he wasn't doing anything confidential. Lucian knocked on the open door, and Alaric looked up, his eyes widening in surprise.

"Lucian," he said. "You're here."

Lucian smiled at him. "I'm here," he acknowledged. "And I want to talk to you. I know you've been avoiding me, but we have put this off long enough, don't you think?"

A look of wariness crept across Alaric's face. "What do you mean?"

"Give me some credit," Lucian said moving inside and examining one of the glass fronted shelves which held some books, his eyes riveted on Alaric's reflection. "We both know that I am here not because I'm suspected of being a spy. If that were true, I would be in a prison. So, tell me the truth, Alaric. Why am I here?"

Alaric looked away. "Lucian–"

"I know something is wrong with me," Lucian said turning to face his friend. "I know my body and my magic, and I can tell when something is wrong with both. Now, either you can tell me, or I'll just form theories of my own." He attempted a smile. "You know me. I'll likely jump into the most erroneous conclusion, the worst scenario possible."

It failed to bring a smile to Alaric's face, who looked like a man condemned to death. He lifted a hand, the door slammed closed, and Alaric whispered a spell of privacy. Lucian waited and he saw Alaric's expression changing, smoothening, as if he was bracing himself.

"There's a curse on you," he said after a long droplet of silence that stretched thin and taut. "It will kill you if not broken, except no one knows how to."

"What does it do other than kill me?" Lucian asked, his voice even, and he was proud that he could keep it so.

"It made you attack me when you first regained consciousness," Alaric said. "We, the healer and I that is, assume that it is triggered by the presence of people you care for, and is meant to make you harm them. As long as it is allowed to fulfil its purpose, it won't harm you."

"I need to sit down," Lucian said, and this time his voice was shaking.

Alaric came around the desk, and led him to it, helping him sit down, which Lucian couldn't have done by himself, considering how much he was shaking. He tried to make sense of what he heard. A curse that made him attack and possibly harm the people he loved, and if he was not allowed to do it, it was going to kill him. Under the circumstances, he couldn't blame Alaric for choosing to keep him confined to the house.

"Lucian." Alaric sounded alarmed.

Lucian stared at Alaric, not knowing what caused him to have that tone, that look in his eyes, that worry. He wanted to say something to reassure Alaric, to make it go away, but what came from his lips was, "Show me."

"What?" Alaric looked baffled now.

"You said I tried to attack you," he clarified. "Show me."

Alaric was still for a droplet before he unlaced his tunic, letting it fall open, revealing his torso. It was so familiar to Lucian, that body, and that was why he noticed the new scar almost immediately. It was on his chest, a long gash across it; It was healing, but no less visible.

"It's not that I don't trust you," Lucian said as Alaric laced his tunic back. "I just..." Why had he asked to see that?

"You're a desperate man, looking for a way out," Alaric said quietly.

"Would you think me a coward if I told you I want to live?" Lucian asked. "Would you think that I'm terribly selfish?"

"Not at all." Alaric sighed. "You're human, Lucian, and no one really wants to die. Everyone wants to live. It doesn't make you a bad person."

"Even with so much at stake?" Lucian whispered.

"Even then," Alaric said. "But you have to remember that

you're here and still alive. His Majesty and I wouldn't have decided to do that if we didn't have hope for you, hope that this curse can be broken. We have been contacting every Serenian mage who has taken refuge here, and not as spies either. We have also been in touch with every one of our spies left in Sarian."

Lucian swallowed. It was too much, and he wasn't sure that his life was worth it. But the fact was that he wanted to live and wanted it very badly. He had just started to mend his relationship with Alaric, not to speak of his relationship with his siblings. He was young, and he was healthy. Even when he was a prisoner of the Serenians, he hadn't actually thought he would die.

"I don't want to die," he repeated. "But I don't want to hurt anyone I love either... Alaric... How can you even stand to look at me? I tried to kill you."

Alaric shrugged. "It wasn't you. Besides, it was only a graze."

"Because I was too weak," Lucian muttered.

Alaric shook his head. "No, you were stronger than I expected. But it seemed like you were fighting yourself as well. I trust you, Lucian. This hasn't changed that."

"And if I cannot be saved?" Lucian asked.

Alaric set his jaw. "Even if I have to go to Sarian and interrogate them one by one to find a cure, I will do that, but I will not let you die, Lucian. Nor will I let you hurt anyone you love."

Alaric meant it, Lucian knew. He should probably be relieved, and he was, but more than anything, he was alarmed. He appreciated Alaric's words; they meant more than Alaric could possibly imagine, but Lucian didn't want Alaric to waste his life and time trying to find a cure when it might not even be possible.

"It must have been her," he said aloud. "There was a woman... I think it was her who cursed me."

She was the only one with magic, after all. Isolde, the spymaster of Sarian. It had taken time for Lucian to recognise her, but now he knew.

"We're trying to find their tracks," Alaric said. "But like I said, even if they're in Sarian, it won't make a difference. We will find them, Lucian. You have nothing to worry about."

Lucian said nothing, nodding along. Alaric looked even more worried now, but Lucian hoped that he wouldn't suspect what Lucian planned to do. He hoped that Alaric would chalk up Lucian's uncharacteristic responses to the stress of the droplet, to his fear of death.

If Lucian was going to die, he was damned if he was going to do it, locked up here, like a rat in the hole. It was his problem, and it was for him to find a solution, and if he died in the attempt, at least it would be worth something.

But he was not going to drag Alaric into this, nor cause him to be implicated due to his association with Lucian.

FIFTY SIX

ALARIC HAD KNOWN that he couldn't keep the truth from Lucian indefinitely. Lucian was an intelligent man, after all, and quite capable of working things out for himself, which he had done. Yet, there was really no good way of telling Lucian what had happened, what had been done to him, and Alaric had wanted to protect him from the knowledge and the pain of it for as long as possible.

What worried him the most now was Lucian's reaction, or rather, non-reaction. It could be shock, he reasoned, but he remembered Lucian after Wayan's death. Lucian had always been passionate, and he never hid his feelings, not from him.

We're not those people anymore.

Perhaps Lucian just got used to hiding his true emotions while Alaric was away.

He couldn't help the twist his mouth formed at the thought. Away, as if he had left of his own choice, as if he had not been exiled. The bitterness at everything that happened back then was fading fast, however.

"Alaric," Lucian said quietly. "Are you all right?"

Alaric stared at the other man. This was the Lucian he knew, and there was anxiety in his eyes, and a haunted expression which Alaric hated. He knew why it was there, and he didn't want to see it.

"Am *I* all right?" he asked, injecting disbelief into his tone. "Lucian, you... You're the one dying here, and... Why shouldn't *I* be all right?"

"Ah," Lucian said quietly, lowering his eyes, and sighing as he stood up and half turned away. "No reason, I suppose."

Something was wrong. Alaric frowned.

"Lucian," he said gently. "Tell me how I hurt you now."

Lucian's eyes flew to his.

"What do you mean?" There was tension in his tone, and his posture.

"You know what I mean," Alaric said, rising as well. "I know we're rebuilding our relationship, but that doesn't mean I don't know you. And if you really meant everything you said, perhaps you should be honest with me now."

Lucian stared at him, his eyes wide, and so many emotions

chasing across each other.

"The Alaric I knew would have been worried, hurt, and going out of his mind with worry for me," he whispered finally.

Ah.

Perhaps Alaric too got used to hiding his true emotions while he was in exile. He didn't have anyone to show them to anyway.

Alaric stepped closer and hugged Lucian.

"And would the Alaric you know have let you know it, when you're the one who's really suffering?"

Lucian hugged back, sagging.

"I'm scared," he whispered, his voice trembling, and Alaric felt Lucian's heart racing close to his own. "But yes, you wouldn't have let me see, not when it is me who's dying."

"We'll find a way," Alaric told him. "I will, Lucian. I won't let you die." He drew back his head just enough so he could see Lucian's face, which was buried in his shoulder which was growing wet. "Look at me, Lucian."

Lucian did, eyes moist, which explained the dampness Alaric had felt.

"I won't lose you," Alaric said. "I can't. Not for anything." He drew a deep breath, taking the plunge. "I love you, Lucian, and not just as a friend. I've been in love with you forever. Whatever happens, I will find a way to save you."

Lucian's eyes had widened again.

"You love me?" he asked, as if he couldn't believe what he heard.

"Yeah," Alaric said. "Didn't you know?"

Lucian shook his head, still looking bemused.

"We wasted so much time," he said, sounding plaintive. "I love you too, you know."

Alaric went still.

"What about Dew?" he asked.

He hadn't meant to bring her up. Not her, but it must have bothered him more than he realised.

"I loved her," Lucian said softly, grief in his eyes. "But I was never in love with her... She knew... Somehow she always knew that she was..." Lucian swallowed. "A replacement for you... because she... She resembled you somewhat and had some of the same mannerisms... She never knew it was you, but she knew that she was... not the one in my heart."

"And she didn't mind?" Alaric asked.

"She... She wasn't interested in people that way," Lucian said. "But her father expected her to marry, especially after Keylin and Bertram got engaged. So, it suited her because she knew I wouldn't make any demands on her that she abhorred. We never even kissed... She wasn't into any of that, and that was all right for both of us."

"But you..." Alaric shook his head. "You're not like that."

Lucian grimaced. "I know, but I didn't want her that way, you know? After I lost you, I didn't want anyone that way."

There had been other people before him, Alaric knew. Both men and women, because Alaric was the one who had to listen to Lucian talk about every one of his sexual experiences, the same way that Lucian had listened to Alaric's first crush, kiss, and sex. Once they started sleeping with each other, they had not had anyone else.

Perhaps we should have known then.

"We wasted so much time," he repeated Lucian's words from earlier. "But to be fair, I think we were both trying not to fuck up our friendship."

"Which got fucked up anyway," Lucian muttered.

"Did it?" Alaric asked, and Lucian sighed and leaned in, so their foreheads were touching.

"I suppose not," he said.

They stayed like that, in the circle of each other's arms, and

Alaric wished they could do this forever, that neither of them had to return to the real world or face the truth that Lucian might well be dying. Except Alaric was determined that he would not. He didn't yet know what he could do, but there had to be something. Even if he had to comb every iode of Sarian to find the woman who had cast this curse, he would. He didn't even need her to break it for him, because it was the kind of curse that disappeared with the caster. All he had to do was kill her.

Lucian stirred and murmured.

"Take me to bed? Just to sleep, and please hold me. I've missed you so much."

Alaric nodded and kissed his temple.

"Anything for you," he said.

He meant it. He had always meant it. There was nothing he wouldn't do for Lucian, then or now. Even if the King changed his mind and decided that Lucian was too dangerous to live, Alaric was not going to let that happen. Nothing and no one was going to take Lucian from him again.

They had wasted enough time, and Alaric was determined that they wouldn't anymore.

"I love you," he said again, and Lucian's smile was blinding.

The smile that Alaric loved and missed and the one he couldn't help but kiss.

FIFTY SEVEN

LUCIAN WOKE UP in the circle of Alaric's arms, the other man's regular breathing indicating that he was still asleep. Lucian knew that it wouldn't last. Alaric had always been a light sleeper and any movement on Lucian's part would cause him to wake. It was dark out, and Lucian judged it to be sometime after midnight. He stayed still, keeping his breathing even, and on the next exhale, he whispered a sleep spell. It was not a too potent one, but it would ensure that Alaric would sleep through the next few waves without interruption. It would not affect his normal waking up at dawn. That would give enough time for Lucian to leave.

He got up, slowly extricating himself from the clinging limbs. Lucian felt absolutely wretched, hating that he had to do this, and so soon after their confession. But he was damned if he was going to let Alaric risk himself on finding a cure for Lucian or even going against the King for Lucian's sake. Because Alaric would. Lucian knew it. His friend, his lover, had always been a much better man than Lucian himself. Too stubborn for his own good.

But Lucian couldn't afford to think of that now. He dressed himself and padded to his room on stealthy feet. Once inside, he closed the door and bolted it. Moving to the wardrobe, he picked out a pair of pants and a tunic, both in a drab grey. They used to belong to Wayan, and Lucian had kept them after his death. He used magic to change their size to fit him, even that making him realise the alien entity inside him.

The curse sat like a spider at the centre of its own web, spinning its threads over his magic, and Lucian could feel every strand of it. It wasn't painful as such, but it was uncomfortable, especially when he had to use any magic other than the simplest spells. Magic like changing the sizes of clothing, for instance, which needed both focus and the knowledge of precise measurements and used no spoken incantation. It was more a matter of intent than spoken spells which was what made unspoken spells so much more complex.

Lucian dressed himself in his dead brother's clothes, remembered that Wayan had died in Sarian too, and allowed himself a wry twist of the mouth. The only reason he wore them was because they were the only pair of his clothes that couldn't be traced with magic, other than his work ones, and none of that was here. He didn't know what had happened to the ones he had worn when he was abducted, but he was not going to check. It was likely that they were unsalvageable and hence burned. After all, official uniforms were not something to keep lying around.

He moved to the window. The wards were familiar, but powerful. Any attempt to leave through the window or to break the wards would alert both Alaric and the royal guards. He walked to the door and stepped outside. The only unwarded entry and exit must be the front door. There would be royal guards standing watch, but Lucian was not the Blade of Castrial for nothing. Even cursed and weakened, he had managed to stab Alaric. He was sure that he could take on a few guards. If he could manage to stop them from raising the alarm, that would be great. But either way, Lucian was leaving, not just the house, but Castrial.

He didn't know how he knew where she was, but the curse in him was guiding him. It was like an awareness laid over his own, a seventh sense which told him exactly where to go. He would need to create a portal, and for that he needed one of the portal stones that the royal guards carried. No single mage had enough magic to cast a portal all the way to Sarian on their own. However, the portal stones had enough power in them to send him to the other side of the world, if needed.

Lucian paused at the front door, breathing in and out slowly, and called forth his magic to hide him, to make him unnoticed. No guard worth their salt would miss the front door opening, however, and Lucian wasn't sure he could walk through the door. But if there was a time to try, this was it. Hoping that no guard was leaning against the heavy wooden door, Lucian set to work, allowing his magic to reach out, to wrap itself around the frame of the door before sinking in, making the wood insubstantial by increments, but keeping it visible. Lucian felt his limbs grow heavy, and eyes blur. His left leg ached, and his left eye was tearing so much that he had to wipe it every few moments. At the end of what seemed to Lucian like an aeon—it was actually only a couple of waves—he had managed to make enough of the door insubstantial that he could just walk through it.

Two guards were standing a foot away from the door on both sides, their eyes constantly scanning their surroundings. Four others were patrolling around the house, each keeping the front door in sight at all times. Lucian stepped closer to one of the guards in front of the door, pausing just behind him. A chop to the side of his neck had him crumpling to the ground, and Lucian moved quickly to the other guard, his hands coming down on another chop. He grabbed the portal stone from the pouch on the guard's belt and leapt over the heads of the other guards running towards him, using a little magic to keep him out of their reach. Once he was on the road, he opened the portal to the border with Sarian, and leapt inside, pulling the portal shut.

He stood there, breathing heavily, his eyes scanning for any more guards or soldiers. The border had a guard post, but Lucian was not bothered about that. They hadn't seen him yet, and the portal stone still had enough magic for one more jump. He moved to the cover of the trees before opening another portal, this time, close to the capital of Sarian. That was where he would find her. He was certain of that.

In the days when he had nothing to do but lie on a bed, and go over what he had been through, Lucian had recognised Isolde. He had met her at an official function soon after he had become the Blade, but that had been farials ago. He should have known that neither the Queen of Sarian nor her spymaster would just do nothing, not after the massacre of the Castrilian agent and her family in Sarian, and the quiet retaliation by Castrial.

It was still night when he reached a small inn within the capital. He had money in the currency of Sarian, something he had managed to procure when he was bedridden. It was in a box that he had asked Donald to get him from his house, citing that it was too risky to leave it unattended. Donald hadn't known what it contained, and hence had brought it to him without question since Lucian had told him it was official and important. The box also contained the seal of the Blade, and the coins were in a pouch inside a secret compartment.

The seal was back in Alaric's house, but the pouch was with him. Lucian masked his magical signature as well. He couldn't afford to be found before he had found Isolde and got her to break that curse.

Once, he and his people had thought about counterfeiting the Serenian coins but had postponed the idea for a time when Castrial's economy was more stable.

The inn was not seedy, but that was the best that could be said for it. Paint peeled away at places, and the floorboards creaked. Dust was gathered in corners and under the threadbare carpet. The counter was clean enough, and the man behind it looked bored.

Lucian paid for a room, made up a story about a sister when asked, and climbed into the unfamiliar bed, falling asleep almost immediately. The bed was musty, the sheets slightly damp, and the mattress was lumpy as fuck, but he was too tired to care. Alaric was going to be angry with him. By now, he would have learned that Lucian was gone, and Lucian was certain that they wouldn't be able to find him. His magical signature was masked, and he had abandoned the portal stone. There was nothing on him that could be traced.

It was a kick to his chest that woke him, and Lucian noticed that dawn hadn't broken yet. They had found him quickly, but then, he had expected nothing less. Isolde was known for her efficiency, even if not her humanity.

"Well, well, well," a hated and familiar voice said, almost

purring. "Look who has come all the way into Sarian. I must say I'm impressed. I was thinking that you'd probably die in that cage they made for you. Waste of my time and energy, I'd thought."

Lucian looked at her, taking in the glee in her eyes, and the boot on his chest that prevented him from getting up. It wasn't constricting his breathing just yet, however.

"I don't want to die," he said. "And I was certain that I would have, if I had stayed there." He paused. "What would it take for you to remove the curse on me?"

She looked at him, a gleam of speculation in her eyes now.

"Depends on how badly you want to live," she said.

"Very badly," he said. "Why would I be here otherwise? I am truly a fugitive now. There's no going back."

Lucian swallowed the lump in his throat as he spoke. Saying it made it so much more real than when it was just in his head. He forced himself not to think of anything else but the implications of his actions. He was an outcast from Castrial now, and he had done it himself. He could never go back. He would never see Alaric again or be trusted by Garret again.

But he would be alive.

She removed the boot from his chest enabling him to sit up, rubbing his breast.

"Well?" he asked.

She regarded him, no smile on her face.

"You know what to do," she said. "We need information that only you or the King can provide us, Lord Blade."

Lucian winced.

"Don't call me that," he said tightly. "And you do realise that whatever information that I have could well be outdated now. That the King would have made different plans as soon as I went missing that first time."

She shrugged.

"Plans change, people don't. If you want to live, you can tell us all you know about the people who lead Castrial, their weaknesses, and their strengths, the way they think."

"This is about the war," he said. "You're planning to invade Castrial."

"Of course," she said as if it was a fact of life. She leaned forward. "You know that your country can't withstand it, no matter what you tell us. But if you do co-operate, not only will you get to live, but we also promise to keep alive anyone you want, even the King. After all, there is no need to kill anyone without reason, is there?"

Lucian swallowed again. He should have known she would ask something like this, but he was prepared for it. His only worry was that it was going too well.

"All right," he said. "But I want a binding assurance from your queen and the curse on me to be broken first."

She shook her head.

"You're in no position to be bargaining with me."

"Then I would rather die," he said. "You're right that Castrial is not in a position to withstand an invasion, but that doesn't mean anything. Even animals fight desperately when cornered, and the people of Castrial are brave and strong. Your victory is by no means assured, but with my help, you *will* win."

It was a gamble, a desperate gamble, because he knew very well that Castrial would lose in the event of an invasion. But she seemed to be mulling over his words.

"Take it," she said, taking something from inside her pocket and handing it over.

It was a vial with a colourless liquid that moved sluggishly.

"It's an antidote," she said. "It will block the effects of the curse for seven griels. Within that time, we will decide if the information you have is of any use. If it is, you will have your agreement, and another dose of antidote."

She smiled at him, but it held no mirth.

"I won't be breaking your curse till we are victorious over Castrial."

Lucian bent his head, acquiescing. He had no choice now, anyway. He had chosen this path, and now he had to pretend to turn traitor to his kingdom, to his King, to his family, his friends. To Alaric.

Lucian uncorked the vial and swallowed the antidote. It tasted vile, like snakes slithering down his throat and into his stomach. Pain was next, and he doubled over, biting his lips to prevent the scream that wanted to tear from him.

"Just bear with it," she said. "It will get better over time, but this is the only way."

Lucian's vision blurred as he gasped and writhed.

EPILOGUE

ALARIC SAT ON his chair, feeling exhausted to the bone. It had been a griel since Lucian had disappeared. Escaped. Even though none of them knew where he had gone to, it was easy to guess. Alaric and the King weren't the only ones who guessed, though.

He had been working around the clock since that day, trying to find Lucian. Astra had been put in temporary charge of the

Blade's office while Sylvester was in Sarian, trying to find any trace of Lucian. They had all tried everything. Lucian couldn't be traced magically, and they had found the spent portal stone that he had taken on the boundary between Castrial and Sarian which confirmed Alaric's guess.

The King had raked him over the coals for telling Lucian about the curse.

"You should have known," the King had raged. "Of course, he went to Sarian! It was the only chance of saving his life! Why did you think I asked you to keep it quiet? Now, he has truly turned traitor, and all because you couldn't keep your mouth shut!"

Alaric hadn't refuted or defended himself. What could he have said anyway? What the King said was true. The King had calmed down later, and he, Alaric, Sylvester, and Astra had sat down and made plans for if Lucian had sold out Castrial. The defences of the country had to be strengthened, plans and whichever key people was possible changed.

What was worse was that Alaric was glad Lucian had gone to Sarian. Because that was the only chance for Lucian to live, and Alaric wanted him to live. No matter what the consequences, nothing was as bad as Lucian dying.

As for the future, he would deal with it when it happened.

The front doorbell rang, and Alaric frowned. He heard the steady steps of Donald as he made his way to the door. Alaric was not expecting anyone, and he almost gaped as Keylin entered his field of vision. He hadn't been avoiding her, but despite her and Sylvester's many invitations, he hadn't gone to visit them.

Alaric had been busy, though he could have found time for a visit if he had been so inclined. But he was aware of the rumours about him and Keylin. He would not be the reason her reputation got destroyed, and hence he had stayed away.

But she was here now, and she was alone as far as he could see.

Why would she come to him by herself when she no doubt knew the implications?

"Were you ever going to tell me?" she asked.

He stared at her blankly.

"Tell you what?" he asked.

She made an impatient gesture.

"That you are my brother," she said, her voice tight, and Alaric gaped at her.

"How did you find out?" he asked finally when he could find his voice. "Did Sylvester…"

She snorted. "No, he didn't. But I'll be having words with him too." She paused. "I'm not an idiot," she said. "I should have guessed before this, but I… Alaric, for fuck's sake, why didn't you tell me?"

He sighed, feeling as if a weight was gone from him. She knew. There was no reason for him to pretend anymore.

"May I hug you?" he asked, and she nodded, her smile joyful.

He got to his feet, took a step forward and hugged her. She hugged back, no hesitation, and he breathed her in. Her magic smelled very similar to his own and Sylvester's, and he revelled in that small detail, something he tucked inside, for comfort on a lonely day.

"I wasn't sure how you would react," he said. "And I didn't want to hurt your mother."

"Idiot," she said, her arms tightening around her, her voice muffled by his shoulder. "My mother already knows, you know. I assume Lucian does too, other than Sylvester."

"Yes," Alaric said. "No one else, though. My mother, naturally." He sighed again. "You can tell Bertram, you know."

Her mother probably knew because of the scandal it had caused back then with his mother declaring that Lord Giles and not her master was the father of her child, and the magical test on the infant Alaric that confirmed it.

"I want to tell the whole world," she said. "And my mother likes you... She won't object. I know her."

"You must do as you see fit," Alaric said quietly. "But unless your father acknowledges me, it wouldn't make any difference."

"He's your father too," she said, but there was something in her voice, a hesitation, a wariness.

Alaric released her and stepped back.

"He's the man who fathered me, yes," he said. "But he has never been a father to me, and is not likely to be, even if he acknowledges me."

"He has known all this while," Keylin muttered, her face troubled. "And he has not even told us... Alaric, was that why you said that our family was always the target that first day?"

Alaric grimaced.

"I apologise for how I behaved that day," he said. "I said a great many nonsensical things back then. I hope you can forgive me."

She shook her head, her eyes blazing.

"Don't you dare apologise to me, not when our father has treated you so shamefully! Everything you had endured all your life is because of him, and... We're the ones who should be asking your forgiveness."

"You can't help being his daughter," Alaric said. "Any more than I can help being his son. It's enough for me that you know and care."

She gave him a wistful smile. "Dew would have loved you too," she said.

Alaric felt a sharp ache in his chest. He couldn't grieve for a person he barely knew, but he grieved for what he could have had.

"I wish I had known her too," he said. "I'd met her a few times, and she seemed a good person."

"Can I meet your mother?" she asked, as if he would deny her.

"I want to apologise to her, and I know my mother would want to as well."

"You and your mother have nothing to apologise to either of us for," he said firmly. "Hamin is the only one to blame in all this. Not you, not us. We were all his victims in a way."

"I have another brother," Keylin murmured, almost to herself. A blinding smile appeared on her face. "I'm so happy, even though... Do you know why Lucian left?"

Alaric shook his head. It was so difficult to lie to her, but he had to. There were some secrets that were not his to reveal anyway.

He couldn't help but wonder if Lucian had meant what he said to him that night. Had he lied to lull Alaric into a false sense of security, to allay his suspicions, or had he been telling the truth? Did Lucian decide to confess as a distraction or because he knew it was the last chance he was going to get?

"I'm sorry," she said softly. "You love him, don't you?"

"Always have," Alaric said quietly. "I just wish he had trusted me... That he had stayed."

That was partly a lie too, because he was glad Lucian left, that he had taken a chance to live. But he did wish Lucian had trusted him. Alaric would have helped him, no matter the consequences to himself.

Perhaps that was why Lucian left without a word.

Keylin took his hands in his and said quietly. "I'm here, you know. You don't have to keep everything to yourself now. You have a family."

Alaric swallowed past the lump in his throat and blinked his blurry eyes to smile at her. His sister. His family.

It was all he had to hold on to now, and he was determined to cherish it, and protect it for as long as he could. No matter what, he would never allow anything to happen to her again.

"We're family," he said softly, echoing her words, and she

smiled at him, warm and comforting.

He hugged her again, because it felt good, and because he could now. Without any deception or misunderstanding.

My sister!

He smiled.

ACKNOWLEDGEMENTS

This is the first time I'm doing this. Not because there wasn't anyone to acknowledge, but because I'd never felt like I'd written a good enough book to link with names other than mine.

When Lucian and Alaric first walked into my head, I didn't expect their story was going to be like this. My initial idea only had Lucian betraying Alaric and the repercussions of that to their relationship and to Castrial.

That iteration was never written, but when I envisaged it, I thought Garret would be a villain.

He might not be much different in many readers' minds, but he isn't in mine. He's a man with the lives of millions to think of, and he has to make hard decisions. Even then, he tries to be fair, to do his best.

The character was inspired by the various emperors I'd seen in several C Dramas. I took them and improved on them to make Garret.

The first draft of Blade Broken lacked focus. There was not a central plot thread or a cohesive plot. It was a jumble of scenes, and there were no stakes or tension.

It is thanks to my awesome betas, Susanne Schmidt and M.C. Burnell that it became this version. I had to delete almost 25k words and add more than that to create this book that you have in your hands.

Most of that 25k words is Keylin and Betram's story which really didn't have a place in Blade Broken as it stands now. Someday, I might put them together, revise them and make a book of its own, but not today.

A lot of the credit for this book goes to my cover artist, Artscandre, whose cover for this book is simply breathtaking.

Thanks also to Labyrinth designs who created the title frame, and Leigh Cover Designs whose interior graphic of a broken blade fits this book so perfectly.

I'm also immeasurably grateful for Luca who has not only ARC Read this book in one day and left a five star review, but who has been sharing my posts on Bluesky, who has even paid me for the free character art of Lucian and Alaric on my Ko-fi shop. You're a rockstar, my friend.

Susanne and M.C. have both read various versions of this book, and Susanne is also the creator of the blurb to this book. I suck at blurbs, but she came up with the perfect one based on my terrible attempts.

There are many, many, more people I want to thank.

Kate Ramsey who beta read the revised version, my ARC readers, especially Paul G Zereith and Ellie Yarde who both kept shouting on Bluesky how much they were enjoying it. It's such a huge confidence boost and also helped boost some pre-orders. Everyone who pre-ordered this book, who bought a copy after release, who has taken the trouble to read it and got this far.

Thank you all.

It truly takes a village to bring a story to life. Being an introvert, it's hard for me to speak about my books. (Writing is different). And yet, somehow, me forcing myself out of my comfort zone for this book has helped immensely because of the support of so many people!

Thank you all once again from the bottom of my heart.

Niranjan

Support me by leaving a review at the retailer site from which you purchased this.

If you want extra cookies, leave reviews at Goodreads and Bookbub.

Subscribe to my newsletter for more updates on new releases, discounts, free books and more.

Follow me on Bookbub for new release alert and price promotions.

Find me at Bluesky.

Buy me a coffee!

Join my discord server!

ABOUT THE AUTHOR

An author and editor, Niranjan's biggest ambition is to have a character named Garth in every book they write. Niranjan writes books rooted in mythical worlds, and their stories are often a combination of magic and futuristic technology.

When they are not writing or editing, Niranjan can be found cooking or just lying on their couch watching or rewatching C Dramas and writing fanfiction.

More about them may be found at https://authorniranjan.in/

They have a ko-fi shop where you can get free maps and character arts as well as purchase their books.

ALSO BY NIRANJAN

NOW AVAILABLE FOR PRE-ORDER

www.ingramcontent.com/pod-product-compliance
Ingram Content Group UK Ltd.
Pitfield, Milton Keynes, MK11 3LW, UK
UKHW040949240325
456642UK00001B/52